PASSION NEVER DIES

PRAISE FOR ANNA DURAND'S BOOKS

Other Books by Anna Durand

from Jacobsville Books

THE MORTAL FALLS (UNDERCOVER ELEMENTALS, BOOK ONE)

DANGEROUS IN A KILT (HOT SCOTS, BOOK ONE)

WILLPOWER (PSYCHIC CROSSROADS, BOOK ONE)

INTUITION (PSYCHIC CROSSROADS, BOOK TWO)

REBORN TO DIE (REBORN, PART ONE)

REBORN TO BURN (REBORN, PART TWO)

REBORN TO AVENGE (REBORN, PART THREE)

REBORN TO CONQUER (REBORN, PART FOUR)

THE FALLS: A FANTASY ROMANCE STORY

from The Wild Rose Press

TEMPTED BY A KISS

PASSION NEVER DIES

THE COMPLETE REBORN SERIES

ANNA DURAND

PASSION NEVER DIES

ISBN: 978-1-934631-78-2 (pbk.)
ISBN: 978-1-934631-81-2 (ebook)
Library of Congress Control Number: 2016956933

Manufactured in the United States.

Jacobsville Books
www.JacobsvilleBooks.com

Publisher's Cataloging-in-Publication Data
provided by Five Rainbows Cataloging Services

Names: Durand, Anna.
Title: Passion never dies : the complete reborn series / Anna Durand.
Description: Lake Linden, MI : Jacobsville Books, 2016. | Series: Reborn.
Identifiers: LCCN 2016956933 | ISBN 978-1-934631-78-2 (pbk.) | ISBN 978-1-934631-81-2 (ebook)
Subjects: LCSH: Man-woman relationships--Fiction. | Amnesia--Fiction. | Reincarnation--Fiction. | Magic, Egyptian--Fiction. | Love stories. | BISAC: FICTION / Romance / Paranormal / General. | FICTION / Romance / Suspense. | GSAFD: Love stories. | Occult fiction. | Romantic suspense fiction.
Classification: LCC PS3604.U724 P37 2016 (print) | LCC PS3604.U724 (ebook) | DDC 813/.6--dc23.

REBORN TO DIE

CHAPTER ONE

SHE WOKE UP DROWNING. HER LUNGS BURNED AS SHE struggled to suck in a breath, but got liquid instead. Warm liquid that burned like acid. Viscous, acrid liquid filling her lungs. She tried to flail her arms and legs, to get above the water. Something restrained her. She tried to scream, but sucked in more liquid. More burning. Oh God, she was going to die. And it would hurt like hell.

The restraints on her arms and legs popped free. Hands reached into the water to grasp her upper arms, lifting her out of the liquid. She coughed it up, hacking over and over, almost vomiting from the pain and effort. Then, with one long gasp, she breathed in clean, dry air. It tasted like salvation.

The hands that had rescued her let go, leaving her sitting up with her legs stretched out in front of her. She clung to the edge of the pool. Her entire body shook with a violence that rattled the glass.

She blinked. Glass? Her vision was blurred. She blinked repeatedly until enough of the bleariness cleared that she could make out her surroundings. She sat inside a glass coffin—at least that's what it looked like—with wires attached to her chest and head, held in place by sticky pads. Her head pounded. Her heart beat so fast it hurt. The lighting, though dim, seemed too bright for her eyes. She squinted, blinked some more, and tried to make sense of what she saw.

The glass coffin was filled with a pale blue liquid, the thick, acrid-tasting stuff that had nearly drowned her. The coffin sat atop a table or dais. The wires attached to her body stretched down from the coffin, draped across the concrete floor, and snaked upward to a bank of electronic equipment along the nearest wall. Lights flashed on the equipment. Beeps echoed through the room. More equipment populated the rest of the room. A video camera on a tripod stood several feet from her glass coffin, its lens pointed directly at her. She felt it watching her, as if an evil spirit inhabited its circuits and chips.

Mirrors lined half of one wall of the room. An instinct told her those were two-way mirrors, designed to let people on the other side view this room without being viewed themselves. The mirrors revealed a wet, bedraggled young woman hunched inside a glass coffin. It was her, she realized. Long, dark red hair hung limp and wet, stopping just short of her breasts. Her fair skin looked even paler in the sterile lighting. For some reason, her own image seemed unfamiliar. She was too far away from the mirrors to see the color of her eyes, yet she felt they must be hazel.

Now that the warm liquid had run off her arms and torso, a chill seeped into her flesh. Goose bumps prickled her skin. She shivered a little, rubbing her arms. That's when she noticed it.

She was naked. Not half naked either. Completely, one hundred percent naked.

Before she had time to ponder that, she noticed *him*. A man hunched beside her coffin, bent at the waist to gaze at her from her eye level. The liquid from her glass coffin dripped from his hands, which grasped the coffin's lip. The man had light brown hair, cinnamon-colored eyes, and light skin. His arms were wet—dripping actually, with the pale blue liquid from her coffin. His features were well proportioned and smooth, reminiscent of ancient statues of virile young men she'd seen…someplace. Couldn't recall where. She could picture the statues, though. Men with trim bodies and angelic faces who held staffs in their hands and appeared to be walking with great purpose and confidence. She could picture this man as one of those statues. The only difference was his expression. His face was pale, his mouth open, eyes wide and tinged with red.

He leaned closer to her, fixing his gaze on hers, and said, "Can you hear me?"

She tried to speak, but wound up hacking again. Her throat burned. She wanted water but couldn't say it. He repeated his query and she nodded. She pointed at her throat, then gestured with her hand as if it held a cup. He seemed to get the idea. The shock—or was it terror—on his face softened into an expression more like concern. He trotted to a nearby table, grabbed a bottle of clear liquid, and brought it back to her. After unscrewing the cap, he offered her the bottle. She took it in her trembling hands, lifted it to her lips, and tilted the bottle to spill cool, tasteless liquid into her mouth. The water felt so good on her throat that she took another sip, and then another, and another. The burning in her throat subsided. She decided to test her voice with a simple word.

"Thanks."

It came out as part croak, part whisper. The man gave her a tight-lipped smile, though his eyes widened even more, if only for a second. She took another, longer drink of the water.

The man raised a hand. "Take it easy. You don't want to overdo it."

She rested the bottle on the coffin's wide rim. When she spoke this time, her voice sounded less scratchy. "Who are you?"

He arched his eyebrows. "The better question is, who are you?"

His question stopped her. She stared at him, her brain spinning in circles, like a car's wheels in deep mud. Her voice quavering as she said, "I don't know who I am."

He didn't look at all surprised, which sent a shiver down her spine. Or maybe that was from the lukewarm air tickling her damp skin. Might've been a little of both. Questions bubbled in her mind, and she struggled to arrange her thoughts in some semblance of order. Hard to do when nothing around you made sense. She took in more of her surroundings in an attempt to order the chaos within her. Tall ceilings with inset lights that cast a sterile glow on the room. Lots of equipment with lots of flashing lights. The video camera. A row of widescreen computer monitors on a table. The monitors faced away from her, so she couldn't tell what they showed.

A laboratory. This was a laboratory.

The realization came out of nowhere. She didn't know how she knew this place's function. Somehow she just did. Why the hell had she been drowning in a glass coffin inside a laboratory?

She focused on the man again. He must know. Another shiver coursed through her. She was sitting here naked with a strange man who clearly knew more than she did about her situation.

The man glanced down at her body, blushed, and averted his gaze. Guess he'd finally realize she was au naturel. He scurried away, retrieving a backpack from under one of the tables and snagging a long coat from a hook on the wall. The presence of other hooks indicated that other people used this room, someone other than the strange man with her now. Returning to her, he dropped the backpack at his feet and unzipped its main compartment. He dug out a pair of socks and set both the coat and socks on the floor before offering her his hands. She knew he was offering to help her out of the coffin. Still, she tried to stand on her own. Apparently, she was stubborn and suspicious. Good to know. Her feet slipped and she almost tumbled over, taking the coffin with her. The man caught her by the waist, hoisting her out of the coffin in one swift motion.

The coffin teetered but stayed in place.

He set her down on her feet. She teetered a little too and grasped his forearms for support. He held her elbows until she steadied, then plucked the electrode pads off her body one by one as fast, she imagined, as any human on earth could've managed. At the same time, he avoided looking at her naked flesh as much as possible. Once he'd finished his task, he picked up the socks and coat and thrust them toward her without glancing at her body or her face.

"It's the best I can do," he said, shrugging. His gaze stayed fixed on his own feet.

She took the items and slipped them on, feeling less than well dressed. It was better than naked.

"Thank you, Jake," she said.

His head jerked up. He gaped at her with a bug-eyed expression.

She scrunched her brow. "What?"

"How do you know my name?"

Her heart skipped a beat. She had called him by name. She had no answer for his question, and quite frankly, she didn't know what to say. He seemed equally stumped. After several seconds she managed to form a single question. "Do you know my name?"

"Um…" He glanced around the room and refused to meet her gaze as he asked, "How are you feeling?"

"Headache. Otherwise okay, as far as I can tell."

He retrieved a tablet computer from a nearby table and handed it to her. She glanced down at the text displayed on the screen.

"Can you read this?" he asked.

"It's a bunch of scientific gobbledygook, but yes, I can read it. I'm not illiterate." Well, she did have amnesia. She couldn't fault him for wondering if she could read. Yet an instinct warned her there was more to it than simple concern for her faculties. "Who are you?"

"Jake. Have you forgotten? You spoke my name—"

"I know that." She frowned at him. "What's your last name? Where are you from? What are you doing here? What am I doing here?"

"Long story." He checked his watch. As he stuffed the tablet computer back inside his pack, she glimpsed a small revolver tucked into a pocket sewn into the pack's lining. He had a gun? Before she could ask about it, he told her, "If you can walk, then we need to go. Quick."

"Why?"

"I'll explain later."

He reached for her arm, to urge her to walk. She shook free of his grasp.

"Explain now," she said, crossing her arms over her chest. "I'm not moving until you tell me something that makes sense."

Wow, she was plucky. She was starting to like herself.

Oh great. Was she also egotistical? Maybe she shouldn't get too fond of herself after all.

Jake met her gaze as he took hold of her shoulders. "I know you're scared. And confused. I will explain everything, I promise, but for now you have to come with me. If they find out you're alive, they'll kill you. Understand?"

No, she didn't really understand, not in the broader context. In terms of what killing meant, oh yeah, she understood that all right.

She had two choices that she could see. Stay here in a creepy lab where unknown people had stuffed her in a glass coffin and tried to drown her for unknown but surely terrifying reasons. Or go with Jake, the attractive man who saved her from drowning but refused to explain anything—yet.

"I'll go with you," she said.

Though he smiled, the expression was tight and seemed more relieved than cheerful.

An alarm buzzed.

She jumped.

Jake grabbed his backpack and ushered her across the room toward a large metal door that stood shut. She saw no knobs or levers for opening the portal. Jake pulled a badge out of his pocket and swiped it through a reader mounted beside the door. A mechanism clunked and the door slid open with a grinding noise.

The alarm buzzed again.

"Hurry," Jake said, shoving her through the doorway. "They're coming."

She had no time to ask who or why. He grabbed her arm and dragged her down a hallway toward a T intersection, where this hallway ended at a set of huge metal doors that must've reached ten feet in height and twenty in width. Ignoring the doors, he swerved left. His hand still gripped her arm, a little too tightly. Grimacing, she tried to get her bearings as they rushed headlong toward an unknown destination. Doorways opened off the hallway here and there, each one labeled with an alphanumeric designation. Nothing gave any clue about what this place was. She knew only that she'd woken up in some kind of laboratory. Not comforting.

The alarm buzzed faster now, striking a rhythm almost as fast as her heartbeat.

CHAPTER TWO

J AKE HAULED HER AROUND ANOTHER CORNER, INTO A hallway identical to the previous ones. Despite her socks, the concrete floor chilled her feet as they ran. This hallway dead-ended at a single door, smaller than the others and equipped with a knob. A red exit sign glowed above the door.

The alarm fell silent.

Jake muttered a curse under his breath. The wall beside the door held a card reader like the one on the laboratory door. Jake swiped his badge, a mechanism chunked, and he twisted the knob, pushing the door outward.

"They're almost here, let's go," Jake said, urging her to walk through the doorway.

She didn't move. Couldn't move. Or maybe her subconscious simply wouldn't allow it.

A scowl flashed across Jake's face, then vanished. He pursed his lips, as if struggling to not yell at her. His frustration seemed to roil in the air, palpable on a psychic level. The emotion driving his frustration was not anger, she realized, but rather fear. This man was terrified. Of what? Or whom?

"Please," Jake said, his tone almost pleading. "Explanations later. Escape *now*."

She fled through the doorway. Jake followed her out, and then took the lead as they raced through pitch darkness toward a destination that, she hoped, at least he knew.

As her eyes adjusted to the darkness, she spotted a shape ahead of them. A large, boxy shape. A vehicle. Jake halted beside the vehicle, an SUV, and flung open the driver's door. She noticed a logo etched onto the SUV's door, a symbol that struck her as familiar, though she couldn't quite place it. For some reason the word redeo popped into her brain. She had no idea what the word meant. It sounded like a foreign language.

Jake motioned for her to climb inside the vehicle. She crawled over the driver's seat and center console onto the passenger seat, settling in as Jake slammed the door. He jammed a key in the ignition and cranked it. The engine grumbled to life. He shoved the gear shift lever into drive, floored the accelerator, and spun the car rightward. They rocketed through the night, the headlights cleaving the darkness ahead of them, revealing a gravel road. She twisted around to look out the back window. The outline of a building was visible thanks to the moonlight that filtered through thin clouds. She could make out no details on the structure.

"Fasten your seatbelt," Jake said.

She did as commanded. He'd already snapped his seatbelt into position and turned on the heater. After several long minutes, the lukewarm air turned into a warm current that blasted over her feet. It felt so good she wanted to cry, but that probably wouldn't go over well with her scared and frustrated savior. She bit her lip to stave off the tears.

The car bounced over a pothole. Her teeth clacked together. Pain lanced through her jaw and straight into her brain. The headache she'd already had ratcheted up a couple notches. She rubbed her temples. Maybe the headache stemmed from her brains attempt to catch up with events. She felt numb, in more than the physical sense. The warm air from the heater took care of her frozen flesh. The other numbness came from somewhere deep inside.

She glanced sideways at Jake. "Where are we going?"

"No talking. Not until we're clear of the perimeter."

"What perimeter?"

"Quiet." He'd practically shouted the word. In a softer tone, he said, "Please. I need to concentrate. These roads are full of holes and channels carved out by the rains we had last week. I can't risk slowing down, but I don't want to flip the Jeep either."

She gulped against a tightness in her throat. Flipping the Jeep sounded like a good thing to avoid.

"Okay," she said. "No talking."

He relaxed a smidgen, though enough tension remained to keep his entire body rigid. His fingers gripped the steering wheel with such force she half expected the wheel to pop off in his hands when they skimmed over a rock that lay in the road.

The headlights glanced off a metal barrier up ahead. It was a chain-link gate, set into a chain-link fence. And they were barreling toward it at high speed. She waited for Jake to hit the brakes, but he didn't. The gate loomed closer and closer as her heart pounded faster and faster. She gripped the edges of her seat, squeezing her eyes shut. If she had to die, she supposed smashed to bits in a car wreck was better than drowning.

They hit the gate with an explosive thud. The car shimmied. Something—the gate, presumably—bounced over the car.

She cracked her eyes open to peek through her lashes. They were speeding down the gravel road again, across the desert landscape that she caught glimpses of in the headlights. The windshield was cracked on her side. Although the car must've suffered at least a few major dents, she couldn't see any other damage in the darkness. They'd made it.

Twisting around in her seat, she stared out the back window. It revealed nothing but the gloom of night. Even the shape of the structure they'd fled from was no longer visible.

She faced the windshield. No lights. No sign of another living thing. She looked at Jake.

"If we're in so much danger," she said, "why don't I see anyone chasing us?"

Although he kept his attention on the road ahead, his lips compressed into a line. He stayed silent for so long she thought he wouldn't respond. Finally, he said, "It'll take at least ten minutes for them to get inside the lab and figure out you're gone. After that, they'll need some more time to check the security cameras and find out I helped you escape. At that point, they'll mobilize the pursuit."

"Are you in the military?" she asked.

"No, I'm a grad student. I used to be a Boy Scout, if that helps. Always be prepared. It's a motto I've tried to live by."

"Is that why you have a gun?"

"You saw it?"

"Uh-huh. Your bosses let you have a gun at work?"

He squirmed a little in his seat. "They don't know about it. Most of the personnel at the lab have weapons provided by Redeo Biotech, the company we work for. I decided I should have one too. Since they don't bother with metal detectors, because only authorized personnel are allowed inside the facility, I was able to sneak my contraband weapon inside."

She studied his face for a few seconds, but she couldn't glean any information from his impassive expression. "How do I know you're telling the truth? Maybe nobody's coming after us. Maybe you put me in that tank and tried to drown me because you have a sicko fetish thing about drowned girls. For all I know, you like to kidnap and torture women."

He slammed on the brakes. The car's momentum thrust her forward against the seatbelt, making it dig into her flesh. She gasped and braced herself against the dashboard. The Jeep fishtailed, then jerked to a stop.

Jake reached into his pants pocket. "I'm sorry. I didn't want to have to do this, but you're leaving me no choice."

"What—"

He jammed something into her neck. She felt the sharp stick of the needle and then...

Nothing.

JAKE STARED STRAIGHT AHEAD THROUGH THE WINDSHIELD AS THE Jeep hurtled down the gravel two-track. He avoided looking at the unconscious woman slumped in the passenger seat because it made his gut twist. Sedating her had seemed like his only option. She'd been too upset to handle. If he were totally honest with himself, though, he'd sedated her mainly because she wouldn't stop asking questions. He couldn't tell her certain things, no matter how much she pestered him. Things she wouldn't understand. Things she wouldn't believe. Soon he would have to reveal everything to her. For now, though, he simply couldn't deal with it.

He was a coward. He knew this.

Before she'd woken up this evening, he'd spent hours simply gazing at her and wondering what kind of person she had been before she became a test subject. He'd looked at her naked body, of course—he was a man, after all—but eventually, his attention had shifted to her face and he no longer paid much attention to her lovely body. Her face captivated him. Those hazel eyes especially. He got to see her eyes only when one of the scientists pulled her eyelids open to examine them, which they did once a week. He lived for those moments, when he spied those light brown irises flecked with green. He swore he'd seen a spark of life in those eyes, despite the scientists' assurances that she would never awaken.

Everything had changed the moment she opened her eyes.

He had one choice—run. If they didn't, they would both die.

CHAPTER THREE

S HE WOKE IN A FOG, OF THE MENTAL KIND. HER BRAIN FELT fuzzy, her eyelids too heavy to open. Her mouth was dry. She forced her eyelids to part, with an effort that seemed out of proportion with the task. Her vision was blurry, so she could make out only vague shapes. A machine hummed nearby.

Back in the lab?

She jerked upright. No, not the lab. Although her vision got clearer, now she saw two of everything. Two beds, two pairs of her own legs lying on the bed, two television sets, two Jakes. She stared at her quadruple feet, waiting for things to settle down in her brain. By the time the double images recombined, she felt less fuzzy headed. Propping herself up with both arms, she stared past her outstretched legs, beyond the foot of the bed on which she sat, toward the man standing between the bed and the low dresser. Jake had taken off his T-shirt, baring his smooth, muscled chest. Her stomach fluttered. She couldn't stop staring at him. At his chest. At his muscular but not muscle-bound arms. At his tapered waist. At the rivet on his jeans.

Jake slipped a long-sleeve shirt over his arms and started buttoning it up, blocking her view of his toned flesh.

She felt warm all of a sudden, and tingly. Damn, did male flesh always have this effect on her? She wished she could remember. Maybe all women felt this way when confronted with a bare-chested man. Maybe it was only her. She might be a wanton woman. Jake caught her gaping at him and arched an eyebrow, his lips twitching in what threatened to turn into a smile.

"What are you staring at?" he said.

A touch of humor lightened his brusque tone. Her cheeks flared hot. As she averted her gaze to the bedspread beneath her, she touched a fingertip to her cheeks. The warmth she felt made her wonder if her whole body turned pink when she looked at Jake's bare skin. Better not risk it. No more staring at the beefcake.

Jake cleared his throat. Leaving his shirt half buttoned, he settled onto the foot of the bed near her sock-shielded feet. She felt the warmth flushing through her again. Dammit, this man had knocked her out with an injection of who-knew-what. She refused to let his physical charms seduce her into forgetting that.

"It's later," she said.

His brow furrowed.

She scooted backward to lean against the headboard. "You said you'd explain everything later. Well, this feels like later to me. And first off, I want to know what the hell you did to me in the car."

"I gave you a sedative. Brought it along in case you became agitated." He raised a placating hand when she opened her mouth to balk at his statement. "It's to be expected, I imagine. You did come back to life only a few hours ago. And I'm sure waking up inside the tank didn't help matters."

Come back to life. His words stuck in her brain. She woke up dying, so she must've been alive. Yet she had no memory of anything before that moment.

She shook her head. "That's not good enough. I want details. All of them."

He let out a long sigh. Then he looked her square in the eye and said, "Your mummified remains were discovered five years ago in an untouched tomb in Egypt's western desert. You died in approximately 1750 BC."

She opened her mouth, and though she struggled to speak, no sound emerged.

Jake continued. "You—or rather, your remains—were brought in as the final stage in a ten-year-long scientific experiment. The goal was to prove desiccated tissue could be returned to a near-living state. The tests began with microscopic life-forms and gradually progressed to plants and finally animals. When those tests proved successful, the next logical step was to try the process on human tissue. They started with small tissue samples, but eventually moved on to whole organs, and then..."

Despite knowing the answer, she had to ask. "And then what?"

He cleared his throat, his eyes focused on the curtains that hid the window. "Then you. The final phase of the experiments was reviving your mummified flesh."

She laughed. The sound started out as a harsh noise, but quickly escalated into giddy, uncontrolled guffaws that made her ribs ache and her eyes water. She couldn't stop it. Her mood was nothing close to happy, and yet the laughter tore out of her, sounding more like the wild cries of a hyena than the laughter of a human being. Although what Jake had said was ridiculous, it wasn't funny, not in the ho-ho sense. His claims had slid far beyond funny-strange and straight into clammy hands territory.

Wiping her damp palms on her coat, she said, "You have a sick sense of humor. What you're saying is not possible. If I'm an ancient Egyptian, why do I speak English and know about modern technology, like TVs and cars? I don't think King tut had a computer, but I know what a computer is. And how do I know your name?" She threw her hands in the air. "None of this makes sense."

"I know." Jake shook his head. "I can't explain any of it. You weren't supposed to even be alive, much less regain consciousness."

She folded her arms over her chest, lifting her chin as she said, "Your story doesn't add up."

Maybe she shouldn't have felt so proud of herself for pointing out the inconsistencies in his story. If Jake turned out to be a psychopath, then she might do better by placating him. She couldn't help it, though. Guess she was reckless, on top of her other flaws.

Jake's expression brightened. He almost smiled again as he raised a finger in triumph. "Of course. You understand the English language and modern technology because you could hear us talking. And I would leave the television or radio on for you when I left for the day. You must've absorbed the information you heard. They say coma patients can hear what's happening around them."

"According to you, I was dead until—" The bedside clock read 1:30 AM. Jake had said she'd woken up several hours ago, an unhelpfully vague estimation. "—until I woke up in your delightful tank. How could I have heard anything?"

"The electrodes on your body monitored electrical activity, including brain waves. The scientists saw barely perceptible activity, but they dismissed it as a calibration error. Your brain could've been alive, on a level that modern science doesn't recognize yet."

"You keep saying they, like you're not one of them, whoever they are."

"I'm not." He squirmed a little, fingering a loose thread on the bedspread. "I'm a grad student working on a master's in communications at the University of Nevada. A year ago, a group of scientists employed by Redeo Biotech contacted me asking for my help in documenting the final stages of their experiments in tissue regeneration via DNA repair. I had to sign a nondisclosure agreement, swearing me to secrecy until they make the experiments public—if they make them public."

A draft from the room's air conditioner wafted over her, sending a shiver through her body. She pulled her knees up so that the coat shielded them from the cool air. Her toes poked out from under the coat. Like her hands, her toes were freezing. She hugged herself, but gained only a modicum of warmth.

Jake picked up a plastic bag from the floor, tossing it to her. She caught the thin white bag, and it rustled from her touch. The bag featured the logo of a discount store, a name she didn't recognize. If she believed Jake's fairy tale, that would mean he and his scientist buddies never talked about this particular store while in the laboratory.

If she believed him. Which she absolutely did not.

Inside the bag, she found a pair of jeans, a powder-blue cotton shirt, white athletic socks, a pair of sneakers, pink cotton panties, and a tan bra. As far as the color choices, she assumed he'd grabbed whatever he saw first, most likely from a conveniently placed clearance rack. But the bra stopped her. She lifted it out of the bag, twirling it on its skinny plastic hanger.

"How do you know my size?" she asked.

Jake blushed. "The scientists took your measurements several times, to track the progress of the tissue regeneration and to watch out for any swelling or shrinkage that might indicate a problem with the process."

He spoke so rapidly she had to really focus to keep up with his words. She frowned at the bra. "And was it always men who took my measurements?"

"Um, uh, yes." He cleared his throat, his gaze virtually nailed to the loose thread on the bedspread. "The scientific team included two women, but they had other responsibilities."

"Right. Somehow the onerous duty of fondling the comatose woman always fell to one of the guys."

"It wasn't like that. They saw you as a test subject, closer to a colony of bacteria than a genuine human being."

Yeah, that didn't make her feel any better. Her stomach knotted. She gritted her teeth in an attempt to stop herself from chastising Jake. He looked earnestly ashamed of his colleagues' behavior.

The whole thing was ridiculous anyway. She was not a reconstituted mummy.

"You still don't believe me," Jake said. He grabbed his backpack off the floor, unzipped a pocket, and pulled out a tablet computer. It looked like the ones she'd seen in the lab. He queued up something on the screen and offered the tablet to her. "Maybe this will trigger your memory."

CHAPTER FOUR

SHE ACCEPTED THE TABLET, HOLDING IT WITH BOTH HANDS. THE screen displayed a photograph of an underground chamber that she recognized as an Egyptian tomb. She knew that from watching the History Channel or reading National Geographic, didn't she? She used her fingertips to pan the image and zoom in and out on portions of it. She scanned past objects in a far corner of the tomb. A familiar shape jumped out at her and she panned the image back to it. A chill washed over her. The object was a statue of a youthful man striding forth holding a staff in one hand.

And the statue's face resembled Jake's.

Not perfectly. Not as if they were the same person. Minor details differed, yet left enough in common that anyone looking at the statue, if they knew Jake, might remark on the similarities.

She stared at the image of the statue. Her mind went blank and fuzzy, although her eyes stayed sharply focused on the carved and painted wooden face.

Rahotep.

The word popped into her brain and she knew instantly it was a name. His name. The statue in the photo represented a man called Rahotep. No, it couldn't be true. She must've heard the name somewhere, probably from the chatty scientists in the lab. Like Jake had said, if coma patients could hear conversations around them, then she might have too.

Despite fearing the answer, she had to ask a question. She tapped the image on the screen and said, "Is this a statue of Rahotep?"

Jake glanced at the screen, and then at her, his eyes wide. "Yes it is."

"You guys must've talked about the statue, right? That's how I know the name."

He shook his head. "No one ever talked about the statue inside the lab. The scientists don't care about Egyptian artifacts. I know the name only because I talked with the archaeologists who found the tomb, but their data is still unpublished and unknown to anyone outside of the discovery team or the scientific project. The archaeologists signed a nondisclosure agreement, like I did." He pointed at the tablet screen. "You have no way of knowing that statue's name except by remembering it from when you were alive the first time. In ancient Egypt. You still have your memories, you simply can't access them at will."

"No. You're wrong."

"How do you explain it?"

She couldn't, and he must've realized that because a faint smile curved his lips.

Dropping the tablet on the bed, she snatched up the bag of clothing, leaped off the bed onto her feet, and scurried around the foot of the bed past Jake and into the bathroom. She shut the door, closing herself into the tiny space. Jake's words echoed in her brain, bouncing off the walls of her mind in an ever-increasing cacophony. She focused on removing her coat and socks, and then slipping into the items Jake had bought for her. They fit perfectly and they were comfortable. The shoes had cushiony insoles the felt like miniature clouds under her feet. Lord, it felt wonderful.

Well, she had to give Jake credit for one thing. He knew how to dress her.

Probably because he'd seen her naked.

A warm tingle danced down her spine. The thought of Jake looking at her nude body didn't bother her as much as she'd thought it would. In her mind, the picture switched from Jake's admiring gaze to the faces of all those scientists leering at her through her glass coffin. Ew. She didn't want to think about *that*.

Coffin. Why did she keep thinking of the tank as a coffin? Sure, the tank was shaped somewhat like a coffin. But it had been filled with pale blue liquid that tasted of chemicals, and it had sat inside a sterile scientific laboratory. Every time she thought of the tank, however, the word coffin sprang to mind.

Maybe because, until recently, she'd lain trapped inside a coffin.

She'd been dead. Dead people couldn't remember their own coffins.

Opening the door, she marched out of the bathroom and halted in front of the small sink area.

Jake took in her appearance and nodded. "Much better."

There went that warm tingling again. She bit her lip, choosing to stare at the wall behind Jake.

"Your hair needs work, though," he said, tossing her a hair brush.

She caught the brush and, thankful for an excuse to turn away from him, spun around to face the mirror above the sink. Her hair looked tangled and ratty. She fought to pull the brush through her locks, and eventually managed to tame the mess, at least a bit, so her hair no longer resembled a furnished apartment for rodents.

By the time she returned to the bed, taking a seat a few feet from Jake, he had queued up another image on the tablet. He tilted the screen toward her and said, "This is another tomb that was attached to yours by a corridor that had been sealed off sometime after construction. The archaeologists think the second tomb may have belonged to your husband or father."

The photo showed a tomb jam-packed with funerary objects, from statues to chests to canopic jars housing the deceased's embalmed organs. If she had seen other burials during her original lifetime, then that might explain why she thought of the glass tank as a coffin. On a subconscious level, she knew she had died. Therefore, she knew she must've wound up in a coffin inside a tomb.

It made sense. If she accepted that she was a reborn ancient.

"If that was my tomb in the other photo," she said, "how come you don't know my name? Egyptian tombs always had decorations naming the dead person. Right?"

"Yes. But sometimes the names were scratched out later. That's the case with your tomb and the adjacent tomb belonging to a male. He might've been Rahotep, the man depicted in the statue found in your tomb."

"Why would anyone scratch out our names?"

"The archaeologists told me it happened occasionally in ancient Egypt. Sometimes it was done for political reasons, sometimes for religious ones, and sometimes for reasons no one can determine yet. But erasing the name meant taking away the person's identity and essentially condemning their soul."

She was condemned. Wonderful. She wondered what a girl had to do to get her soul condemned. Then again, she probably didn't want to know. Right now, ignorance felt like a nice cozy blanket she intended to cling to for as long as possible.

Jake had left out one vital bit of information. Her stomach had already twisted into knots based on everything he just told her. She supposed the last piece of information couldn't be much worse.

Looking straight at him, she asked, "How did I come back to life?"

He shrugged.

She scowled.

Clearing his throat, he worked his lips as if trying to figure out how to speak. After a few seconds, he said, "I don't know. Not for certain. Maybe—I guess there could've been an electrical surge that jumpstarted your heart. I'm not a doctor or a scientist."

She thought back to the image of her tomb, and the canopic jars that held her embalmed organs. Clearly, her organs were in their proper places and working. Another hole in his story. She also recalled that Egyptian mummies had their brains removed. Yet another hole.

"Egyptian mummies," she said, her tone a little more condescending than she'd intended, "had their brains removed. Clearly, I've still got mine."

"You were a rare case of a mummy with its brain intact. Nobody knows why. When you were discovered, so intact and well preserved, the scientists at Redeo jumped on the opportunity."

"Okay, but what about my organs? Mummies had their internal organs removed and mummified separately—except the heart, which they left in place. I think I've got all my organs, or I wouldn't be walking or talking."

"Yours were the human organs the rehydrated before moving on to the final phase of the experiments." He pointed at her abdomen. "You can still see the scars from when they returned the organs to your body."

She glanced down at her belly, lifting her shirt. Several scars, faded now, slashed across her flesh in the appropriate places. She froze, her hand over one of the scars. Her ears rang. Darkness flickered at the edges of her vision. How had she gotten the scars? Multiple organ transplants or surgeries to repair damaged parts? Or was Jake right about her? The darkness crept closer and closer. She felt weak, lightheaded, and paralyzed. The ringing in her ears drowned out everything else.

Hands shook her. She heard Jake's voice, faint behind the ringing, urging her to breathe.

Breathing. Yes. She should be doing that. She sucked in one breath, then another.

"Slowly," Jake said, nearly shouting to make her here him over the ringing in her ears. "Deep, slow breaths."

She inhaled a careful breath and released it with equal care. She kept up the slow, deep breathing until the ringing subsided and the darkness retreated.

Jake sat right in front of her, inches away, his hands grasping her upper arms. She gazed into his eyes as she felt the warm tickle of his breath on her face. It triggered a wave of heat inside her that swept through her like a tidal wave. She looked at his mouth, and the thought of pressing her lips to his raced through her mind. She imagined the softness of his lips, the warmth of his flesh.

Jake let out a ragged breath.

She looked into his eyes again and she knew, in a way she could not explain, that he wanted to kiss her too.

He released her arms, sliding backward to get some distance from her. The indefinable aura of desire left him as quickly as it had come on, replaced by his favorite impassive expression.

"I realize the truth is quite a shock to you," he said, "and you've been through a lot today. We can't stay in one place too long, though, or they'll find us. We should get moving."

"Why do they want to kill me?"

"Because you're alive."

CHAPTER FIVE

J AKE WATCHED HER EXPRESSION AS IT MORPHED FROM confusion to frustration. The corners of her mouth tightened and her eyebrows first raised, and then knit together over the bridge of her nose. She looked beautiful even when annoyed, more beautiful than she had looked while lying in the tank, unaware and apparently dead. Oh, she had looked lovely then. He hated to admit it, but he'd found her enchanting in death—or near death, or whatever her true state had been. Hours had passed during which he did nothing but gaze at her face, somewhat blurred by the liquid that surrounded her, and wonder what she must've been like when alive.

She had been a princess, he'd decided. A daughter of the pharaoh, the greatest beauty in all the land, admired by noblemen and commoners alike. Every man had wanted to marry her. Every woman had wanted to become her. She was glorious, incandescent, awe inspiring. All right, he could admit to himself that his musings had turned into a rather sappy fantasy that no real woman could live up to. The reality of this woman, however, had left him flummoxed. She turned out to fall so far from his imagined princess that he wondered how he could still find her so enchanting.

Beautiful, yes, she was that. As for glorious, incandescent, and awe inspiring...

He found himself face to face with the most frustratingly suspicious and distrustful woman he'd ever met. Hadn't he saved her from drowning in the tank? Hadn't he helped her escape the laboratory before the scientists discovered she'd awakened? He'd bought her clothes, brought her to a decent motel where she could clean up a little. He intended to buy her a meal too, and take care of her until this situation was resolved. He had no idea how to resolve it, at least not yet, but he would figure it out. He must. After all he'd done for her, and everything he would do for her, how could she stare at him as if he were the worst kind of criminal?

Well, he had sedated her. He supposed that did give her good reason to mistrust him. And perhaps his fantasy of her, and her failure to live up to it, clouded his judgment a little.

"Why?" she asked, with that distrustful tone in her voice.

For a moment, he couldn't recall to what she was referring. He stared at her with an expression that must've bordered on utter blankness. Then he remembered and said, "Oh, you mean why would they kill you simply for being alive."

She rolled her eyes. "Duh."

He winced a little. No incandescent princess in this room. "There are laws against experimenting on human beings without their consent, so I'm sure that's part of the reason. You might sue them or have them arrested. But I think mainly they believe that if you're alive, it invalidates their research. The company has spent millions of dollars on this project and—"

"Why?" When he just stared at her, she sighed and said, "Why did they spend millions of dollars on trying to rehydrate desiccated tissue? What was the point?"

"To see if they could, I suppose. I gathered from what they said that it would be a huge discovery to find a way to make self-repairing DNA and use it to regenerate tissue. I think it has to do with reversing the aging process."

"Then why kill me? I'm the ultimate proof that they succeeded. The process works."

He gazed into her hazel eyes and realized for the first time that they looked different now. Life sparkled in them, a light that emanated from within her, from something science tried to dismiss but had always failed at explaining. The light came from her soul.

Folding her arms over her chest, she frowned at him. "Well?"

He shrugged. Really, he didn't know why they would kill her. He simply knew they would. Dr. Barnhart had told him as much. One day in the lab, Jake had casually asked what would happen if she woke up from her lifeless slumber. At first, Barnhart laughed it off as impossible.

"But if somehow she did wake up," Jake had replied, "what would happen? What would she be like? How would the world react?"

Barnhart's expression had turned dark. Frowning, the man rubbed his neck and made an odd face that seemed to Jake to convey discomfort.

"Pray she doesn't wake up, son," Barnhart said. "Because if she ever did, we would have to terminate the project. Besides, she would most likely be mentally defective to the point of being uncontrollable."

"What if she weren't? What if she were normal?"

The scientist shook his head. "Doesn't matter. Either way, they would kill her."

"If that's a joke—"

"It's no joke, Jake. They couldn't allow her to exist."

Despite asking more questions of Barnhart, Jake had received no more answers from the man. Barnhart clammed up so tightly it would've taken a crowbar to loosen his lips.

Jake's thoughts returned to the present, and his eyes refocused on the woman seated several feet away from him on the bed. A few minutes ago, he'd nearly kissed her. He'd wanted to, he'd considered it, and he'd chickened out at the last moment. It was wrong. He wanted his fantasy, and this woman had proved quite different from what he'd imagined. His desire probably stemmed from those fantasies, not from any feelings for this real woman.

No, he couldn't convince himself of that. The more time he spent with her, the more he liked this infuriating, suspicious, vibrant woman.

She waved a hand at him. "Are you awake over there?"

Barnhart's explanation had never satisfied Jake. On the surface, it seemed to answer the question. On closer inspection, though, it made little sense. Despite sensing another reason lurking beneath the surface, Jake had accepted Barnhart's rationale because, frankly, he never imagined the body in the tank would turn into a living woman.

"I need a name," she said, in a matter-of-fact tone.

"No one knows your name."

"Do you plan on yelling 'hey you' every time you need to get my attention?"

"I hadn't thought about it."

She crossed her arms again. "I need a name."

"Dawn," he said. "The ancient Egyptians believed the dawn was a time of rebirth. Appropriate, don't you think?"

"It'll do."

She smiled, just a little. Not enough to mean she'd forgiven him for sedating her, or even that she trusted him. Just enough to give him hope.

And more than anything right now, he needed hope.

———

SHE LAID HER HANDS ON THE BEDSPREAD AND STUDIED THEM. THE smooth skin. The creases of her knuckles. The shiny pink nails with neatly trimmed whites. Who had trimmed her nails? The scientists, she supposed. Or maybe her nails hadn't grown during her regeneration period in the tank. She had so many questions, but at least now she had a name.

Dawn.

She might not have chosen that name for herself. Hearing it from Jake, though, she found it appealed to her more than if she'd thought of it. The name sounded plain to her. When Jake spoke it, and told her what it meant, something about the tone of his voice and the look on his face made her feel the name. Feel the truth of it. The rightness of it. She was Dawn.

At least until she learned her original name. Even then, she might keep this one.

"Dawn," Jake repeated, as if the single syllable tasted good to him.

A shiver snaked down her spine. Not fear. Not revulsion. A good shiver. A cool tingling that made her skin prickle. She longed to move closer to him, but figured if he'd felt the same way then he wouldn't have squirmed away from her. He had wanted to kiss her. A few minutes ago, she'd felt certain of it. In this moment, though, she felt nothing close to certainty. About anything. Particularly about Jake.

She folded her legs under her, sitting cross-legged with her hands on her knees. "Why did you leave the radio on for me? When I was, you know, dead."

"I don't know. I guess I thought you might be lonely."

"I was a corpse."

"You looked alive." He stared straight into her eyes. "Sometimes I would talk to you. Read to you."

Another shiver coursed through her, this one less pleasant than the first. Jake had sat beside a glass coffin talking to a dead body. It was sort of creepy, and yet kind of sweet. In a creepy way. This whole situation—dead mummy girl reconstituted and mysteriously awakened, on the run with a strange grad student—was creepy and bizarre in ways she couldn't verbalize.

At the same time, she felt inexplicably comfortable with Jake. And inexplicably drawn to him.

Maybe she did hear everything he said while she was...dead.

A phrase popped into her mind and she said, "Glorious princess, daughter of the sun."

Jake's eyes widened. His face blanched. "What did you say?"

"Is that some ancient Egyptian title? Was I a princess?"

"No," Jake replied, drawing out the word as if unsure he'd chosen the right one. "Not that I know of."

He still looked pale and wide eyed.

"What?" she said. "What's wrong with you?"

"I, uh, well…" He coughed, glancing around the room. After a few seconds, he looked at her. "That's what I used to call you. My glorious princess, daughter of the sun. I—it was—" Words seemed to fail him and he shook his head, shutting his eyes. "I'm sure that makes me sound like the psychopath you think I am."

"I don't think you're a psychopath." And at the instant she said those words, she realized it was true. Damn, how bizarre that she'd begun to trust him. "But I don't understand. Why would you call me that, and why would you talk and read to me?"

He lowered his head, refusing to meet her gaze.

The truth hit her with near-physical force. She gasped. "Did you have a crush on me? Dead me?"

His head jerked up, his intent gaze locked on hers. "I am not a necrophiliac. I don't lust after dead flesh. You looked so alive, as if you might wake up at any moment." He paused, his gaze seeming to bore into her, igniting sparks inside her. "And then you did."

She jumped off the bed and onto her feet. Marching around the foot of the bed, she stopped directly in front of Jake. He turned his whole body to face her, and his knees brushed against hers. She fought against the warmth rising inside her, because she felt completely capable of losing all sense of reason if this man touched her. Still, she didn't back away from him. Her traitorous body refused to move. She believed he cared for her, at least in the way you might care for an abandoned puppy. But how could he have any real feelings for her? Although he might be physically attracted to her, he had really only known her since she woke up in the lab earlier today.

Hell, she barely knew herself.

He took her hands in his, and the warmth of his skin chased away the chill in her fingers. She hadn't even noticed her hands were cold until he touched her.

"Look at me," he said, his tone not quite demanding, yet not quite a request either. When she complied, he squeezed her hands. "I want to help you. I want to protect you. Do you believe me?"

Yes, she wanted to say, but instead she shrugged.

He stood, narrowing the gap between them to mere inches. Though she tried to back away, he grasped her shoulders in his firm grip.

"Sooner or later," he said, "you'll realize I'm on your side. I only hope it's not too late."

He bent his head close to hers. His breath tickled her lips. She stared into his eyes, so close to hers that if she blinked her lashes would probably brush against his.

"You're more than a body," he whispered, "more than the specimen. You're a human being. A woman."

He pressed his lips to hers. Desire flashed through her, hot and liquid, devouring her reason like a fire consuming oxygen.

The door exploded inward.

CHAPTER SIX

J AKE SPUN TOWARD THE DOOR, SHOVING HER BEHIND HIM. THE door bounced off the doorstop as a tall man walked into the room. He stopped six feet away, and two more men entered the room after him, taking up positions slightly behind and to either side of the first man. Two more men lingered outside the door. All except the leader wore military-style camouflage fatigues with semiautomatic handguns strapped to their belts. The leader wore an expensive-looking dark blue suit with a crisp white shirt and dark blue tie. His shoes looked like alligator skin. Wrinkles scored his tanned skin, which accentuated the paleness of his blonde hair. The man squinted, fixing his dark eyes on Jake.

She tried to step out from behind Jake, but he thrust an arm out to hold her back.

"Leave her alone, Saxon," Jake told the man.

Saxon shook his head. "She doesn't belong to you. All test subjects are the property of Redeo Biotech Incorporated."

She saw a muscle tick in Jake's jaw as he spoke through clenched teeth. "She is a human being."

"It is a formerly desiccated specimen returned to a lifelike condition through a series of proprietary chemical, biological, and technological processes. What you perceive as personality and intellect are, in fact, nothing more than random biochemical reactions in the brain that mimic humanity. Those reactions will dissipate the longer she—it—is, for lack of a better word, awake."

"No."

Saxon smiled. The expression sent a chill through her. She met the man's cold gaze and said, "I don't understand. Why are you so hell-bent on keeping me?"

"If the process truly worked, and self-repairing DNA is a reality, then can you imagine the possibilities? Countless people would pay exorbitant prices in order to not simply halt the aging process, but reverse it. Eternal youth, and eternal life, may become possible—at least for those with the money to finance it. Your autopsy will provide all the data we need to move forward with the project."

Jake clenched his hands into fists. "You are not going to cut her open."

"You have two choices, Jake," the other man said. He gestured to his goons, who responded by drawing their weapons, aiming them at Jake and Dawn. "Hand her over to me voluntarily, or be shot in the head and I'll take her anyway."

Dawn looked at the closest goon, meeting his gaze. "Would you really murder someone because your boss tells you to?"

Saxon waved a hand in a dismissive gesture. "They do as I say, nothing more and nothing less."

Autopsy. Bullet to the head. She wasn't sure which option sounded worse.

Saxon pointed at Jake. "Choose. Her or your life."

Jake snorted. "I'm sure if I cooperate, you'll let me go."

"No, but I will keep you alive. Your documentary skills are not indispensible, but it would take time to find another weak-willed fool to take over your duties."

Jake flinched at the term weak-willed. Dawn laid a hand on his still-outstretched arm, the one that barred her from passing him, and squeezed gently. She hoped he understood the gesture as one of support for him, and disavowal of Saxon's comment. She could not think of Jake as weak-willed. He seemed quite certain of, and intent on, his goal—to protect her.

Since she couldn't tell him that right now, she squeezed his arm again. Moving only his eyes, he glanced down at her for a brief moment.

"How sweet," Saxon said. "You've grown attached to the specimen. Is she good in bed? Is that why you want to keep her?"

Jake didn't speak. His entire body went stiff, and he lowered his arm.

"Giving in so easily?" Saxon asked. He took a step closer.

Faster than her brain could interpret what she saw, Jake swung his arm behind his back, reached under his shirt, and pulled out his revolver. He raised the gun at Saxon.

A gunshot exploded inside the room.

Her ears rang from the concussion, drowning out all other sound.

Jake jerked, and seemingly in slow motion, crumpled to the floor at her feet, face-down. His gun tumbled across the carpet. She flung herself toward it.

In the instant her body hit the floor, a pair of strong, hard arms seized her around the waist. Her fingers grazed the revolver's grip as Saxon hauled her off the carpet. Her feet dangled in the air. He clutched her to his body, her head level with his. Those powerful arms pinned hers to her body. Though she flailed her legs, the kicks struck hard muscles that seemed to absorb the energy.

She felt vibrations in Saxon's chest as he issued orders to his men. The ringing still overwhelmed her hearing. As one of the man passed close to her, she noticed some kind of high-tech ear plugs in his ears. Saxon transferred her to the equally strong grip of one of his goons. She struggled against them both, but to no avail. She lacked the muscle strength, probably because until recently she had been a desiccated corpse.

Saxon withdrew a small, flat box from his pocket. Popping open the box, he brought out a syringe.

They were going to kill her. Right now. Put her down like a rabid dog.

She glanced at Jake, lying on his side, motionless, on the floor. A red stain had spread across his shirt. Alive or dead, she couldn't tell.

With more care than she would've expected, Saxon inserted the needle into her flesh and depressed the plunger. Clear liquid was injected into her.

The room spun.

And then she was gone.

WHITE LIGHT BLINDED HER. DAWN SQUINTED AT THE BRILLIANCE, then realized she was not blinded after all. Sterile white lights did burn all around her, but the whiteness she stared into was the ceiling. She tried to sit up. Restraints bound her wrists and ankles, and a strap across her forehead held her head in place.

She lay on a metal table. Though she caught only glimpses of the shining metal, she felt its cold, hard surface beneath her. A ventilation system whirred overhead. She was in a laboratory. Not the same one as before. This one probably lay in the same facility, though, since Jake's boss had brought her here. She was still clothed in the outfit and shoes Jake had bought her.

Jake. The last time she'd seen him, he'd been dead or dying from a gunshot wound.

Sooner or later, you'll realize I'm on your side. I only hope it's not too late.

He'd been right. She realized now he had tried to help her—he'd gotten shot trying to protect her—but she understood it far too late.

A shuffling sound originated from beyond the head of the table, out of her line of sight. She struggled to turn her head. The strap proved too snug.

Someone coughed.

"Who's there?" she said.

A man scuffled into view. He halted beside the table, leaned over her torso, and flashed a penlight in her eyes. She winced. He placed his thumb under her right eye and his index finger on her upper lid, and then peeled her eyelids apart to shine the light in her eye. Giving a little harrumph, he repeated the procedure with her left eye. As dark spots danced in her vision, the man straightened, standing alongside her right arm.

"Pupil response is normal," he said.

She glared at the scruffy, gray-haired man. He wore a lab coat but no name tag, a dress shirt but no tie, and glasses attached to a chain around his neck. Taking off the glasses, he let them flop onto his chest. She felt his cold fingers wrap around her wrist, checking her pulse.

"Ninety-eight," he pronounced.

"Who are you?"

As he released her wrist, the man focused his light brown eyes on her. After several seconds, he shrugged and said, "Won't matter if you know, I guess, considering. I'm Dr. Barnhart."

"Considering what?"

"You'll find out soon enough."

She thought back on everything Jake had told her. "You're going to kill me. Why haven't you done it already?"

Barnhart sighed, and his shoulders sagged. "I needed to run a few tests first. Once I've completed my examination, the specimen will be prepared for dissection."

"I am not a specimen." Spittle peppered him as she spoke. Her heart beat so fast that she felt lightheaded. "I'm a human being. I have rights."

Shaking his head, Barnhart gave her a sad look. "No, my dear, I'm afraid not. You are the property of Redeo Biotech and they need to know whether their process works, and if so, why and how well. Those answers can only come from an autopsy."

A shiver tingled down her spine. Autopsy. Dissection. Oh yeah, she knew what those words meant. And finally, she understood that Jake had told her the truth from the start. These people, these so-called scientists, would kill her.

"It won't hurt," Barnhart assured her. "I'll give you something to knock you out, and then I'll administer the lethal injection. You won't feel a thing. I hope that's some consolation to you."

"No," she hissed through clenched teeth, "it's really not."

Barnhart shuffled to a cart at the foot of the table. He picked up a bottle of clear liquid and a syringe.

"I'm alive," she said, "I'm a person. This is murder."

He glanced at her over his shoulder. "It's not as if you have a soul. That sort of thing doesn't exist. The human psyche is nothing more than biochemical reactions in the brain."

"Bullshit."

The soul existed. She knew it. She felt it. Her own soul, that indefinable thing that made her an individual, she felt it inside her. It *was* her.

The ancient Egyptians had believed in the soul—not merely one soul, but several that combined to make a person. One aspect of the soul, known as the *ba*, wandered among the living after death. The ancients had mummified the dead because the *ba* needed to return to the body at night, reemerging at dawn to walk the living world. If her soul had traveled in the daytime, over thousands of years, then that might explain how she knew so much about the modern world. She had witnessed it firsthand.

Apparently, somewhere between Jake kissing her and waking up in this sterile room, she'd decided to believe she was an ancient Egyptian reborn via modern technology. She didn't believe it because Jake told her to. She believed it because she felt the truth of it, crazy as the truth might have been.

Now if only she could remember her birth name.

Dawn would do just fine for the time being. She liked the way Jake said the name, as if it were a sacred word, yet not so sacred that he couldn't speak it or touch her. Oh yes, he felt free to touch her all right.

An image flashed in her mind. Jake, lying facedown and motionless on the floor of the motel room. Dead? She couldn't say for sure.

"Where is Jake?" she asked.

Barnhart, having drawn a dose of the liquid into the syringe, tapped out the bubbles. "I don't know. Saxon took him away."

"Is he alive?"

Barnhart shrugged.

She must find Jake. She must tell him he'd been right all along. She must tell him...

Nothing. She would tell him nothing, because she was strapped to a metal table about to be put down like a stray dog.

So what, she would lie here waiting for it to happen? Like hell. She did not get resurrected just so she could die again.

CHAPTER SEVEN

BARNHART STEPPED UP BESIDE HER, SYRINGE IN HAND. HE took hold of her arm and rotated it to expose the flesh in the crease of her elbow. He lowered the syringe toward her skin. She twitched her arm. The needle popped out of Barnhart's grasp. It hit the floor with a soft click.

Sighing, Barnhart plucked the syringe from the floor. "Fighting won't help. You're incapacitated, my dear, so please let me get this over with."

Something in the tone of his voice bothered her. It sounded almost like remorse.

He lowered the syringe. Its tip nicked her flesh.

"Archimedes four-five-two," she said.

Barnhart froze. He slowly turned his eyes to stare at her. "What?"

"It's your computer password. Archimedes four-five-two."

"How do you…"

"I know a lot of things I shouldn't, if my psyche is nothing more than biochemical reactions." Her voice morphed into a harsh whisper, imbued with all the desperation roiling inside her. "I have a soul. While everyone thought I was a dead husk, my soul explored this world and this facility. More and more of what I saw and learned is coming back to me. You can't kill me. *I am alive.*"

He stared at her for so long without moving that she wondered if he'd suffered a stroke. When he finally spoke, his voice trembled ever so slightly.

"I don't—you can't—" He stumbled backward, dropping the syringe. "I have to consult with Saxon on this."

"He'll say to kill me, right? But you're a scientist. Don't you want to study a living, breathing example of the soul's immortality?"

Barnhart bumped into the wall. He sagged against it, his face pale.

"Don't you at least want to know," she said, "how I found out your password?"

He said nothing, but his jaw quivered.

She pressed on, praying her words meant something to him. "Imagine what you could learn by studying my living brain."

He trudged toward her, halting near her arm. He bent down, picked up the syringe, and took hold of her arm.

Her pulse thundered in her ears. She felt nauseous and lightheaded, terrified beyond description.

Barnhart tossed the needle aside. It struck the floor, skidding across the smooth surface.

Tears stung her eyes as he unfastened the restraints on her wrists and then her ankles. When he released the strap over her forehead, she felt the tears dribble down her cheeks.

Barnhart backed away from the table. He waved a hand toward the door. "Go."

She leaped off the table. "Thank you."

"Don't. You still have to get out of the building." He slid a hand into his pocket and brought out a badge like the one Jake had used to get them out of the building the first time. "Take this. It might help. The nearest exit is—"

"I know where it is."

She took the badge and fled through the open door.

Footsteps clapped behind her.

She spun around to find Barnhart jogging up to her. He held a semiautomatic handgun, which he offered to her. Taking the weapon, she muttered another thank you, tucked the gun inside her waistband under her shirt, and bolted down the hallway.

Without thinking, she followed a path down the maze of corridors, around corners, and straight to a door marked with an exit sign. It was not the same door Jake had taken her through, but somehow she had known where to find this exit. She no longer questioned the things she knew, because it all made a bizarre kind of sense, now that she'd accepted the truth. During her millennia-long sleep, which modern scientists called death, she had explored the world. Watched its changes. Learned its new ways. And while imprisoned in this facility, her spirit had explored its confines as well.

She reached out to swipe the badge in the reader mounted beside the door.

"I wouldn't," a voice said behind her.

Even as she turned around, she knew whose face she would see. It was Saxon, backed up by his goons. And beside him, hunched and pale, stood Jake.

"Well," Saxon said, a smirk tightening his lips, "you are a persistent specimen, aren't you?"

"I am not a specimen." She glanced at Jake, at his blanched face and slumped shoulders, at his red eyes and pallid lips, and at the maroon stain on his shirt. Her heart thudded.

"Oh, he'll live," Saxon told her. "The bullet hit no major organs or arteries. My men don't kill without my express permission. Actually, they don't do much of anything without my express permission. And I thought Jake might prove useful as leverage, in case Barnhart succumbed to his compassionate side. It's a miniscule component of his personality, but it's there nonetheless. Apparently, I was correct to worry."

She couldn't speak. Her eyes refused to look away from Jake, who met her gaze with his own hollow one. He looked defeated. Half dead. Not from his wound, apparently, but from resignation.

Saxon shook his head in mock sympathy. "The specimen is in love. How sad. Do you really think Jake—or any man—could love you? After all, you're not entirely human anymore, not after we inserted foreign DNA into your genome. You've got a bit of tardigrade, a hair of nematode, a touch of frog—"

"Shut up," she hissed.

"Go back to your tank," Saxon said, "and I'll have someone patch up Jake. I'll even let him leave the facility, go back to his normal life."

Dawn scowled at him. "Sure you will."

He shrugged. "That's the deal, take it or leave it. If you leave it, be advised that Jake will die."

One chance. She had one solitary, insane chance to escape from this hellhole.

The insane had turned out to be right so far.

She thrust a hand under her shirt, yanked out the gun, lifted it in front of her, and fired straight at Saxon's chest once, twice, three times.

The man jerked, crumpling to the floor.

For a moment, the goons didn't move, their expressions stunned. In that moment, Jake sprang to life. He raced toward her, snatched the badge from her hand, and swiped it through the reader. The door unlocked with a thunk. Jake shoved the door open.

Dawn grasped his hand. They rushed out the door, slamming it behind them.

They had exited into a parking lot illuminated by dim sodium-vapor bulbs perched on squat poles. No wonder she hadn't seen the lights from the other side of the building. The structure itself had blocked them from view. Within the lot, neatly parked inside the outlined spaces, stood two rows of black SUVs, each emblazoned with the Redeo

Biotech logo, the same logo she had recognized on the vehicle Jake appropriated for their first getaway.

Jake dragged her to the nearest vehicle. He tried to get in on the driver's side, but she motioned for him to go around to the passenger door. When he balked, she said, "You're in no condition to drive.'"

Without a word, he trotted to the passenger side door and got in. She jumped into the driver's seat, pulling the door shut after her. She knew to find the keys tucked under the sun visor. Jamming the key into the ignition, she cranked it. The engine started with a grumble.

The exit door they'd just come out of burst open, unleashing a swarm of armed guards. As she yanked the gear shift lever into drive and floored the accelerator, shots exploded outside the vehicle. The SUV lurched forward. The tires found traction, and the vehicle rocketed across the parking lot.

The side window in the backseat shattered.

In the rearview mirror, she watched the human figures and the boxy vehicle shapes recede. Headlights popped on, telling her the guards intended to pursue them. She knew a trick or two, though, now that she'd stopped fighting the truth about herself. Knowledge gleaned from her spiritual expeditions returned to her faster and faster each moment. She knew this world. She knew it better than most of the people who had lived in it their entire lives. Her afterlife of exploration gave her unique access to, and a unique perspective on, this world.

Down the gravel road they sped. Jake slumped in the passenger seat, cradling his right arm. The blood stain on his shirt was on the right side. The bullet must've hit near his shoulder, the way he was holding his arm.

"Are you okay?" she asked.

"I'll make it."

"I'm taking you to a hospital."

He jerked upright, wincing. "No, they'll report a gunshot wound to the police."

"Good, we need the police involved in this." She swerved off the gravel road, heading across the desert, avoiding cactuses as the vehicle rushed onward. They had lost their pursuers, she felt certain. She knew this desert better than they did.

"Where are you going?" Jake asked, his tone wary.

"I know a shortcut." When he scrunched his eyebrows at her, she smiled. "Trust me. I trusted you to get me out of the lab the first time. It's my turn to help you."

"Okay." He gave her a weak smile. "I trust you."

She glanced at him sideways. His color looked better, but still she worried. "Are you sure you're okay?"

"Yes." He stared at her in the way that sent hot tingles through her. "I'm feeling much better since you rescued me."

Resisting the urge to lean over and kiss him, she said, "You still have a bullet in you. I am taking you to a hospital."

"First, we need to make a stop."

"Where?"

"I'll show you." He settled back into his seat. "I buried something under a freeway overpass not far from here, just in case."

"Buried what?"

"Evidence." He flashed her a real smile. "A flash drive that holds all the video recordings I made while working at the laboratory. Plus a few files I purloined from their computer systems. It should be enough to convince the police that Redeo Biotech is up to no good."

Dawn maneuvered the car onto a two-track road, veering left. Then she leaned over to plant a kiss on Jake's lips. As she returned her attention to the road, he laid a hand on her thigh.

"Saxon was wrong, you know," he said. "Someone can love you."

She didn't dare speak. The tears that stung her eyes might overflow into a fit of weeping if she tried.

"You are more than a human being," Jake said. "You're a beautiful, amazing woman."

"With tardigrade DNA."

"I don't care."

The car jounced over a pothole. She gripped the wheel tighter. "Tardigrades are microscopic creatures that—"

"I know what they are." He squeezed her thigh. "I just don't care. Whatever you've got in your DNA, you wear it well."

A blush fired up in her cheeks. In a hushed voice, she said, "Thanks."

He leaned his head back against his seat's headrest, leaving his hand on her thigh.

She bit the inside of her lip, then asked, "What if I turn into a zombie or a vampire or something?"

Jake chuckled.

"It's not so far-fetched," she said. "I am a resurrected ancient mummy with frog DNA. Anything seems possible at this point."

He took a deep breath, leaned close to her ear, and murmured, "Whatever happens, I'm with you. Forever."

"That's a long time, especially for a reconstituted mummy girl."

His lips grazed her ear as he said, "Reconstituted mummy *woman*."

She stared straight ahead at the road, knowing exactly where it led and what turns she must execute, though not knowing precisely when she'd gained the knowledge. It felt strange to trust instincts that seemed to stem from nowhere. She was getting used to feeling strange. And she was getting used to having Jake with her.

"We'll get your flash drive," she told him. "Then we're off to the hospital, whether you like it or not. And after that we go…"

"Into the future. Together."

She smiled. "Sounds good to me."

REBORN TO BURN

CHAPTER ONE

HANDS CLAMPED ON THE STEERING WHEEL, DAWN stared out the windshield at the interstate unrolling beneath the SUV and marveled at how a three-thousand-year-old woman such as herself could understand so little about life. Maybe because she was dead for most of those years. Mere hours ago, she'd languished inside a glass tank in a scientific laboratory, a specimen devoid of life. Now she hunched in the driver's seat of a stolen SUV. A fugitive. Confused, adrift.

But not alone.

She glanced at her companion. Her heart sank into her stomach. Jake's muscular body slumped in the passenger seat, his pallor tinged with a jaundiced overtone. "How's the shoulder?"

"Fine." He shifted position, twisting his shoulder, and winced. Raking a hand through chestnut hair, he winced again. "I told you it's a flesh wound."

Images unreeled in her mind—a motel room, Jake's lips on hers, the door bursting inward. Commandos flooding into the room, driven by orders from Redeo Biotech. A gunshot exploding. Jake tumbling to the floor. Blood on his shirt, near his heart. Then Saxon, a vicious man, shoved a needle into her neck, plunging her into darkness.

She checked the rearview mirror. Nothing there. Yet the hairs on her neck stiffened, as goose bumps prickled her arms. Maybe she was paranoid. Then again, a team of brutal pseudo-soldiers pursued them at this very moment, and despite her success in shaking them off her tail, they would be back.

Jake's cinnamon-colored eyes focused on her, though with a bleariness that shot ice through her veins. He nodded toward her right hand. "How's your cut?"

"Screw my itty-bitty cut. You've got a bullet wound, for crying out loud." But her finger did burn like someone held a lit match to it. Paper cuts were evil. In the future, she'd exercise more caution when handling road maps. She wiggled the finger, spotting a bead of blood on the cut, and shoved it in her mouth to lick it clean. When she withdrew the finger, she froze.

The blood was gone, yes. But so was the cut. More than healed, the wound vanished with no trace, not even a faint scar. Impossible.

Oh for heaven's sake. The cut had been teeny, more of a scrape than a slice. She couldn't see a mark because it had been nothing to begin with.

"Everything okay?" Jake asked.

The tension in his voice reeled her back into reality. "Relax, I'm fine. Where is this flash drive of yours anyway?"

"I told you, I buried it under a freeway overpass, along with some cash and a few other supplies. When we get to the right place, I'll tell you."

"And you're sure the flash drive has enough damning evidence to shut down Redeo."

"Yes, I'm positive."

She steered the car up the onramp, onto the interstate. A handful of other vehicles fanned out ahead of and behind their SUV. The night unfurled all around them, into the sky glittering with stars, and out toward the cardinal directions in a desert landscape concealed by the darkness. The streetlamps posted in the vicinity of the onramp retreated behind them, and the night swallowed everything beyond the reach of the headlights. The other traffic dwindled, abandoning them on the interstate.

Exhaustion settled over her, heavy and inescapable. She hauled in a deep breath. She couldn't rest. One of them must remain in control, and with Jake's injury, that left her in charge.

Crap. What qualified her to take command, of anything? A reconstituted mummy girl with vague recollections of a past life in ancient Egypt. Her knowledge of the modern world, gleaned from the her wanderings as a disembodied soul, proved much sharper. But she might not recall as much she'd need to if she intended to keep them both safe.

Headlights popped on close behind. She threw up a hand to shield her eyes. What was this idiot doing? He must've driven with his lights off until he got within yards of their SUV.

Her pulse raced. No one would do that unless —

Shit.

Jake lurched forward, grimacing as he twisted his body to squint at the back window. "It's them."

"Why don't they kill us and get it over with?"

"They need your brain undamaged. An auto accident would be...messy."

"Charming. But a few hours ago, you said they'd kill me simply for being alive."

"That's when Saxon was in control. He's gone."

A chill shimmied through her. Saxon was gone because she'd killed him, to save Jake. Her finger had pulled the trigger, and a part of her wondered whether she'd swapped his life for her own.

"Trust me," Jake said, "the other scientists at Redeo understand the importance of examining an intact, resurrected brain."

"Great, I feel much better." She pushed the SUV harder. The other car, its shape invisible behind the glare of the headlights, receded in the mirror.

"It won't be that easy."

"I know," she snapped. Redeo Biotech had created her, in a way, and they despised giving up anything they owned. "What would you like me to do?"

"Drive faster."

"You said that wouldn't help."

"No, I said it wouldn't be that easy." When she opened her mouth to protest, he laid a hand on her shoulder. "Use your knowledge. Most of us born into this world don't know it as well as you do. Tap into what you learned during your soul journeys." He gave her shoulder a light squeeze. "And *drive faster*. It'll buy us a little time."

She rammed her foot down on the accelerator. The car shot forward, pinning her to the seat. The steering wheel shimmied, and she gripped it tighter. The headlights of the other vehicle shrank in the mirror. She released the breath trapped in her lungs.

Headlights surged closer. A powerful engine snarled behind them.

Electric ice zapped through her, clenching her hands and quickening her breaths. So much for buying time.

She stomped her foot on the accelerator.

The other vehicle snarled, revving its engine.

Blood thundered in her ears. Every muscle in her body went rigid.

The other car slammed into them with an explosive crunch. The concussion flung her forward. She clung to the wheel as it jerked in her hands. *Christ, no.* The seatbelt gouged into her, radiating pains through her chest. She gasped, gritted her teeth, and held on.

An object thunked in the center console. Her gaze flicked to the cup holder, and Jake's gun stashed there.

The attacker barreled his car into them a second time. Their SUV fishtailed. She fought to control the wheel, but the SUV fishtailed again. Skidded sideways. Thwacked over a bump.

And spun out into the night.

CHAPTER TWO

THE METALLIC ODOR OF GUN OIL SATURATED JAKE'S SENSES as he roused from near unconsciousness. Thoughts wavered in his brain, ghosts of memory and recognition. He squinted into the gloom inside the car. The dashboard lights had extinguished, the headlights too. A blunt object poked into his temple. He lay crumpled on his side, hips twisted, one arm entangled in the seatbelt, which had popped free of its latch.

He sensed toxic threads wending their way through his bloodstream, eating away at his body. Infection? No, the Redeo doctors injected him with antibiotics—or so they'd said. They might've given him anything and he wouldn't have known the difference. Strapped to a table, he couldn't stop them either.

He struggled to move, to touch the object jammed into his temple. His muscles ignored his commands. He gritted his teeth, willing his body to move. Nothing. If he were injured to the point of paralysis, wouldn't he experience pain?

A blade of ice lanced through him. *No pain.* Even his limited medical knowledge, gleaned from listening to scientists chatter to each other, warned him what a lack of pain meant. A hard ball congealed in his gut.

"Jake?"

His name jolted him back to the present, dragging his attention to the driver's door. Craning his neck, the only part of his body he could move, he strained to see in the moonlight bleeding in through the open door. A figure slumped there, arms outstretched across the driver's seat. The pale light shimmered on Dawn's dark red hair, igniting streaks of fire within the locks. Her creamy skin glowed, as if lit by a heavenly gleam. He couldn't make out her expression, but the frantic way her fingers clawed for him set off a blistering chill.

He rasped, "Are you all right?"

"Yes." She hauled herself up a little, close enough to slide a hand across his cheek. Her skin burned on his. Lord, his body temperature must've plummeted more than he realized. Her fingers trembled, questing for signs of injury. "What about you? Your gunshot wound. The accident." She exhaled a shaky breath. "You're so cold."

The naked fear in her voice made his jaw clench harder, shooting pangs through his head. The rest of him floated in a cloud of eerie numbness. Though he despised needing to tell her, she must know the truth. To prepare for the inevitable. "I can't move. Or feel anything, except in my head and neck."

Her fingers, her entire body, stilled. "Oh."

The utter blankness in her tone made his heart ache. He should've protected her. He should've formulated a plan, instead of running off one-tenth cocked, fleeing into the unknown with a woman hunted by his former employers. A woman who'd been born and died in ancient Egypt, gotten mummified, and three thousand years later wound up as a specimen in a scientific laboratory. The woman he adored.

Yet he'd known her for a matter of hours.

He longed for her skin on his, even a light caress, to experience the thrill of familiarity that always coursed through him at her touch. A connection bound them, on a level so profound he couldn't fathom its depths.

Dawn crawled over the seat and bent to peer down at his face. Her long hair brushed across his skin. It smelled of soap—and blood. His blood.

He ground his teeth. She'd risked her life to rescue him from Redeo. And he thought he could save her? Getting shot, yeah, that protected her all right. Now he lay paralyzed. He was useless.

She lifted his head and deposited it on the arm rest of the center console. The plastic chilled his cheek. Her hand dived down into the cup holder, snatching up the object his face had rested on a second earlier. The semiautomatic handgun looked blocky in her delicate hand.

Odd how he'd stopped worrying about his paralysis. The world drifted further and further from him each second. Though his surroundings hovered as close as ever, his attachment to the world weakened. He sensed his energy, his life, siphoning out of him little by little.

Dawn stuffed the gun in her waistband and grasped his face in both hands. "Don't you give up on me. I won't allow it."

The depth of emotion electrifying her voice astonished him. He probed the vague, pale shape of her face, but the gloom foiled his efforts to make out her expression. Why did she trust him? Or care what happened to him? When they'd first met, he'd knocked her out with sedatives because she asked too many questions he couldn't answer.

No, he could've answered. Fear held him back, fear of what she'd think of him if she knew he'd sat by her tank in the lab, talking to her lifeless remains. So he drugged her. Hauled her off to a motel. And then, finally, confessed everything.

He was a coward. He knew this.

"Do you hear me?" she demanded, jiggling his head, jarring his brain. "You cannot die on me."

"Blood loss doesn't mix well with blunt-force trauma, but I'll try."

A shaft of moonlight illuminated her face as she bent nearer, her eyes narrowed but glistening with unshed tears. "Do more than try, dammit. You're all I've got, and you are not leaving me."

Regret stabbed into him at her words, at the anger and desolation of her tone. She was begging him to stay, and God, but he wanted to. But the numbness overtook him again, swallowing the impulse to act. Her eyes transfixed him with their gleaming golden irises, flecked with emerald dust. The eyes of a princess. Or maybe a commoner. He had no idea what her station was in her first life, but in this one she perched atop a throne he'd erected for her. His incandescent princess. Dawn. He'd christened her with the name, when she demanded to have one. The memory tugged at his lips, almost forming a smile.

A tear dripped onto his mouth. Salty. Bitter.

"Don't look like that," she hissed.

"Like what?"

Her nose bumped his, and her lashes fluttered across lids. "Like you're about to say goodbye. I told you I *won't allow it*."

"Yes, ma'am." Strange how his words slurred. "But I'm afraid I can't comply with..."

His voice trailed away, as his mind tumbled toward darkness.

Dawn slapped his cheek. "Wake up, dammit!"

His lids flew open. Her eyes locked on his, and something inside her plunged into him, towing his consciousness back from the brink. At least it felt that way. Did she possess supernatural abilities? Gazing into her eyes, mesmerized and yet enlivened by them, he wondered.

Pain flashed in his chest, spiraling out from the gunshot wound. An intense ache bit into his legs and gnawed its way up into his torso. He sucked in a breath. Not paralyzed after all. Spikes of agony racked his body. Paralysis sounded damn good as he squeezed words out between his teeth. "God almighty."

"What is it?"

"I can feel again." He fought to keep his tone calm, despite his panting breaths. "I need a minute to get used to having nerves again."

She stroked his hair, infusing him with her warmth, engulfing him in her scent. Sweet. Earthy. Wonderful. Relaxing into her touch, he managed to catch his breath at last.

"We have to get out of here," she said. "Those Redeo creeps will find us any minute."

"I know." He cradled his arm. Pain sliced through his shoulder, stealing his breath. "We'd better get moving again, fast."

"The car won't start."

Shit. "We have to walk."

Her fingers slipped into his hair, massaging his scalp. "Can you walk?"

"Yes." Conviction toughened his voice, despite the quivering in his limbs. "There's no other way."

She brushed a kiss across his lips. "Let's get moving."

In the distance, an engine grumbled, louder every second, creeping closer.

CHAPTER THREE

DAWN CINCHED HER ARM AROUND JAKE'S TORSO AND hooked his arm around her shoulders. A portion of his weight settled onto her. She resisted the urge to lean into him for support, because the point was for her to brace him. Though he'd roused, and could move now, she refused to risk him tumbling to the ground, possibly injuring himself worse, just to assuage his newfound macho streak.

A coyote howled in the distance.

Shuddering, she hugged Jake closer. He grunted. She loosened her grip. "Sorry. Didn't mean to squish you."

"That's not the problem." The tension in his voice pricked her heart. It was the tightness of pain, suppressed but inescapable. "I thought I could...I'm not sure anymore. Standing up was more difficult than I expected." He tried to pull his arm away, but she clamped her hand over his on her shoulder. "You should leave me here, Dawn. Run. As fast as you can."

"Like hell I will."

The vehicle engine rumbled louder, nearer, advancing on them with relentless precision.

She urged Jake to move, half leading and half dragging him away from the SUV. "What happened to 'always be prepared'? Don't you have a plan for scenarios like this?"

"No." He gasped.

"I'll think of something. Just hold on." Adjusting her grip on him, she forged ahead. No choice. They must keep moving. And to ensure they did, she must distract him from his pain. "I've pretty much decided you're a CIA agent, sent to scope out Redeo Biotech and take them down."

"I'm a simple grad student, not a spy."

Simple? Yeah right.

Something bleeped behind her. She froze.

A radio crackled, and a voice echoed from the interior of the SUV, emerging through the open door a dozen feet away. "Time's up. We're coming and you'd better cooperate, or things will get rough."

Dawn shot a glance over her shoulder. "Was there a radio in the car?"

Jake gave a halfhearted laugh. "I suspect there was."

Biting her lip, she considered the options. Escaping from the car, with Jake's weight slowing them both down, would demand a massive effort. Could they get away before the Redeo goons closed in on them?

Headlights flared on, blinding her for a heart-stopping second.

The other vehicle had zoomed far closer than she expected. Within a handful of heartbeats, the Redeo team would swarm over them. All their options had evaporated.

She eased Jake onto the ground. He didn't fight it, which knifed panic through her.

Bolting for the car, she dived inside and dug around for the radio. She found it in the storage compartment inside the center console. Her fingers fumbled for a hold. The radio clattered to the floor on the passenger side. She nabbed it and sprinted back to Jake.

He sprawled on the ground, eyes open but vacant.

Jesus, no. Falling to her knees, she took hold of his shoulder and jostled him.

"I'm awake," he said, though with a mild slur.

The Redeo vehicle rolled to a halt, its headlights blocked by the SUV, their former getaway car.

Thrusting her arms under Jake's, she hefted him onto his feet, with a bit of help from him. He pushed her arms away, shuffled half a step, tottered, shuffled another step.

His legs crumpled.

She seized him, and his full body weight bore down on her. She choked back a cry. Her legs threatened to give out too, her body trembling from the labor of bracing him. He lurched away, flailing toward the SUV, and collapsed against its hood. His chest heaved with each wheezing breath.

The Redeo vehicle advanced on them, closer, closer.

"Go," Jake said. "Hurry."

She strode to him, her nerves crackling with awareness of the other vehicle lurking several car lengths away, yet so close a glimpse of its outline triggered a surge of adrenaline. The sight of Jake's face, even paler than before, wrenched her heart. Tears stung her eyes.

Jake raised a hand to her cheek, his fingers millimeters from her skin. "Please go. I can't make it out on my own, and I won't stand by while Redeo takes you prisoner and turns you back into a lab specimen. If you stay, I'll die fighting them."

If she left, he'd die anyway. A tear rolled down her cheek onto her lips, tainting her tongue with its bitter salt. An odd clarity overwhelmed her, as if she'd slipped on a pair of eyeglasses that heightened her acuity in every sense.

Redeo needed her brain undamaged, according to Jake. They *needed* her.

She dug the radio out of her pocket and punched the transmit button. "Stop right where you are or you will lose your precious specimen."

The headlights jounced. The vehicle barreled toward them.

She ripped the gun out of her waistband, flicked the safety off, and stepped away from Jake, exposing herself in the headlight beams. Raising the gun to her temple, she spoke into the radio. "I know you can see me. Stop your vehicle right now or I pull the trigger. I doubt your bosses would appreciate their specimen being returned to them without a brain. And it'll be rather difficult to collect mine once it's splattered all over the sand."

The vehicle slowed. The male voice she'd heard before growled through the radio. "You wouldn't. You don't have the guts."

"I've got nothing to lose. My life ended three thousand years ago, and I can't go home again. You've got five seconds stop your vehicle and shut off the engine. One, two—" She tensed her finger over the trigger, her heart hammering, every breath a battle. "Three, four—"

The other vehicle skidded to a stop. The grumbling of its engine died.

"Stay," she told Jake, and turned to confront their pursuers. She gripped the gun tighter.

The Redeo vehicle hunkered there, unmoving.

A breeze ruffled her hair. She swiped a lock from her eyes and squinted at the Redeo vehicle, but the glare of its headlights obscured her view. She swallowed. Watched. Waited.

Come on, come on, do something already.

The front passenger door swung open. A figure clad in dark clothing exited the vehicle, sauntering into the beam of the headlights. The silhouette loomed there, a few car lengths away, tall and erect. The man lifted something to his face, and a calm voice intoned through the radio, "There's no need for violence, my dear, we have no intention of killing you. Either of you."

She pressed the transmit button on her radio. "Uh-huh. I should believe you why?"

"Because I am not Saxon." The man strode further from his vehicle, beyond the blinding radius of the headlights, but still illuminated by their glow. "My name is Anton Vahl. My man overreacted to your demands, and I apologize for his crudeness."

"Gee thanks."

Vahl strolled toward them, one arm dangling loose at his sides, the other holding the radio near his face. The closer he approached, the more details she discerned on him. His black hair hung in loose curls around his face, and the glare of the lights turned his glasses opaque, concealing his eyes. His dark suit blended into the shadows. He shook one foot, casting off a cascade of sand.

She didn't recognize Vahl. Though dead for most of her stay at Redeo, she'd traveled beyond the confines of her mortal remains to explore the world as a disembodied soul. In her soul travels, as Jake dubbed it, she'd observed the scientists at Redeo, enough to know their computer passwords. Yet the man watching her now was not one of the scientists she'd known.

Of course, she didn't recognize Saxon either. Her memories weren't perfect.

Waving toward Vahl, she asked Jake, "Do you know him?"

"Dr. Vahl is the molecular biologist who founded Redeo Biotech. I've seen him, but I never had any real contact with him." He stretched one hand up to grasp hers. "Be careful. Vahl's an unknown variable. I don't trust what I can't quantify."

"I agree. Mystery men are bad." She closed her fingers around his. The frigid feel of his skin sucked the warmth out of her, dragging her heart down into a black hole. "You're the only mystery man I'd stake my life on."

The radio in her pocket warbled. She rose to stare at Vahl, who lounged against the SUV, one hip braced on the hood. Though she couldn't see his eyes, she sensed his attention boring into her with an unsettling intensity. She swallowed, rolled her shoulders back, and hit the button on the radio. "What do you want, Dr. Vahl?"

She suppressed a flinch when Vahl's smooth baritone voice answered. "I see Jake is alive, but I know for a fact his condition is worsening."

"What makes you think that?"

"Barnhart told me you remember a great deal from your out-of-body experiences. If that's true, then you surely know how ruthless and cunning Saxon was. I don't condone his actions."

Her stomach lurched. Barnhart. The scientist had been ready to autopsy her, at Saxon's orders, until she'd blurted out personal information about Barnhart, which she'd learned in her soul travels, and convinced him she was alive. Without his help, she and Jake would've died at Redeo. Though she lacked any afterlife memories of Saxon, she had enough brains to keep that fact to herself right now.

Vahl continued. "Saxon administered a slow-acting poison, and I have the antidote."

CHAPTER FOUR

POISON. THE NIGHT WHIRLED AROUND HER, SPINNING and blurring, threatening to rip the earth out from under her feet. She clutched the radio. "Tell me what you want, Vahl."

"You, naturally." He paused, and her skin itched with a wicked anticipation. "But I am no barbarian, like Saxon. He believed your corpse would suffice. I realize to prove the regeneration process is a success, we need you alive, healthy, and conscious. Turn yourself in, and we will take care of you both."

He sounded too reasonable, too calm. Her nerves twanged in warning. "No thanks. I prefer the nuclear option—blowing my brains out so you'll never get what you want from me."

"Don't make this harder than it needs to be."

"I don't care to be autopsied alive."

He ran a hand over the SUV's hood. "No one said anything about an autopsy. We wish to prove the regeneration process works. A living specimen is the best evidence." He observed her across the distance without expression. "Rest assured, there will be no autopsy today. So please, my dear, return to the fold and I promise I'll take care of you and Jake personally."

"Give me the antidote for the poison first."

Plucking an object from his pocket, Vahl wagged it in front of him. It looked like a vial. "Here it is. Come to me and I'll administer it myself."

Jake clawed at her ankle. His voice croaked. "Don't do it. You can't trust anyone from Redeo."

He was right, but she had no choice. Tucking the gun inside her waistband, she clasped the radio to her chest and crouched to slip a hand through Jake's hair. His scalp chilled her skin, and when she lowered her fingers to his lips, it was like touching permafrost.

No. Her jaw trembled, her eyes burned, and her throat constricted. She could not lose him. Not now, not ever. In the space of hours, he'd burrowed into her soul like no one in her entire life—the first life, or the second one.

"He's dangerous," Jake said. "We have no idea what his end game is."

"I know." She kissed his forehead, his skin freezing her lips. He needed a hospital. Right now. She rose, lifting the radio to her mouth. "I will turn myself in to you."

Jake gasped, scrabbling to get to his knees, and clutched her hand. She clamped her teeth down over lips, hauling a breath in through her nose to stave off tears. He tried to stand, lost his balance, and slumped against her leg. She squeezed her eyes shut, determined not to cry, willing her heart to toughen, until her jaw stopped quivering. "We'll come to you, Vahl. But your men are staying in the other car."

"I accept your terms. With one caveat." He gestured toward her midsection. "Toss your gun on the ground before you walk over here."

Get rid of the gun? Hell no.

Jake went limp against her, his eyelids drifting shut. His weight dragged her down to her knees, with him cradled in her embrace. His face had gone deathly pale, the fever gone, driven out by an icy cold. It could not end like this. Not after everything they'd endured together. Not here, not now.

His head lolled to the side. Lifeless.

No, goddammit.

She slapped a palm on his cheek and jerked his face toward her. His lips had gone blue. Her body trembled with contained sobs, and she clenched her teeth. *No crying.* It was weakness, and she'd vowed to stay strong for him. To guard his life. To save him. But how? Cradling his lifeless form, overwhelmed by the coldness of his flesh, she scrambled for an answer. None came. Ice crystallized around her heart, yet an ember burned deep inside. She needed him, wanted him, in a way she'd never experienced before.

He could not leave her. She refused to allow it.

Shutting her eyes, she fluttered a kiss across his cold mouth and rested her forehead against his. Hushed words tumbled from her lips. "Please don't die, please don't die, please don't die."

A tight ball of anger and fear weighted her down. She bent her head back and, summoning all her willpower, fired a prayer straight into the heavens.

The ball exploded.

In her heart, the ember erupted into a blaze. Tears flooded out of her, dripping onto Jake's face, trickling down to dampen her palm. Whimpers burst out of her. *Come back to me, please, I need you.* The power of the plea resonated through her entire being, stoking the fire of anger and fear and desperation. She'd been so alone in her first life, and treated as a test subject in this one, but in all her centuries on this earth one thing and one thing alone imbued her with a sense of worthiness, completeness, purpose.

Jake.

She mashed her lips to his again, propelling her breath into his mouth, overcome with the need to transfer her life into him. An instinct once dormant overpowered her rational mind, and she relinquished control to it, lost in a soaring sensation of freedom and power. She injected another breath into him. The heat in her chest combusted, racing up her throat, singeing her tongue. The energy poured into him, transported by her kiss. As tears dribbled from her eyes onto his face, his skin warmed beneath hers. His body quivered.

Wake up, oh God please, wake up.

A breath hissed out of him, into her. The taste of him, sweet and spicy, thrilled her beyond reason. With a gasp, she tore her mouth from his. Supporting his head between her hand and her chest, she scanned his face, his body, for another sign of life. Her pulse pounded in her ears, in her veins, drowning out everything else.

His eyelids peeled apart. His bleary gaze roamed, as if he couldn't quite recognize his surroundings. After a couple seconds, his attention rolled toward her. "Hey."

A sob burst out of her. Between wrenching gasps, she said, "Hi."

The tears blurred her vision, but she glimpsed enough to realize his color had returned.

He pushed up into a sitting position. "What's wrong? Did Vahl hurt you?"

"No." The word squeaked out. The relief scorching through her incinerated every last ounce of tension, until she sagged into him, her head falling onto his shoulder. "I thought I'd lost you. Forever."

Jake caressed her back, murmuring wordless sounds, soothing her more than any declaration he might've uttered. He stroked her hair, kissed her cheek, lifted her face to his. Her tears dissipated, leaving only a single flame smoldering inside her. His virile body pressed against hers kindled the flame into a fire that licked at her skin from the inside. A trace of the power she'd tapped into lingered, but the ache burgeoning inside her now stemmed from an altogether different need. A hunger for him.

The radio crackled. "Is everything all right over there?"

Vahl's voice fractured the moment, extinguishing her fire. She extricated herself from Jake and stood. "We're coming to you now, Dr. Vahl."

"The gun first, please."

"No," Jake said. "You can't give up our only advantage."

"It's not our only advantage," she told him. "We have brains, you know."

"Yours is worth a lot more than mine."

She tossed the gun onto the ground.

Jake levered his body off the ground, more awkward than usual, but far stronger than moments ago. His hand on her arm expressed more than any words. His fingers tensed. His eyes searched hers.

She flattened her palm on his chest, relishing the warmth and firmness of him. "You said you trust me, and I'm asking for that faith again. Please do this for me."

"We're in this together. Where you go, I go. Even into Hell." His hand enfolded hers. "But I might pass out soon."

She clenched a fistful of his shirt. "What?"

"I feel much better, but I'm exhausted, like I haven't slept in days." He rubbed his eyes, swaying a little. "I'll make it to the car."

"Maybe your body fought off the poison. Can that happen?"

"Damned if I know."

Without another word, he led her toward the other vehicle. Thoughts twirled in her brain, but she couldn't latch onto one. Something important had happened, and Jake seemed better, but the details flitted away each time she tried to comprehend. And then he told her he'd pass out soon. Better, and yet not better? As for what happened a minute ago, when she kissed him...

Nothing made sense.

Jake's feet dragged in the sand, kicking up little sprays of earth. He slouched his shoulders forward, his head too, and though he retained his healthy color, shadows darkened the skin under his eyes. All the clues pointed to exhaustion, yet Vahl claimed Jake was poisoned. Until a minute ago, she'd believed it. His ice-cold skin and complete weakness convinced her. Now, she didn't know.

Vahl had taken up a position by the backseat door when they arrived at the SUV. He arched an eyebrow at Jake, but said nothing as he swung the door open. Jake halted in front of Vahl. He glowered at the scientist, who assessed him with narrowed eyes clouded by the reflections on his glasses.

Jake climbed into the backseat and sprawled out across its width.

Vial in hand, Vahl strode past her toward the car's bumper.

She snagged his arm, and he paused. "The antidote please."

"Later."

"Now." She dug her nails into his arm. "You said you'd give it to Jake when we gave ourselves up."

"I've altered the terms of your surrender."

He marched around the front bumper to the driver's door. By the time Dawn clambered into the passenger seat, Vahl had installed himself behind the wheel. "Thank you, my dear, for making this easy on all of us."

"Where the hell are you taking us?"

"To a hospital, of course. When we drop Jake off there, I'll give him the antidote. Not before."

"Shut up and take us to the damn hospital."

He gave a curt nod.

The ride to the interstate elapsed in silence. Jake indeed passed out a few minutes after lying down. He slumbered now, looking vulnerable and yet masculine, in the way she imagined no one else could have. Gnawing her lip, she studied him for several minutes, her left arm draped over the seat back, twisted in her seat to face the rear. He should've died, or at least continued to worsen. Instead, he'd rebounded.

She dropped back into her seat and asked Vahl, "If you poisoned Jake, why is he feeling better?"

"Are you certain he is?"

"I—" She threw a quick glance at Jake. "Yes. I am."

"He'll need tests to confirm your diagnosis." The car bounced onto the interstate, and Vahl swerved left into the empty lane. "My men will have called for backup by now, and they'll catch up soon. Once Jake has been released, we'll all head back to Redeo." He tapped his fingers on the steering wheel. "Thank you for trusting me. Everything will go much smoother if you continue to cooperate."

His words rewound in her mind, and she slapped her palms on her thighs. "What do you mean we *all* will head back?"

"You, me, my men, and Jake."

Her heart thudded. "Let him go. He's got nothing to do with this."

"I'm sorry, but he knows too much." Vahl massaged the steering wheel with one hand, stroking it like a lover. "If it's any consolation, I'll make sure no one harms him."

"He stays with me."

"No, I'm afraid Jake will spend his days in another facility, far from you. He's contaminated my research enough."

"You said you'd take care of us both."

"And I will." He smiled, a cool expression devoid of empathy. "My way."

Bastard. Vahl proclaimed no one would harm Jake, and that he needed her alive, conscious, and healthy. But he'd never once claimed no harm would come to her. A shiver convulsed her body. He could cut her open, slice out tissue samples, and stitch her back together, leaving her alive, conscious, and—in relative terms—healthy.

Her gorge leaped high in her throat. She choked it back. At least Barnhart would've killed her with a painless injection first. But Vahl meant to prolong her life, her suffering.

Autopsied alive.

———

JAKE LISTENED TO THE TIRES HUMMING DOWN THE ROADWAY, A hypnotic sound, but he felt nothing close to sleepy. Not anymore. Since waking up a few minutes ago, he'd come to a shocking conclusion.

He was healed.

His shoulder no longer ached, and his body thrummed with newfound energy. He would've jumped right up and throttled Vahl, but he needed more of a plan before he attacked. Dawn was in the front seat, and he would never do anything to hurt her. Strangling the driver might hurtle them into a crash, risking her safety. Not an option.

Dawn cleared her throat. "You said you need me conscious. Why?"

Jake tensed. She was talking to Vahl.

"To test your faculties," the scientist replied. "No one will pay for a process that fails to produce a healthy, viable result."

"So now I'm a result. I suppose that's slightly more flattering than specimen."

Jake stifled a chuckle. That was his girl—sarcastic, suspicious, and wonderful.

"You should be flattered," Vahl said. "Or perhaps honored is a better word. We chose you as the prototype for our regeneration process."

She snorted. "Jake told me how you chose your test subject. I was the only mummy with an intact brain you could get your hands on, because the Egyptians removed the brains during the mummification ritual. I'm not special, I'm an anomaly."

Something in her tone gripped his heart. Anomaly? Maybe. But to him, she was a miracle. The impulse to leap up and hoist her out of her seat into his arms rushed through him, but he stamped it out. Wrong time, wrong place.

"If you'll let me," Vahl said, "I can help you, Dawn."

"What did you call me?"

"Dawn," Vahl repeated. "That is what Jake calls you, isn't it?"

Anger flashed through him so hard he grappled for self-control. His fists itched to connect with Vahl's jaw. How dare this asshole speak her name. It belonged to her, and to him, no one else. It was…sacred.

Which may have been the dumbest idea he'd ever dreamed up.

Yet it felt right and true.

Fabric scritched on fabric. Jake risked peeking over his shoulder, and saw Dawn squirming in her seat.

"Do you know how I woke up?" she asked Vahl. "What triggered it, I mean."

"No." The car jounced over a pothole or a bump in the road. Jake's body listed backward, but he grabbed the seatbelt dangling near his head, halting his fall. The scientist in the front seat said, "But now that you are alive, my dear, it opens up a whole new world of possibilities. Once we figure out how you were reborn, we can do more than reverse the aging process. We can sell resurrection."

Vahl's tone resonated with awe—and a dark thread of glee.

Jake rolled onto his back, careful not to squeak the seat's framework or rustle his clothes. Dawn's eyes darted in his direction, bulged for a second, and then she switched her attention back to Vahl. "What happens to me after you get your answers?"

"That remains to be decided."

"You'll kill me."

"Mm, no. I doubt it." Vahl patted her thigh. "You are the prototype, after all. Investors will clamor to get a look at you."

"I'm not your pet monkey."

"True. But you are the property of Redeo Biotech, which means I own you. Your fate rests in my hands and mine alone." He scraped his palm across her thigh. "I'm sure we can reach some agreement."

Jake clenched his jaw. Dawn cringed, her face a stoic mask. But underneath her mask simmered a terror she would never expose, a desperation visible only to him. He knew her better than he knew his own family, and he would do anything for her. Anything.

Vahl let out a dramatic sigh. "The choice is yours, my dear. Live a life of luxury with me, or be locked in a cell at Redeo for the rest of your life. However long that might be."

"And what about Jake?" Her gaze flitted to him, and he tried to smile, to reassure her. She didn't respond.

Vahl returned his hand to the wheel. "Oh yes. Jake. Well, as I told you, he'll live out his remaining days in his own cell. You will never see each other again."

Like hell they wouldn't.

Jake sprang off the seat. He lunged forward, clamping his arm around Vahl's neck. The scientist shouted, but Jake's arm strangled his cry.

The car swerved.

Jake growled into Vahl's ear. "You're never touching her again."

He crushed the man's windpipe. Vahl gurgled, flailed, scratched at Jake's arm, unable to reach his face. The car rocketed off the interstate, bouncing over obstacles, careening through shrubs.

Dawn scrabbled for the wheel, half out of her seat.

As Vahl slumped, his eyes closing, Jake glanced out the windshield.

Up ahead, in their direct path, towered a boulder the size of a motor home.

Dawn screamed.

They barreled toward the rock wall, straight into disaster.

CHAPTER FIVE

DAWN SCRAMBLED ONTO VAHL'S LAP, HEART POUNDING, breaths gasping. The gigantic rock loomed closer and closer as the SUV bounded over the landscape. She forced her leg down between Vahl's and stomped on the brake. The car slowed. But still it barreled toward destruction.

She hugged the steering wheel, using it as a lever to brace herself in a semi-standing position. A whimper exploded out of her. She slammed all her weight into standing on the brake pedal.

The tires froze up. The car skidded, bounced, veered left and then right.

She pushed with all her strength, arms burning, sweat stinging in her eyes.

With a jolt, the SUV stopped.

Dawn collapsed against the door. She closed her eyes, panting for air, her arms trembling.

"Are you okay?"

She cracked her eyelids open. Jake stared at her, face pinched and pale, though not with a deathly pallor this time. A normal, scared-shitless pallor.

Her face must've mirrored his, because he hurled himself onto the center console, ignoring Vahl's limp form, and seized her hands. "Are you okay?"

Vahl. She sat in a heap on his lap, back to the door. Her skin crawled at his proximity, but with Jake in front of her, she was stuck.

"I'm fine," she said. Eyeing Vahl, she added, "Is he dead?"

Jake jammed a finger into Vahl's neck. "No. Unfortunately."

"What the hell were you thinking?"

"I won't let you go back to Redeo."

Her jaw dropped open. "Seriously? You couldn't come up with a better escape plan than plowing into a huge freaking rock?"

"I—" He ducked his head. Crouched on the console, one leg in the backseat and the other bent under him, he looked stuck too. "I couldn't stand him touching you like that."

"Again, you couldn't come up with anything better than a fiery car wreck?"

"I wasn't thinking. I—had to stop him. Get his filthy hands off you."

"Christ, Jake, I can deal with a little fondling from a scumbag. Getting us both killed is not helpful."

Head still bowed, he rolled his eyes up to look at her. "I'm sorry."

She reached behind her, grasped the door handle, and shoved it down. The door popped open. She clung to the steering wheel, easing her feet out onto the ground.

Leaning into the open door, she said, "What now, oh hero of mine?"

He grimaced. "I said I'm sorry."

"Stop apologizing, it's okay. Got any plans now?"

"Yes." He crawled over Vahl, sliding out to stand beside her. "We dump him here and get as far away as possible. But first, we retrieve the flash drive."

"Won't they track this car?"

"Yes, but not until they find Vahl and realize what happened. By then, we'll have a new, clean vehicle."

She scrunched her eyebrows. "How are we going to do that?"

"Trust me. This is one scenario I'm prepared for."

———

DAWN PEELED HER EYELIDS APART, ROUSED BY THE BLARING OF A horn. Beams of light slashed over her. She sat forward, squinting at the pickup truck roaring past them. Beside her in the driver's seat, Jake studied the asphalt road ahead, lips tight, brow creased.

The taillights of the pickup disappeared into the night.

Jake swerved their car around a corner, onto a narrower paved road. The momentum flung Dawn to the side, straining her seatbelt. She gripped the arm rest and prayed this old clunker would survive Jake's aggressive driving.

"Hang on," he said, "we've got another corner here."

She clutched her seatbelt as the car slalomed around the corner. Her weight slung toward the other side of the car. She held on with every ounce of strength left in her.

"Jeez," she huffed. "Take it easy, would you?"

"I'll take it easy when we're safe."

The car straightened out. The tires rumbled over gravel.

Through the windshield, she watched the slender road unfurl before them as the car raced through a wooded landscape. The tree branches curved over the two-track, not quite meeting over the center. The sky flamed in shades of red, pink, and purple. The sun, out of sight, must've hovered just below the horizon.

Sunrise. She was witnessing her first sunrise in over three thousand years. The knowledge hit her like a powerful wind, and she grasped the driver's seat for support. Twenty-four hours ago, she'd lain dead. With the memories of her first life concealed from her, everything she saw and experienced shined with the newness of a freshly minted coin.

Dawn snagged the duffel bag that rested on the floor at her feet. Jake had prepared after all, though not for the exact circumstances they'd encountered. He'd prepared to run.

Bits of dirt and grass rubbed off the canvas fabric onto her jeans. Unzipping the main compartment, she peered into the depths of the bag. Four wads of cash, each an inch thick and composed of hundred-dollar bills, sat atop a pile of folded clothes. A handgun, quite like the one she'd dumped in the desert at Vahl's behest, nestled among the clothing. She fingered one of the cash bundles. When he'd said he stashed "some cash" with the flash drive, she'd envisioned a couple hundred bucks, not thousands upon thousands. He really was a man of mystery.

She glanced at Jake. "You've got the flash drive, right?"

"You saw me put in my pants pocket."

"'But it might've fallen out."

He patted his pocket. "Still there."

"Good."

She leaned toward him and scrutinized his face. A healthy glow colored his cheeks. His clear eyes darted sideways to squint at her. She stretched out a hand, sliding it under the neck of his T-shirt to explore the gunshot wound. Her fingers skated over muscular flesh, tickled by short, silky hairs. Warmth swept through her, a gentle flow of relief and desire. She wanted to pull him closer, to peel his shirt off and run her lips over his flesh.

Just to verify he wasn't injured anymore. Strictly a medical examination.

Her heart skipped a beat. *He's not injured anymore.* How was that possible?

As her fingers probed his flesh, a smirk played across Jake's face. "You're much sexier than any nurse I've ever met."

The warmth rushed through her anew. Sexy? Her? No. She must've misheard him. "Yeah sure. I bet you say that to all the formerly mummified girls you meet."

"You're a woman. That's all I need to know." He dropped one hand off the wheel, draping it over her thigh, and a tingle trickled over her skin. "Have you finished your examination yet?"

She stilled her hand, relishing the heat of him. His skin chased away the chill that lingered within her. She withdrew her hand, with great reluctance. "I don't get it. You were shot. A few hours ago, you almost died."

"Not almost." He fell silent for a moment, his face unreadable. "I died. I felt it."

"Obviously, you didn't die."

He slowed the car, turning his head to stare straight into her eyes. "My life ended out there in the desert. You brought me back."

"What? You're insane." She hugged herself, shaking her head. "That is not possible. I may be a reconstituted mummy girl, but I don't have magical powers."

A frown etched lines on his face, but he said nothing.

Revived him? Her? No, he was wrong. She couldn't do that. But oh God, when he'd almost died, a strange fire blazed inside her, spreading into him, and then he'd come back to her. It was a miracle, for sure, but it had nothing to do with her.

Her gaze wandered to her finger, and the absence of a cut.

"You did it," he said. "You burned it out of me."

"Burned what out?"

"Death."

Her finger. She stared at it, heart pounding, ears ringing, incapable of breathing or moving. Her finger had burned. And it healed.

You brought me back. Jake's words thundered in her head.

"I couldn't have healed you, it's impossible." Words gushed out of her now, in a wild torrent. "For all I know, Saxon was right and I'm nothing but a bunch of random biochemical reactions that mimic life. I shouldn't be alive anyway. Death is the end, the final stage, the doorway to the afterlife, and nobody should come back from that. I'm a specimen, a thing, someone's property, not a human being. *I shouldn't be alive.*"

He launched an arm out in front of her and jammed his foot on the brake. The tires spun. Gravel sprayed up around the car. If not for his arm, she would've collided with the dashboard. He unhooked his seatbelt, looped his arms around her waist, and hauled her onto his lap, positioning her between the steering wheel and his body, with her back to the wheel. They huddled face to face, their breaths mingling, his hands clasped at the small of her back. Every inch of her skin tingled from his proximity, his presence. Her lungs struggled to take shallow breaths. Her lips craved his mouth.

His brown eyes locked on hers with an intensity that ignited fireworks inside her, low down, in the most intimate parts of her. She ached for his touch everywhere, in every way, consumed by a blazing need. Her head dipped toward his. Their lips grazed each other. The blaze roared hotter, a scorching hunger for him.

A sensual smile teased his lips. He lunged a hand between their mouths, easing her away.

Her stomach lurched at his refusal. Maybe he'd fibbed about her being sexy after all, if he could reject her this way. How could he want her? He'd seen her desiccated body, before the scientists at Redeo restored her. He knew what she'd been. How she was revived. No man could desire a thing like her.

That's what she was. A thing. A creature. An abomination.

"What are we doing?" she asked. A faint tremor wavered in her voice, matching the unsteadiness of her thoughts and her heartbeat. "You shouldn't be risking your life for a thing like me. An ex-mummy. A monster."

"Stop that," he snapped, and his lips flattened into a line. His gaze riveted to hers, as if nothing else in the world mattered but her. The lines of anger smoothed out of his features. "You are not a mummy, a thing, or a monster."

"But I—"

He splayed his fingers over her mouth, silencing her. "You're a woman. And you are alive."

She couldn't move. Couldn't speak. A ringing started in her ears, warning her to breathe—but she couldn't do that either. The world seemed to have stopped, as if they hung suspended together inside a snow globe, minus the snow. The fever in their bodies, the passion sizzling below the surface, would've vaporized a glacier.

Inhaling a ragged breath, he dragged his fingers over her jaw, down her neck, across the swell of her breasts. "Don't ever believe you're anything less than a living, breathing, red-blooded woman. That's all I see." His hand on her back nudged her tighter into his hard body. "I risk my life for you because you're worth it."

In this moment, tangled up in him, she knew he meant it. He would risk death—for her.

Cuddled so close to him, she fought to catch her breath, to catch a coherent thought. But she willed her mind to clear, dared to flatten her palms on his chest despite the intoxicating feel of him, and told him what she most needed to say. "I can't let you keep endangering yourself on my account. We have to go our separate ways. You have to leave me."

"No."

The determination on his face scraped her nerves raw, because she knew he was too damn stubborn to walk away. Which left her one choice. "I'm leaving you then."

Before he could respond, she grabbed the handle of the driver's door, hurled it open, and twisted out of his embrace. Her right foot touched down on the roadway. Her chest constricted as grief wrenched her to the core. She could do this. She *must* do this. Bolstered by her resolve, she straightened her spine, lifted her chin, and with a blast of will that grated inside her, she erased the pain from her expression.

"Dawn, no."

She vaulted out the door.

CHAPTER SIX

J AKE SNARED HER THIGH, HALTING HER ESCAPE. WITH ONE leg outstretched over his lap, she balanced on the other foot, planted on the gravel road. No, dammit, he would not allow her to give in to her fear. A monster? A thing? If she believed he saw her that way, then by God, he'd prove her wrong—whatever the cost.

Clinging to the door frame, she cast him a sidelong look rife with such anguish it shredded his anger. She shook her head, eyes pleading with him. "Please, Jake. Let me go."

Never. He must act, to make her understand what his verbal assurances failed to communicate. *Show her. Prove it to her.*

He hooked a finger in a belt loop on her jeans and urged her back toward him. She acquiesced, all but collapsing onto his lap, her thighs straddling him. A tear trickled down her right cheek, and her teeth clamped down on her lower lip. He slipped his hands around her waist, up her back, easing her into him until their bodies melded.

"Jake, please—"

He smothered her plea with his mouth, capturing her bottom lip between both of his, and licked her ripe flesh. Her sigh teased his skin like butterfly wings, enveloping him with her scent, a heady concoction of earth and soap and feminine allure. When he skimmed his tongue across her lip, she broke. Any reserve she'd harbored evaporated, and she opened herself to him, inviting him to taste and touch, her lips and her body and her essence. He savored the sweet taste of her, the softness of her mouth, the willingness of her surrender, awed at the way he cherished and craved her with equal measure. Everything about her enthralled and excited him on levels far deeper than mere lust.

Folding his arms around her, he plundered her mouth, and she dissolved into him. The kiss consumed them both, inflamed their desire, until her body writhed against him. He groaned, plunging deeper into her. She succumbed to his every demand, yet he surrendered to her too, driven by the compulsion to claim her for his own.

Her hips sank into him. She plowed a hand into his hair, her flesh yielding to his as their hands groped each other with reckless abandon. His passion for her escalated with each stroke of her fingers, each thrust of her tongue, scorching away the tatters of his inhibition. He caught one breast in his palm and flicked his thumb over the nipple.

She flinched.

The lust flushed out of him in an instant. She'd flinched in pain.

He grasped her upper arms and pushed her away.

Her back bumped into the steering wheel. Breathless, she regarded him through a haze of desire and confusion. "What's wrong?"

Afraid to move or touch her, despite the fact she still sat astride him, he did the only thing he could. He glared. Not at her, but past her shoulder at the road. He'd been such a fool, thinking he could save her when all he'd ever wanted was to lose himself in her. When she'd lain in the tank at Redeo, he'd dreamed about her awakening and what those incredible eyes might see in him. But it had been a masculine fantasy. He'd rescue her, of course, and spirit her away to a little love nest where he'd demonstrate his devotion to her in every way imaginable and she'd fall instantly in love with him. Her gratitude would forge a lasting connection.

What bullshit.

Except she did fall for him. She trusted him. Wanted him. And unless his fantasy warped his perceptions, she needed him. He wouldn't dare suggest, even within his own thoughts, that she loved him. But God, he needed her too.

And—insane as it was and as dangerous as it might prove to be—he loved her. He'd adored her the moment she looked into his eyes back in the lab.

Here in the present, she rested a hand on his cheek. "You're angry again, which means it's time for me to go."

Her voice hitched on the last word. Her eyes glistened. She crimped her mouth, as if struggling to not cry.

Christ. He couldn't saddle her with his baggage, his fantasy. But neither could he sit still while she bolted into the unknown, alone and unprotected. If he accomplished one task before he died, it would be to get her to safety.

She shifted on his lap, leaning toward the open door.

He slammed the door shut. "No one's leaving anyone today."

———

DAWN RECOILED, STARTLED BY HIS VEHEMENCE. "EXCUSE ME?"

He ground his teeth, his jaw muscles popping from the effort.

She frowned. "What on earth is wrong with you?"

"Nothing." He yanked her to him, scooped her up in his arms, and deposited her on the passenger seat. She gaped at him as, without a word, he fastened her seatbelt and withdrew to his own seat. His expression had gone blank. She raised a hand to touch him, but hesitated an inch from his arm.

He floored the accelerator. The car shot forward.

She gripped the edges of her seat. "What the hell are you doing? Kidnapping me?"

"No," he hissed through gritted teeth. "I'm taking you somewhere safe."

"Gee, thanks. I feel safer already, after your charming display of macho bossiness." Her own anger seethed hotter, on the verge of boiling over. Bossiness was an inadequate term for his behavior, which jarred her more than she cared to admit to him. Jake was nice, and sweet in his own way. He could be decisive, yes, but never a hothead.

Right. She knew this after one day with him.

Except she did. After everything she'd experienced post-rebirth, she no longer enjoyed the luxury of doubting her instincts. But he had no right to treat her like a runaway child.

Drumming her fingers on the arm rest, she focused on the dashboard. "*You* kissed *me*, which means you have no right to be mad about it."

"I'm not mad."

He still sounded it, though, and he glared at the road as if it mocked him with its very presence. When they reached an intersection, he veered the car onto the other road. Gravel sprayed up around their vehicle, ticking and cracking on the undercarriage.

"I may have been reborn yesterday," she said, "but I'm not stupid. You are mad."

"Only at myself."

"I don't understand. And if you don't explain, I'm jumping out of this car right now."

Seconds ticked by on the countdown clock inside her. How much time did they have? Could he find a safe place where Redeo and Vahl wouldn't track them down?

When Jake spoke, his tone conveyed tenderness and regret. "It's not you."

"You really don't like to explain anything, do you?"

He tightened his fingers on the steering wheel, then slackened them. "I have to protect you, above all else. Anything between us is…irrelevant. *I have to protect you.*"

"That's sweet, in a very annoying way, but why are you so hell-bent on protecting me?"

"I drugged you. Have you forgotten?"

"No, of course I haven't."

He steered the car around another corner, onto a narrower dirt road, this time exercising more care in his maneuvers. "I dragged you out of Redeo's facility, sedated you, and carried you away to a motel. You deserve better than that, better than me." He strangled the steering wheel, intent on the road. "I had no plan beyond getting you away from Redeo. 'Always be prepared' flew out the window, and in spite of my best—or maybe worst—efforts, I failed you."

"We got away from Vahl and his minions. I'm safe. With you."

"You're wrong. I'll fight to save you until my dying breath, but in the end..." He shook his head. "In the end, I'll get you killed."

"No. I will never believe that."

He slammed his fist into the wheel. "Dammit, stop the hero worship. How can you trust me? I drugged you."

The sheer self-loathing in his voice tore at her, and she flung out a reflexive hand to grasp his arm. "I know what you did. But when you drugged me, I was kind of freaking out and you were scared and we were being chased by Redeo scumbags. I don't like what you did, but I understand. And I forgive you."

Utter grief racked his features and he drooped his head.

"Yes," she said, praying she'd imbued her voice with enough sincerity to convince him. She had forgiven him, in an instant, back in the motel room. Without consideration or regret. He'd liberated her from Redeo, taken a bullet for her, and then dived back into the fray once again to free her from Vahl's clutches. How could she *not* trust him?

"I'm a coward," he said, "I took the easy way out. Instead of talking you down, I shoved a needle in your neck, just like Saxon did later. I'm as bad as he was, as Vahl is."

"No. You're the one who saved me."

JAKE NAVIGATED DOWN EVER-NARROWER ROADS CLOGGED WITH trees and bushes and grass, his attention tied to the view in front of him, doing his damnedest not to look at Dawn. If he did, the reverence on her face would ruin him. His resolve would liquefy. He'd pull her into his arms for another scorching kiss, and this time he wouldn't let go.

For the past twenty minutes, ever since she pronounced he'd saved her, their conversation had dwindled into nothing. At first, she'd prodded him with tentative questions, but he refused to answer. To her, his reticence must've seemed like anger. In reality, he feared what might come out of his mouth if he opened it to speak. Her forgiveness, the love in her eyes and in her touch, breached a dam inside him. Words—ridiculous, flowery stuff about how much he cherished and craved her—threatened to tumble from him. Macho men did not confess their undying devotion in poetic terms. Of course, no one ever accused him of being macho—except for Dawn. Most women dismissed him as, at best, too scholarly.

But with Dawn, the testosterone-drunk beast within him stirred.

He hadn't decided yet if that was a good thing.

She coughed. Smoothed her blouse. Rested her arm on the center console. "Where are we going?"

"A safe place." He hoped. Or rather, he prayed.

"Uh-huh. Care to elaborate?"

"Not particularly."

She huffed.

He couldn't help smiling, just a bit. "We're almost there, and I promise I'll explain when we get to the cabin."

"Cabin?" Interest lightened her voice. "Sounds cozy."

"I wouldn't know. Only been there once."

Overhanging branches concealed the driveway he sought. But even after ten months, he recognized the landmarks that indicated the turn—a gnarled, dead tree and a small pile of rocks. He swerved the car around the corner, down the pothole-infested driveway. The bumps rattled his teeth. He clutched the wheel, fighting to maintain control but unwilling to slow down. Reaching the cabin became the sole focus of his existence.

"Is this it?" she asked. "Kinda spooky, out here in the middle of nowhere."

"That's the point. It's remote."

The trees parted, revealing the log cabin nestled in a small clearing. He parked the car in front of the porch steps. The knob on the cabin's front door captured his gaze, its brass shine tarnished but reflective enough to glint in the single ray of sunlight beaming down on the cabin. He dragged in a deep breath. Dropped his hands from the wheel. Shut his eyes. And at last spoke to her. "Why do you go wherever I take you? Don't you worry I have ulterior motives?"

Anticipation loomed over him as he awaited her answer, like the razor-sharp pendulum in that Edgar Allen Poe story, swinging back and forth, lower and lower. He chanced a peek at her. She chewed her lip, as if mulling her response. A bad sign, he decided. Very bad. *Drop the blade already.*

She tipped toward him, fixing those glorious eyes on him. Something sharp scraped across his thigh, through the fabric of his pants, and he glanced down to discover his own fingernails burrowing into his flesh. He pried them loose, forcing himself to relax.

"Look at me," she commanded, and he obeyed. She gazed at him not with reverence, but with a look of serene certainty. "You may not believe this, and I can't explain why it happened so suddenly, but I know it's true and real. I trust you, yes. And I'm grateful for everything you've done for me."

"That doesn't sound unbelievable to me. Foolish, maybe."

"Shut up. I'm not finished."

"Yes, ma'am."

A slight smile brightened her face, yet the tender determination remained. "You want to know why I stick with you? Why I let you drag me wherever you want, even when you refuse to explain where we're going or why?"

He didn't want to know. He needed to know. His life seemed to hang on the answer, dangling him above a yawning abyss.

Her smile broadened, beaming with the light of a thousand suns. "I do it because I love you."

At those words, the ground dropped out from under him. But instead of plummeting into the depths of despair, he soared into the clouds. Yet a frisson of tension lingered inside him, a doubt made manifest in his flesh.

She squinted at him. "Did you hear me?"

"Yes."

He shoved the door open, leaped out, and marched around to the passenger door, tearing it open. Dawn's wide eyes scrutinized his every move, and her parted lips begged for him to devour them. Scooping her into his arms, he carted her up the porch steps and into the cabin. When he set her down on the wood floor of the living area, a few feet inside the door, she slanted into him, her hands gliding over his chest.

He towed her to him, enthralled by the feel of her warm, supple body. "I love you too."

She grinned.

He kissed her. And this time, he had no intention of stopping.

CHAPTER SEVEN

D AWN SAILED ON A BLUSTERING PASSION, LOST IN THE rapture of Jake's kiss. His hands roamed her back, seeking and finding the exact spots where his fingertips could set off a firestorm on her skin. A bolt of liquid fire shot through her entire body, settling down low, where she throbbed with need for him.

His mouth covered hers, coaxing more fire out of her with each swipe of his tongue. She wrapped her arms around him and let her hands explore his back, relishing the firmness of his muscles. He slid his hands into her hair, inclining her head, forging deep into her mouth. Desire shuddered through her so hard she trembled. He dropped his hand to her waist, sweeping it under her shirt, skating his palm up her side. His fingertips grazed her breast, eliciting a moan of pleasure.

He tore his mouth away from hers. Eyes dark with passion, breathless from their kiss, he whispered, "You're perfect, just perfect." He brushed his lips over hers, across her cheek, to skim her earlobe. "I'll never leave you."

Joy surged in her heart, quickening her pulse. A giddy sensation whirled in her mind, as if her soul had taken flight once more, but this time her spirit would not wander. His love, his passion, rooted her here, and she never wanted to leave him.

She clung to him as words spilled from her lips. "I'm sorry, so sorry, I should never have tried to run away. I didn't want to, I was afraid, just so damn scared I—"

His mouth silenced her. When he peeled his lips away, trailing them down her throat, her body tightened in readiness. He scorched kisses across her collarbone, then straight up her throat, where he raked his teeth over the hollow where her neck met her jawbone. She clung to him, unable to speak, unwilling to let him pull away even one millimeter. She belonged with him, to him, forging a bond time itself couldn't sever.

He ravaged her with a kiss of such fire, such intensity, it obliterated all thoughts, vanquished her inhibitions. She flung one leg around his, winding her herself around him. He groaned into her mouth. His hand under her shirt sought her bra clasp, and as she arched into him, he popped the clasp free. He slid his hand around her side to cup her breast. When his thumb began to move over her flesh, she moaned again.

Their lips still fused, he backed her into a piece of furniture upholstered with cushions that gave under the light pressure of her thighs. A sofa, she realized hazily. The gloom of the cabin's interior masked everything, but she didn't care about the decor. Her thoughts revolved around him, his hands, his body, and the urgency to feel his skin on hers, everywhere.

He ducked to the side, clicked something, flooding the room with muted light. Peripherally, she noticed the lamp, its bulb hooded by a lacy shade, perched on a table next to the sofa. Her mind went blank, though, when he dipped his head to her neck and dipped his tongue in the hollow of her collarbone. His big fingers fumbled with the button of her blouse. Breathing hard, he muttered a curse.

Her breasts strained against her bra, and her clothes constricted her. He fumbled some more, but his unsteady fingers slipped off the button. Oh God, if he didn't get this blouse off her, she'd burst.

"I'm sorry," he murmured, his voice raw.

To hell with this. She took the shirt's hem in her fingers and flipped the garment up over her head, freeing herself. The cool air swept over her bare flesh, arousing her almost more than feel of his body. He whipped his shirt off too, as she tore the rivet of her jeans open and kicked off the pants. By the time she'd shed her socks, he'd rid himself of every stitch of clothing.

She froze. The sight of him naked paralyzed her with a hunger so intense her breath caught in her throat. His muscled chest she'd glimpsed before, but now she soaked in the panorama of his powerful thighs, taut abs, and oh yes, the unmistakable evidence of his arousal. Her body hummed, as if his presence flipped a switch inside her, tuning their bodies to the same frequency.

With swift motions of his hands, he sent her panties and bra floating to the floor. She kicked them aside. He settled his hands on her hips, the weight of them so sensual she wanted to drag him onto the sofa right then, but he skated his hands up her sides to pull her against him. He grasped her buttocks, hefted her up, locking her legs around his hips. She hooked her arms around his neck. Whatever he was doing, she didn't care, as long as he kept touching her.

Spinning around, he dropped onto the sofa. She landed straddling him, both of them seated upright on the thick cushions. The velvety material rubbed her sensitized skin, driving her insane with the titillating sensation. He kneaded her breasts, stroked the nipples, and a wave of heat inundated her. She nibbled his earlobe, then drew it into her mouth to lick it. He groaned. She nipped the wet lobe and sucked it into her mouth again. He grasped her hips, lifting, positioning her just right. His lips devoured her nipple, suckling until she let loose a primal cry, throwing her head back.

He thrust her down onto him, his length filling her. She cried out, overwhelmed by the friction and power of him, inside her at last. He thrust his hips, driving deeper, urging her to move with him. And she did, motion for motion, moan for moan, their bodies entwined and united, the pleasure mounting higher and higher. He flipped her to the side, onto her back lengthwise across the sofa, and drove into her again and again, ramping up the pressure inside her, stripping away her thoughts until nothing existed except him and the panting of their breaths, the sweat dribbling over their bodies, their moans and cries overlapping. His breaths rasped in her ear, showering her with sultry air. The pressure mounted inside her, a flaming rapture so intense her heart pounded and her ears rang. The world vanished as she writhed under him, their cries joined in a frenzied chorus tautened with a craving neither one could slake. When the pressure drove her mad, she clutched his shoulders. He slapped his palms on the sofa arm above her head. Breaths gasped out of him and he groaned as his eyes rolled shut. She locked her legs around his hips, desperate for more of him. With a feral cry, he plowed into her, hurtling them both over the edge.

Her body clenched tight as pleasure shot through her in waves of molten ecstasy. He collapsed beside her, wedged between the sofa and her body. She sagged against him, spent and satisfied.

His fingertips danced along her arm. "I think we proved beyond any doubt you are alive."

Words deserted her. She could do nothing but gaze into his eyes, absorbed by the bliss of the afterglow. His arms around her waist, he tucked her head under his chin, and she let the beautiful intimacy lull her until her eyelids drifted shut.

Pure love washed through her—from him, from her, she didn't know—lightening a burden she hadn't realized held her down, until now. He knew her. He loved her. And he'd spoken the truth. She was alive, and at last, the power of her own life force surged in her veins. He unearthed it. She knew this, with a soul-deep conviction. Tonight, when he demonstrated his love and desire for her, he roused the red-blooded woman buried inside her. But more than that, yesterday back in the lab, he awakened her in the most literal sense.

His willpower brought her back to life.

CHAPTER EIGHT

DAWN DOZED FOR A WHILE, HALF AWAKE, REVELING IN the luscious glow left behind by their lovemaking, floating on a cloud. When she at last descended to earth, everything eased back into focus. She snuggled a little deeper into the velvety fabric of the sofa cushions. The scent of burning logs teased her senses. He must've started a fire, sometime after ravishing her in the most satisfying manner. An orange glow flickered through her eyelids, and a crackling sound issued from nearby. A soft fleece blanket swathed her, caressing her flesh when she wiggled beneath it. Jake's taste lingered in her mouth, and her body felt empty without him near her, inside her, filling her in ways beyond the physical.

She yearned to cuddle under the blanket forever, but suppressed the urge to beckon Jake and seduce him into joining her. Instead, she pried her eyelids apart.

The firelight shimmered across the polished wood floor and danced over her bare skin. The warmth of the fire radiated over her, matching the embers smoldering inside her. Halfway across the living room, Jake leaned his nude body against the frame of a picture window, his gaze alert, his posture relaxed but infused with latent tension. With one finger, he lifted the heavy curtain to peek through the gap. Ever the watchful warrior. Recognition shimmered through her. In her own tomb, she'd seen statues that bore a striking resemblance to Jake. He mirrored them in so many ways—from his physique to the set of his jaw and his purposeful gait, and even the length of his fingers.

Her head grew light, buoyant, her mind hovering in a mist of memory, spiraling backward in time to a murky chamber hewn from bedrock. Torches flickered their light across the walls and over the painted surface of a wooden coffin. A man hunched over the coffin, head bowed, the torchlight gilding his bare torso and tinging his white linen kilt with shades of yellow. He cursed the gods, pounding his fists on the coffin. She yearned to touch him and offer comfort, but she couldn't, for her spirit lacked form.

He threw his head back and bellowed.

Dawn lurched back into the present, her mind spinning. The man's face. She recognized him. Hell, she knew that face better than she knew her own. It was Jake.

Except it couldn't be. The memory came to her from thousands of years ago, during her original lifetime. Jake hadn't been born yet.

But she'd witnessed it. The truth of her vision resonated in her soul. Certainty brought a revelation that whirled through her like a strong wind, and at last she understood. Her trust for Jake, her sense of knowing him so well, her love for him—it all stemmed from a shared destiny. A shared past. Her first life, and his past life.

She roamed her gaze over the present-day version of him, positioned at the window. He belonged to her, forever. Her heart swelled with the knowledge. Now, how to explain it to him...

Sunlight leaked in around the edges of the curtains. It was daytime, though here in their sanctuary midnight reigned. The ghosts of flames that licked the floor cast an evocative glow on his bare flesh, highlighting the hard curves of muscles and accentuating his natural endowments. A sense memory unreeled inside her—the slickness of sweat on flesh, the pressure of him filling her, the sweet friction of his thrusts.

Her body awakened with a rush of desire. As she pushed up onto one arm, half sitting, she let the blanket drop to pool around her waist. It still covered her hips and legs, but the cool air on her breasts made her shiver, though not from the cold.

Jake withdrew his finger from the curtain. He canted his head, running his gaze over her body. The attention aroused her like a physical touch, spurring her to rise and go to him. He welcomed her into his arms with a smile and a stroke of his hand down her spine. She shivered again, as a tingling raced across her skin in the wake of his touch.

"Good afternoon," he said, his voice a husky murmur. "I thought you'd sleep all day."

"Mmm, I could have." She couldn't tear her focus away from his eyes, until he tugged her tighter against him. God, he felt so good. Her gaze wandered to his lips, kindling a deep craving. "I, uh, meant to ask you last night. What is this place?"

"My safe house."

For the first time, she noticed the stone-lined fireplace, the open kitchen delineated by a bar, and the woven-twig chairs situated on the opposite side of the room, around a small table. "Why does a grad student need a safe house?"

"Because I work—or worked, rather—for Redeo Biotech. I told you, I'd known for a quite some time they were dangerous." His gaze flitted around the room. "In case I needed it, I tracked down a safe house. This cabin is owned by a wealthy family who stopped coming here after their patriarch died. It's a good hideout. Totally unconnected to me."

"How'd you find out all that stuff about the family?"

"Research. It's amazing what you can learn online these days."

She regarded him with a renewed sense of wonder at his prowess in all things covert. *Simple grad student, my ass.* "Are you sure you're not a spy or something?"

"Positive." He slid a hand into her hair, cupping the back of her head. "I told you I was a Boy Scout. Always be prepared."

Her body melted into him, and she exulted in his warmth and hard planes. "I don't think the Boy Scouts taught you about safe houses."

"I learned that from movies." His fingers stroked her scalp, trailing down to the nape of her neck. "While you were resting, I used my burner phone to contact a TV reporter at a station in San Francisco. After I e-mailed him a sampling of the Redeo files, he got very, very interested. He wants the story. *Your* story."

Dread snaked through her, cold and brittle.

"Don't worry," Jake whispered into her hair, his mouth grazing her earlobe. "I won't let anyone exploit you." His tone took on a harder edge. "No one touches you. Not as long as I'm around."

"I know." She traced a finger over his collarbone, nuzzling his neck. "I trust you. One hundred percent."

The dark tension sluiced out of him, and he shifted his head to kiss the corner of her mouth. "Let's not talk about serious things anymore." His lips found hers, burning into her, disintegrating her thoughts. "In fact, let's not talk at all."

"Mmm..."

His lips closed over hers in a hard, searing kiss. She clutched at his arms, pressing into him, aching for more. He grasped her buttocks to hoist her onto her tiptoes, and she hooked her arms around his neck, clinging to him as he groaned into her mouth.

A knock sounded at the door.

Jake hustled her backward, drew the curtain aside an inch, and glared out at the porch. "Vahl."

He uttered the name in a hushed voice laden with disdain.

She hugged herself, scanning her surroundings for her clothes, which lay crumpled on the floor by the sofa. "Should we—"

"Get dressed."

Snatching his gun from the windowsill, he strode to the doorway buck naked.

Dawn scrambled to gather her clothes and pull them on, while Jake took up a position beside the door, gun raised in his right hand.

Vahl shouted through the door. "I'm alone. Check the driveway and you'll see."

She trotted to the window, parting the curtains a hair. "I don't see anyone else. Just a sedan with no one inside."

"They could be hiding a little ways down the drive."

"I'm alone," Vahl said. "I only want to talk, and I knew if I arrived with a small army again, you'd never listen to me."

She expected him to throw on his clothes, but instead he swung the door open and stepped in front of it, blockading the room with his naked body. "We still won't listen to you."

Vahl caught sight of Jake and his eyebrows shot up. "Am I interrupting something?"

"No." Jake aimed the gun at Vahl. "How did you find us?"

"I planted a tracking device on Dawn, right before you tried to strangle me." Vahl massaged his neck, careful to avoid a series of purple bruises.

Dawn thought back on her encounter with Vahl in the SUV. He'd fondled her thigh, which she interpreted as a sexual move because for most men it was. Oh damn. That must've been when he tagged her. Clever bastard.

"You can't have her." Jake widened his stance, legs spread, shoulders squared. "I'll fight you to the death if necessary."

"She doesn't belong with you."

"And you think she belongs with you?"

"No. She belongs *to* me." Vahl waved a dismissive hand. "Never mind that, however. I'm here to appeal to your civic nature."

Jake's lip curled. "My what?"

"Think about it. Our regeneration process worked, better than I'd dreamed. She is proof that we can bring the dead back to life, as viable entities. Do you understand what that means?" Vahl rolled his eyes. "Of course you don't. Think, Jake. We could cure death."

"You're insane."

Vahl turned his head toward Dawn. "You understand. And you know you aren't a part of this world, you never will be. Come with me and I will make you a hero. The woman who ended the worst plague the earth has ever known—mortality." He smiled, scraping a shiver down her spine. "I will protect you, my dear, as Jake never could."

Protect her? Only one man had earned that job, and it wasn't Vahl.

"What do say?" Vahl asked her.

She folded her arms over her chest. "Go to hell."

"I urge you to reconsider, Dawn."

At the mention of her name, Jake pulled his fist back and walloped Vahl in the jaw. The man staggered backward. Palpating his jaw, he straightened and chuckled. "You are not the meek young man I took you for."

Dawn took a step, and tripped over Jake's pants lumped on the floor. She teetered, flailing her arms. Jake sprang out to catch her.

And that's when Vahl attacked.

Dawn saw the syringe first, as the sun glinted off the clear plastic. Cradled in Jake's arms, she watched in horror as Vahl stabbed the syringe down toward Jake's neck.

She shoved Jake to the side, tumbling them both to the floor. Her head bumped the end table, bursting stars in her vision.

Vahl smacked onto the wood floor chin first, his cry muffled. The syringe skittered across the room to land near the fireplace.

Jake leaped onto Vahl's back, pinning him. "What the hell was that? More poison?"

"A sedative. To get you out of the way."

Jake shoved the gun's muzzle against Vahl's head. "I dare you to make a move."

Vahl glowered at Jake.

Padding over to the men, Dawn knelt beside Vahl. "It's over, doctor. We're leaving and you won't hunt us down. How do I know that?" She ducked her head close to his, leveling their eyes. "Because you're smarter than Saxon was. You won't come after me again until you have a surefire plan to take me down."

"You need me."

Jake crushed his knee into Vahl's back.

The scientist sputtered, coughed, and scowled. "You want to remember who you are, don't you? I can help you regain those memories."

She scoffed. "I don't need you for that—or anything." Sitting back on her heels, she looked at Jake. "I think we're done with him."

"Yes." Jake slapped the back of Vahl's head. "We are done."

Crawling across the floor, she retrieved the syringe and handed it to Jake.

"Wait," Vahl croaked.

Jake stabbed the needle into Vahl's neck, depressing the plunger. The man slumped, unconscious.

"Let me get dressed," Jake said, "and then we'll get the hell out of here."

"Do you have a pair of pants I could borrow?" She plucked the fabric of her jeans with her thumb and forefinger. "These are way too trackable."

"I've got something for you. Thought it might be kind of big on you."

"Fashion is a low priority for me."

He gave her a smile that flushed warmth through her entire body. "But beauty comes naturally."

Twenty minutes later, they'd driven far enough from the cabin that Dawn allowed herself to relax a little. She leaned into the seat, rolling her head to admire Jake. He wore the determined look again, but when he met her gaze a tenderness softened his resolve. The ball of anxiety knocking around in her stomach settled. He brushed the back of one finger across her cheek.

"Don't worry," he said. "We've got the proof. And once we're in San Francisco, we can contact the FBI. I'm sure they'll be very interested in what Redeo's been up to out there in the desert. Holding a woman hostage, for starters."

Maybe she ought to worry about the future, but as long as she traveled with Jake by her side, she knew everything would work out. Something inside her confirmed the notion, something rooted in a past she'd yet to uncover—her own past. Or maybe she was a fool, like Vahl said. Either way, she belonged with this man.

His features cinched up in confusion. "Why are you looking at me like I single-handedly saved the world from total annihilation?"

She grinned. "Maybe not the world, but you definitely saved me. And I'm not talking about today. I mean yesterday, in the lab."

Concentrating on the road, he shook his head. "I don't understand."

Of course he didn't. Until today, until he'd unleashed the deeper connection between them with his body and his passion, she hadn't understood either. Leaning in, she whispered into his ear. "I know why I woke up. You brought me back to life."

His jaw dropped. His eyes bulged.

The car swerved as his hands loosened on the wheel for a second. He clutched the wheel, easing the vehicle back into the right lane.

"Whoa," she said, "good thing this is a deserted road."

"Sorry, I—" He took several breaths, exhaling through his mouth in huffs. "That is not possible. I have no magical powers of resurrection."

"No," she said, drawing out the word, "but you care. Knowing what the Redeo scientists intended to do with my body upset you."

"Granted. But that's a far cry from—from—"

The car wandered toward the center line.

She grasped his upper arm. "Maybe you should pull over for a minute."

He complied, stowing the vehicle on the wide shoulder of the tree-lined road. His gaze remained fixed on the view out the windshield, his hands locked on the wheel.

"Listen to me," she said, and tugged his right hand free, clasping it to her breast. "I trusted you from the moment I saw you. Which is crazy, right? But an instinct told me I could place my life in your hands, so I did." Still, he refused to look at her, but she plunged ahead. "I know why now. When we made love earlier, something happened between us, like a spiritual bond created from our emotions. You must've felt it too."

His eyes flicked toward her, though his head pointed straight forward, his face blank.

She kissed his knuckles and gave him a small smile. "Admit it, you did. You felt the connection."

He rotated his head in slow motion, facing her without expression. In his eyes she sensed fear, but also a glimmer of hope. He longed to believe her.

Time to convince him.

"That's when I realized," she said, "what happened back in the lab. You told me once how you sat vigil by my tank. You stared at my face, imagining what I might've been like." She pressed her lips to the back of his hand. "You revived me. With your will alone."

"I couldn't. I don't know how."

The disbelief in his voice echoed between them. She climbed across the center console, mounting his lap, and took his face in her hands. Their eyes met. The bond snapped tight, a metaphysical rope tying them together, beyond time and space and death.

"Tell me you don't feel it," she murmured, brushing her fingers through his hair. "You know me, better than you have any right to if you've only known me for a day. Why do you think that is?"

"I don't know."

"But I do." She kissed his forehead, his cheek, his hand. "I had a memory, from my first life. You were my guardian, assigned to watch over me by my father. And you loved me. I saw you pounding on my coffin, angry and grief-stricken." She held his face, willing him to look at her—and he did. "That's why you're so obsessed with protecting me, Jake. On some level, you remember too."

"I..." His chest heaved, his features tensing and slackening, as if he struggled to understand, to accept what she said. "I wasn't resurrected."

"No. But I'm certain you've been reborn, in a different way." She leaned in until their noses touched. "You do feel it, don't you? The connection? The truth?"

He held stone-still for a long moment. Then he pulled her into him, his mouth teasing hers when he spoke. "I feel it. God, do I feel it."

"Then you understand now."

Their breaths mingled as his lips glided over first the corner of her mouth, then the spot just under her lower lip. "I understand. But you've got it backwards." Their lips fused in a slow, sweet kiss. "You saved me. You brought me back to life."

Pure joy swept through her, and she crushed her lips to his, fueling their joining with every iota of passion and adoration she harbored within her. When they pulled apart, his face beamed with a smile as joyful as the emotions overflowing her heart.

He sighed, a wistful sound. "We'd better get back on the road, if we want to make San Francisco by nightfall."

Climbing back onto her seat, she draped her arm over the center console. "Um, it just occurred to me that I don't even know your last name."

His throaty chuckle sent a tingle over her skin. "It's Maxwell."

"Sorry I can't tell you mine, since I don't have one."

"Doesn't matter."

He lowered his hand onto hers, linking their fingers. Whatever happened next, she knew one thing with absolute certainty.

They'd get through it together.

Forever.

REBORN TO AVENGE

CHAPTER ONE

S UPERNATURAL ENERGY SCORCHED THROUGH JAKE MAXWELL'S foot, surging into his ankle in an inexorable march into the rest of his body. He bit back a gasp. Dawn, the woman he adored, kneeled in front of him at the foot of the hard motel room bed with his foot clasped in both her hands, one palm covering the gash on his sole as she employed her healing skills. Eyes closed, she pursed her lips and grimaced. Another surge of power coursed into him.

He jerked his foot away. "That's enough."

She blinked rapidly, focusing in on him. "Are you sure?"

"Yes. It's fine." He wiggled his foot, as if that proved his statement. "You shouldn't do this anyway. We have no idea how healing affects you."

A sweet smile curved her tempting lips. "Please stop worrying. I'm okay."

"As far as we know. You've only had this power for a week."

She rolled her eyes. "What's the good of having this ability if I can't help the people I love? Or the *person* I love." She muttered under her breath, "I don't know anybody else."

His heart ached for her, and he fought the impulse to haul her into his arms for a kiss that would sear them both harder than her healing burned him. He shouldn't. He'd promised himself to keep her at arm's length for the time being.

But it drove him batty, looking at her slender, curvy body and not being able to taste her skin or lose himself inside her. One week ago, he'd made love to her—make that *ravished* her, without a thought for the consequences. Because he loved her. Because she made him feel like a man, instead of a meek grad student. Because she felt so good under him.

"Jake?" Dawn flopped onto the bed next to him, her body close enough he sensed the warmth of her. "Are you sure you're okay, honey?"

"Don't call me that. I hate endearments." He didn't deserve her tenderness. What good was he when he failed to protect her at every turn?

She leaned into him, her breasts pressed to his upper arm, and slid her own arm under his to clasp her hands over his elbow. The heady scent of her mingled with the clean smell of soap, from her recent shower. She rubbed her cheek on his shoulder.

"You know," she said, "if you'd stop getting hurt, I wouldn't need to heal you."

He flinched at her words, though he knew she meant no insult. Her tone conveyed regret and...affection.

Dammit. How had he let things spiral so far out of control?

In spite of himself, he ducked his head to inhale a deep breath of her scent. "And you wouldn't have needed a shower if I hadn't sent us tumbling down a muddy hillside. I should've had a plan ready." He shut his eyes, his throat constricting, her hair still surrounding his face. "I knew Redeo wouldn't wait forever, but I thought we'd have more time. Or at least some backup."

Her fingers massaged the inside of his elbow. "It's not your fault. Even Jake Maxwell, former Boy Scout and simple grad student—who I'm still convinced is actually a CIA agent—can't plan for every eventuality."

But he should've had some kind of strategy for this. Redeo Biotech would never stop hunting Dawn. She was the end result of their secret and sinister project aimed at regenerating long-dead tissue to a lifelike state. Once the mummified remains of an ancient Egyptian woman, Dawn had become so much more than a lifelike corpse. She was a miracle. A living, breathing impossibility.

Anton Vahl, head of Redeo, knew this too. He dispatched his minions to track down Dawn, barely a week after they escaped Vahl's clutches. *We should've had more time.*

He kissed the top of her head. "We can't stay here. We need to get another car and drive the hell away from San Francisco." He'd allowed her a quick shower because, after they fled from their old car while pursued by Vahl's men and taken the aforementioned tumble down a hill, she'd been covered in mud.

"Where do we go?" Her shoulders sagged, and her gaze had gone vacant.

He drew her into his arms, her head tucked under his chin. "I don't know. We'll figure it out on the road. Trust me, okay?"

She lifted her head, her pupils large, those hazel eyes glossy and blazing into him with unblinking directness. "Of course I trust you."

The simple statement tore at his heart. He did not deserve her trust, anymore than he deserved her love.

Dawn extricated her smaller body from his and padded over to the dresser, retrieving her sneakers. Her blue jeans stretched taut as she bent at the waist to slip on the shoes. Her white cotton shirt billowed out, granting him a glimpse of the full breasts hidden beneath the fabric, supported by a lacy white bra. Visions of his mouth on her nipples rushed through his brain.

His pants grew snug in the crotch. He rubbed his hands on his pant legs and tried to banish the fantasy. No such luck.

A veil of dark red hair fell over Dawn's face. She smiled at him through the locks. "I know what you're thinking, but we don't have time." She dropped to a crouch, stealing his view of her bosom. "But it's nice to know you still want me."

Christ. How did she know?

Her gaze flitted to his crotch. He glanced down to see the swelling bulge there. Right. That's how she knew. "Of course I want you. That's never been in question."

Focused on tying her shoe laces, she gnawed her lip. "Maybe for you. But ever since that night in the cabin, you haven't...um..." Her cheeks flushed.

He hadn't tried to seduce her. He thought about it at least twice a minute, but indulging in his hunger for her distracted him from everything else. Like protecting her. Somehow.

"Dawn." He waited until she looked up at him. "I want you. Always. But we need to concentrate on exposing Vahl's experiments to the world, so he'll have no reason to hunt you anymore."

"I know." She tied the laces of her other shoe with trembling fingers. "But I'd understand if you regret being with me. I am a formerly mummified...creature."

They'd been through this already, he thought. "You are not a—"

Banging erupted at the door, which shook from the force of the blows.

Dawn jumped.

Jake leaped to his feet, ripping the 9mm handgun out of the holster fastened to his belt, at the base of his spine. He held the gun muzzle up and crept toward the door.

The banging ceased.

He peered through the peephole. "Shit."

Dawn raced toward him, but he flung up a hand, palm out. She froze halfway to him, her eyes wide, lips parted.

She whispered one word. "Who?"

"Vahl."

Her face pale, she stared at him. "Anton Vahl?"

"You know another Vahl?" The fragile shaking of her head made him want to kiss away her anxiety. He opted for an understanding tone instead. "Yes, it's Anton Vahl."

The scientist responsible for resurrecting Dawn. The man who claimed her as his legal property and test subject. The man Jake would murder if he tried to capture her again.

He raised the gun, targeted at the door. With his free hand, he grasped the knob, curling his fingers around the cold metal.

Dawn threw a hand up. "Stop, Jake, please. Shooting him won't solve our problems."

"Maybe not, but it'll make me feel a hell of a lot better."

Vahl's voice shouted to them. "I know you two are in there. Please open the door. I only wish to talk."

Jake clenched the door knob harder.

Dawn gazed at him with dull eyes and a sad smile. "We've exhausted our options. That reporter thought we were kooks, the cops tossed us out, and the FBI laughed at us." She hugged herself, eying the door. "He says he wants to talk."

"That's what Vahl said last time."

"Maybe it's true. Last week, he did show up alone and unarmed."

Jake strained to curb the fury boiling inside him. "Vahl brought a syringe, full of God knows what, which he intended to inject into you."

She shrugged one shoulder weakly. "We have no choice."

His mind reeled through the memories of all the trauma they'd endured in their desperate attempt to shake free of Redeo and Vahl. The flash drive and its contents—files poached from Redeo's own servers, all related to Dawn and her regeneration—had been their sole hope for salvation, yet it meant nothing.

Her shoes scuffed across the carpeting as she moved closer to settle a hand on his, the one holding the gun. With gentle pressure, and eyes shimmering with tears, she coaxed him to lower the weapon. "You know I'm right, Jake."

Vahl shouted again. "Last chance before I call for backup and we storm this motel. I'd rather not do that. The choice is yours."

A single tear rolled down Dawn's cheek.

Jake tucked the gun in the back of his waistband, under his shirt. Then he cupped her face in both hands and kissed her—a tender, lingering kiss, their lips conveying everything they needed to say.

Withdrawing, he wiped the tear track away with his thumb. "Stay behind me."

She complied.

He faced the door, sucked in a deep breath, and swung it open.

CHAPTER TWO

COLD STEEL TALONS GOUGED DAWN'S HEART AS SHE watched Anton Vahl saunter into the room. He trailed a fingertip across the windowsill on his way to the small table situated there. Pulling out the nearest chair, he lowered his lean body onto the faded fabric of the seat and draped one arm over the table. His fingers tapped the faux-wood surface, in a rhythm reminiscent of Morse code.

Jake slammed the door. He sidestepped to blockade her with his body, and then snarled at Vahl. "If you're here to tell Dawn she belongs to you, save it. We've heard your spiel before."

She took a half step to the right, gaining a view of the scientist.

Vahl stroked the tabletop with his fingers, his dark eyes locking in on her. "I've reconsidered my previous assumptions. You are not property to be bartered for. No, oh no." His mouth stretched into a self-satisfied smile that sent a chill down her spine. "You, my dear, are the embodiment of my every hope and desire, the culmination of my life's work. You are, in a word, proof."

Jake cast a sidelong glance at her, then glared at Vahl. "What the hell are you trying to say?"

"The fact that she lives proves my regeneration process works." He slanted forward, face impassive. "I need the proof, to convince my investors—"

"That you can sell resurrection to desperate, filthy rich people." Jake scowled, shaking his head. "We've heard all this before. Say something new, or..." His voice dropped to a deadly whisper. "I will shut you up for good."

A shudder rattled her. Triggered by fear, yes, because Jake's anger disturbed her. But the shudder also stemmed from a dark pleasure at what he would do to protect her.

My guardian. In every lifetime.

A vision flashed in her mind, of Jake in ancient Egyptian garb—a white linen kilt with leather belt—his muscled chest bare, the sinews of his arms flexing as he wielded a sword.

Vahl's chuckling, soft and menacing, wrenched her out of the memory. For it was a memory, of her first life, before she was murdered and mummified, and after three thousand years reborn, thanks in part to Vahl's experiments. But it was Jake, reincarnated by a mystical process no scientist could explain, who had awakened her from death. Fate brought them back to each other, so he could resurrect her with the power of his will.

"Here's what has changed," Vahl said, still focused on her with an eerie intensity. "I no longer view Jake as irrelevant and expendable. He is, in fact, essential."

Dawn froze. Her pulse thundered in her ears and stampeded in her veins.

Vahl relaxed back against his chair and sighed. "I've been watching the two of you for the past week, since you left me at the cabin."

Jake tensed, his hands fisting at his sides. "That's not possible."

"Come now, Jake, you know that's not true. Modern surveillance techniques provide many and varied ways of utilizing technology to track anyone and anything." Vahl waved a finger toward the ceiling. "Satellites with resolution down to the inch. Facial recognition software. And oh, how convenient it is that so many cities have set up surveillance cameras on their streets, not to mention ATM cameras. It's a veritable goldmine of tracking information. And you simplified the search by taking refuge in a large city equipped with over a thousand surveillance cameras. Add in a judicious use of on-the-ground investigators, and I had all the data I needed to understand you both."

Holy shit. She'd never once thought about the digital eyes observing them. The modern world offered few places to really hide. Had they deluded themselves into believing they could conceal their presence?

Jake shut his eyes, shaking his head.

And she knew, just knew, he was wondering the same thing.

Vahl rose with easy grace, locked his hands behind his back, and began to pace between the window and the bed. His lips pursed, and his brow furrowed. "At first, I was confounded by your bond. You were strangers when Dawn awoke, and yet you instantly committed to shielding each other at any cost. A love of that magnitude does not emerge out of nowhere."

Dawn cleared her throat, fighting back a wave of panic. He knew too damn much. She tried to speak, but her voice foundered.

Beside her, Jake clenched and slackened his fists, over and over, as if trying to pump out—or maybe pump up—his tension. It rippled through him in surges that hunched his shoulders and spurred his jaw muscles to tick.

Vahl stopped beside the table. He turned his head to smile at her. "I know the truth. You and Jake were acquainted in a previous life."

The blood evacuated her brain. The room twirled around her. She staggered to the bed, collapsing onto it. Propped up with one arm, she rode out the dizziness.

Jake had transformed into a living statue. His face blank, his arms slack at his sides, shoulders slumped.

Dawn fiddled with the hem of her blouse. When her wits reassembled themselves, she addressed Vahl. "What could possibly have led you to that conclusion? It's not very scientific."

Vahl turned on his heels, facing her. "Your awakening has no rational explanation. Your consciousness, your healing ability..." He gave a slight shake of his head. "Science has abandoned me, my dear. I've been forced to accept the supernatural plays a role in all of this."

"You didn't answer my question."

"How do I know about your eternal link to Jake?"

The first twinge of a headache pricked at the backs of her eyes. She flicked her gaze upward for a second, and then nodded. The jerk was trying to annoy her by stalling. It worked, but she'd be damned if she let him see that.

"It's quite simple." Vahl reached into the inside pocket of his jacket.

Jake sneaked a hand behind his back, going for the gun.

"There's no need for violence," Vahl said. "I simply want to show you the evidence."

Jake lowered his hand, though his gaze narrowed on Vahl.

The scientist pulled out a small item wrapped in a loose cloth. He unfolded the fabric, revealing a statuette that fit inside his palm. Holding the object upright, he said, "It's carved from the finest alabaster, and was placed inside the linen wrappings that shrouded your remains, right over your heart."

He held out his hand, offering her the statuette.

She glanced at Jake, who squinted at the figurine. His eyes flicked to her, searching, questioning. She had no answers to give him.

Pushing up off the bed, she shuffled just close enough to Vahl to snatch the figurine from his hand. Its finely carved face gazed up at her.

She felt her mouth drop open. The face. *Christ.*

It was Jake.

The fact should not have shocked her. She'd experienced memories from her past life, visions of him huddled over her coffin inside her tomb, cursing the gods and vowing revenge against whoever took her life. She'd already known they shared a bond deeper and stronger than time itself. But this...

Seeing the proof in her hand, it jammed a phantom steel spike into her heart.

Her gaze flitted to Jake's. She held out her hand to him, and he took the figurine. Without expression, he turned the object between his thumb and forefinger. "Where did you get this?"

Vahl leaned his hip on the windowsill, folding his arms over his chest. "I will share all my knowledge with you freely—after you both agree to my terms."

As his gaze shifted from the figurine to Vahl, Jake curled his lip, a dark glint in his eyes. "What terms?"

She beat down the impulse to run to him, fling her arms around his neck, and devour his anger with her mouth on his. Seeing him like this prickled her from the inside out.

"My offer is simple." Vahl glanced out the window, between the slats of the partly open blinds. "Dawn moves into my compound outside Las Vegas. You may visit her whenever you like and do whatever you like within the confines of her quarters."

Dawn rubbed at her arms and wished like hell she were anywhere but here. He couldn't seriously be suggesting conjugal visits. As if she'd feel comfortable so much as kissing Jake, knowing Vahl undoubtedly planted a video camera in her room.

Jake strode two menacing steps closer to Vahl. "Tell us the rest."

The scientist smiled that creepy little smile. "She will submit to any and all tests I require of her." Jake's mouth opened, but Vahl raised a hand. "I give you my word she will not be permanently harmed. Some of the tests may cause discomfort, but I'll do everything in my power to ensure she does not suffer needlessly."

"Forget it."

"The choice is not yours." Vahl's eyes focused on her face, and she scuffled backward a step. "It's hers."

A bead of sweat on her forehead slithered down her temple. "What happens if I decline your generous offer?"

"My men are waiting outside—hidden, of course. They will take you by force, and I imagine Jake will intervene, with serious consequences to his health."

"You'll kill him."

Vahl shrugged. "That depends upon how much he fights."

Ice frosted over her heart. He'd fight to the death, she knew it. For her, he'd risk anything. She loved him, more than reason allowed, and she loved his protective instincts. But not when they put him in danger.

She studied Jake, at his chiseled profile taut with contained fury, until he sensed her attention and his eyes rotated toward her. His expression softened a little, his eyes shimmering with empathy, but his tight smile betrayed his concern.

Let him die? Hell no. They hadn't come this far to lose each other now.

Despite rifling through her brain for a better plan, she came up empty. So that left her with one choice. One terrifying, unthinkable decision.

Jake's anger disintegrated into muted horror. He shook his head.

She prayed her face revealed to him her sorrow and love. She prayed he'd understand, someday, somehow, why she did this.

Facing Vahl, she said, "I'll go with you."

"No!"

Jake's exclamation resounded in the tiny room, a bellow of such magnitude, filled with so much grief and rage, it rattled her eardrums and rent her soul. *No, Jake, please don't fight this.*

His body quivered, his jaw grinding. He glowered at Vahl with enough heat to melt steel. "You. Can't. Have. Her."

The softness of his voice carried a deadly threat.

Dawn rushed to his side, seizing his arm in both hands. "Please, Jake, please. Don't do this. I've made up my mind, I'm sorry, I can't lose you."

The quaking in his jaw bled into his lips. A pallor seeped into his skin, yet his expression remained stony.

She wrapped her arms around his neck, hugging him tight, and whispered in his ear. "I'm sorry. Please forgive me."

He made no response, in voice or body, his every muscle stiff. She withdrew, biting her lip to stave off the tears burning in her eyes. Then she confronted Vahl.

"Are you ready, my dear?" he asked.

"Yes."

He rose and placed a hand on the small of her back to guide her toward the door. Jake blocked their way, a pillar of granite flesh and stone-cold eyes. Dawn beseeched him with her gaze, and somehow he knew what she wanted, because he took one wide step to the side.

Vahl swung the door inward. "My men will instruct you on how to contact us. As I said, you're welcome to visit her."

Jake fixed his scalding glare on the wall. He blew a breath out through his nostrils.

Dawn let Vahl escort her through the door. As she passed Jake, his fingers sprang out to brush hers. She clasped them briefly, her throat constricting, then shuffled outside to the silver sedan awaiting them.

Inside the car, settled into the passenger seat, she buckled her seatbelt and looked out the windshield. Jake stood in the doorway. Tall. Tense. Impassive.

She watched him while Vahl backed the car out of the parking space, craning her neck to see him when the vehicle swung left, coming up parallel to the building. And she kept watching until the doorway shrank out of sight.

Vahl patted her knee. "Don't worry, child. You are in my care now."

A weight bore down on her chest and she fought to breathe. "You told me once you could help me regain my memories."

"I can. I will." He flipped on the radio. Classical music emanated from the speakers, some kind of string piece. "No one knows more about your body than I do, Dawn. Together, we will unlock its secrets—and the memories buried within you."

Remembering who she'd been. That's what she wanted, so badly, and yet trusting this man with her mind and body may have been the dumbest thing she'd ever done. What choice did she have? To stop Jake from getting himself killed, she had to take Vahl's offer. More than herself, though, she worried about Jake. *Oh God, don't do anything crazy for me.*

"The first task," Vahl said, "is to explore your brain."

She gripped the arm rest. *Explore your brain.* Another scientist who'd worked for Vahl told her they would autopsy her alive.

The car veered around a corner, heaving her toward the door. She'd made the right choice, hadn't she? If not…

All she could hope was they'd kill her before they gutted her.

CHAPTER THREE

J AKE MOUNTED THE STEPS TO THE FRONT DOOR OF THE sprawling adobe mansion. The sun glinted off the coy pond to the left of the steps. A breeze wafted the scent of jasmine over him, and the heat of the summer day sizzled on his skin. At the door, he stopped to mop sweat from his forehead with the back of his hand.

His heart thudded as he punched the doorbell. Six days without her. Phone calls left him empty, pain echoing in his heart. How could he have let Vahl take her?

He knew why. She'd begged him to, with her eyes and her somber expression. His gut wrenched at the memory of her walking out of the motel room with Vahl, and of the smug little smile on the creep's face.

I won, the scientist had been saying.

Jake shoved his hands in his jeans pockets. Shifted his weight first to one hip, then the other. Scratched his neck. Raked a hand through his hair, the nails scraping skin.

The door swung inward.

A gray-haired woman, petite and plump, smiled at him with genuine geniality, crinkling the skin around her eyes. "Mr. Maxwell, hello. I'm Gladys Henderson. We've been expecting you."

Because he had to call ahead for permission to come. Vahl relished lording his power over Jake.

His throat went dry. In what ways did Vahl exercise his power over Dawn? *Christ.* He had to see her. Now.

Gladys Henderson scrunched her manicured brows. "Are you all right?"

With intense effort, he relaxed his hunched shoulders and let his arms fall slack at his sides. *Show no fear, it'll only egg Vahl on.* "I'm fine, Ms. Henderson. I'd like to see Dawn, please."

"Of course. And call me Gladys." She turned sideways, waving him inside. He strode past her, and she shut the door, sealing out the heat in favor of the blessed cool of air conditioning. "I'll show you to the young lady's room. She's been anxious to see you too."

Anxious? His jaw tightened. If she'd been hurt, if he found one scratch on her...

"This way." Gladys led him through the foyer and down a hallway lined with abstract paintings of desert landscapes and cow skulls.

It figured a twisted bastard like Vahl would like skull art.

They passed one door on the left, and another on the right. Gladys escorted him to the end of the hall, to the second and final door on the left side. It stood shut. Jake raised his hand over the knob, desperate to grasp it and fling the door open, but paralyzed by the cold spreading through him.

"Go on, honey. She's waiting." Gladys gave him a maternal smile.

Honey. He swallowed hard. Dawn called him that back in the motel, right before Vahl stole her away from him. He'd chastised her for using the endearment. What an ass he'd been.

Gladys patted his arm. "Would you like me to knock for you?"

"No, I..." He drew in a breath, releasing it slowly. "Thank you, I can manage."

With another pat, she turned and left. He lifted his fist, hovering it an inch from the wood. A sensation tingled over his skin, almost like a touch grazing him. He swore he felt her around him, in him. *She's right inside this room, idiot.*

He knocked.

The door flew inward as his fist contacted the wood for a second knock.

Dawn gawked at him, lips parted, eyes wide. Her cheeks flushed. She stumbled backward, and in a breathless voice, said, "Jake."

He rushed into the room, banging the door shut. A couple feet separated them, and he longed to crush her to him, claim her mouth, expose exactly how much he'd missed her. He couldn't move. His heart pounded, his head light. A wave of euphoria knocked him off kilter, until all he could do was gape at her. "Are you...okay?"

She nodded. "You?"

"Fine."

Her gaze shifted down, toward his chin or maybe his mouth. She licked her lower lip, and hunger scorched him. "Are you, uh, planning to kiss me?"

Oh hell yes.

In one stride, he reached her and dragged her into his arms. She gasped, her tongue visible between her open lips. He covered her mouth with his, plunging his tongue inside to savor the taste of her—sweet, salty, with a hint of dark spices. His need for her obliterated reason, and he thrust a hand into her hair, catching her head to tilt it back, then plundering her even more deeply. She melted against him and moaned. Her breasts were mashed into his chest, and even through both their shirts and her bra, the hard tips of her nipples pushed against his chest.

Her arms wrapped around his waist. She reciprocated his kiss with equal ardor, her passion inflaming his. They kissed forever, as time froze around them, the only sounds his hammering pulse and her little moans.

She ripped her mouth away from his, panting. "Jake, we're probably being watched."

Damn, her throaty tone was hot. He dipped his head to trail kisses down her throat and slipped his hand under her blouse. The softness of her skin drove him wild, impelling him to lunge his other hand beneath the fabric. He skimmed both palms up her sides, rewarded by her little groan and the way she arched into him. God, he wanted her. Right here, right now.

He cupped her breasts, rubbing her nipples through her bra with his thumbs.

"Jake." She threw her head back, her hips rolling into him. "Please, we can't. Not here."

Kneading her breasts, he skated his teeth up her throat to the sensitive spot just below her ear. Her nails dug into his back. He nipped her earlobe.

"Please," she gasped. "He's watching."

"I don't give a damn," Jake hissed. "Let the prick have a good show."

She wrestled out of his arms, staggering backward to the bed. Her chest heaved, and the rosiness in her cheeks had deepened. Her lips were swollen, branded by his kiss. She collapsed onto the mattress, looking so adorably befuddled and absolutely gorgeous.

He shut his eyes for a heartbeat, then stared at his palms, which still smoldered from her skin on his. He'd nearly ravished her. In Vahl's house. No conversation, no foreplay. What kind of cretin had he turned into?

Jake scrubbed his face with his hands. "I'm sorry. I don't know what I was thinking."

He hadn't been thinking at all, not with his head anyway.

"It's okay." She grinned, her eyes alight. "That was the best greeting I've ever been given."

"But Vahl…" He searched the shadows and corners, the crevices and walls, for evidence of cameras but spotted none. A clever man like Vahl knew how to conceal such things. He zeroed in on Dawn's eyes. "You were begging me to stop."

Her grin morphed into a tender smile. She patted the mattress beside her. "Sit with me. Please."

"You're begging again."

Her lips twitched, almost a smirk. "I'm extending a polite invitation. When I plead, you'll know. It sounds more breathless."

She patted the bed again.

Helpless to resist any request from her, he settled onto the plain white blanket—cheap acrylic—an arm's length from her. His body ached to slide closer, to pull her into an embrace and kiss her senseless, again. He braced his body with one hand on the bed, resting the other on his knee. The springs in the hard mattress crunched under his weight. "Are you really all right?"

"Fine." She studied his face, her lips sinking into a sad downward curve, not quite a frown. She murmured, "You're so angry."

Heat fused his muscles into iron, his fingers had latched onto his knee, and he itched to hurl something at the wall. Right. This was anger. He'd endured it for six days, until the acid burn of it scarred over, stripping away his nerves, leaving behind a numbness. "I'm not angry with you."

Her hand fluttered up, suspended so near his face the hairs on his cheek stirred.

The tightness in his chest escalated into a searing pressure. He longed to lean into her hand, drown his fury and anguish in her caress, but he couldn't. When he saved her from all this, then he might allow himself to bask in her ecstasy. Only then. When he deserved it.

Her hazel eyes entranced him, and the sheen of unshed tears in them stabbed his heart. *Damn Vahl.*

"What's he done to you?" Gravel scoured his tone. "Tell me."

"Nothing much." Her fingers tentatively lighted on his jaw, near his chin. "Blood tests. An MRI, a CT scan, stuff like that." She gave a faint laugh. "An eye exam too. And an IQ test. Guess he's like you in one respect—he needs to quantify everything." When Jake stiffened, she spread her palm across his cheek, the fingertips feathering over his skin. "That's the only thing you two have in common. He's a megalomaniac, and you—" She cupped his face in both hands. "You are the most honorable man I've ever known. And considering I was born three thousand years ago, that's really saying something."

He strived to smile, to reveal the seed of joy blossoming in his heart, but he couldn't pull it off. "He hasn't hurt you?"

"No."

Relief poured into him, sagging his shoulders. Her palms warmed his cheeks, like the sun beaming onto a snow-capped landscape. But doubt winnowed its frozen tendrils through the warmth. "Has he told you what else he has planned? What other tests?"

She pressed her lips to his in a gentle, chaste contact, then withdrew from him. Hands clasped on her lap, she sighed. "He mentioned testing my physical condition and advanced mental functions. I'm not sure exactly what he meant by that, but I think he believes I've got ESP or something."

Or something. Vahl couldn't know about her healing power. Could he?

Dawn would've said "healing power" if she believed Vahl knew about her ability. Her vagueness implied she suspected Vahl had an inkling about her power, but that she wasn't sure and therefore did not want to clue him in, should he be listening to their conversation. Smart girl. *His* girl.

God, she was amazing.

She cast him a sidelong glance. "Why are you smiling?"

"We're not alone."

A shake of her head. "Tell me something I don't know."

"I'm better at showing than telling." He slid a hand up her thigh, over her hip, higher still, his palm molded to the side of her breast. Her delicate blush set off a matching heat in him. "I wish..."

She let out a shaky sigh, her lips slanting into a suggestive smile. "Me too."

Getting her out of here was his sole goal. He had some ideas, but the help he required might prove difficult to track down. And it would drag him further away from her.

Dawn leaned closer, her lips grazing his ear, and whispered, "If you need to travel, don't let me hold you back. I can handle Vahl."

He stilled, right down to his soul. Could she read minds? ESP may not have been a flippant remark after all.

Nah. She couldn't—No.

"If there's an emergency," he said, quiet as a breath, "I need to be close by."

"Wrong. You won't find answers while holed up in a cheap motel twiddling your thumbs, waiting for your next conjugal visit."

She was right, and he hated it. "Conjugal visit?"

Her teeth captured his earlobe, tugging gently, her tongue slick and soft. "It could be. If we turn the lights off and shut the blinds, it's almost pitch dark in here."

A flashback hauled him into the past, to their first and only sexual encounter. She moaned and panted at his every touch, and he'd responded with a wild hunger. How much noise had they made? He couldn't—wouldn't—risk anyone else eavesdropping on their intimacy. Her passionate cries belonged to him and him alone.

He eased her away. "Wrong time, wrong place."

Disappointment erased her sensual smile. "I know. First, I begged you not to, and now I'm pushing you into it. Sorry."

"Don't apologize." He skimmed a thumb across her lips. "That's my line, remember?"

Even his joke failed to coax a smile from her. She pulled further away, hugging herself. "Let's go for a walk."

"That's allowed?"

"As long as we stay on the grounds, yes."

She rose, offering him her hand. He clasped it and stood, then followed her out the door.

As he crossed the threshold, his gaze flicked back to the window. The sun shining in cast rails of shadow on the backside of the curtains. Shadows cast by metal bars on the window. This was a prison, and one way or another, he would break her out of it.

Dawn ushered him out of the house, via the back door, and across a lush lawn crafted by irrigation and fertilizer. The green stretched out from the house, an expanse of several acres, a stark contrast to the reddish-tinged brown of the desert beyond. To the west, the tiny shapes of the skyscraper hotels and casinos of Las Vegas poked up from the horizon.

On their way across the lawn, they passed a concrete-block building the size of a two-car garage.

"What's that?" he asked, pointing at the building.

"Not sure. I heard one of the guards mention a power station, so maybe that's it. Apparently, Vahl doesn't trust the grid and generates his own electricity from a combination of solar and wind energy."

"I don't think windmills would fit inside that little building."

"Ha-ha." She elbowed him in the side. "If you really want to know, the guard said Vahl's a prick—his word exactly—about not having to look at the solar panels and wind turbines. They're somewhere past the wall of palm trees that surrounds the house and lawn. Vahl owns five hundred acres."

"Fascinating." It wasn't, but he preferred blathering on about Vahl's power station to thinking about abandoning her. Again. "How many kilowatts does the station produce?"

"I don't know. Enough to power the house and the electric fence around the perimeter."

When he looked closer, he made out thin, stick-like objects protruding from the ground in the distance, at the lawn's edge. Fence posts.

"That's all I know," she said.

"It's a lot." He bumped her with his shoulder. "And you think I'm a spy."

She aimed a shy smile at him. His chest tightened, and he turned his head away to avoid doing something unmanly, like crying.

They halted under a tall palm tree. A wind swayed the fronds overhead, slashing shadows and light across them in equal measure. Dawn grasped both his hands, suspended between their bodies. Her lips were compressed, her eyes shimmering. The wind whipped her auburn hair over her face, but she made no move to brush it away.

He tried to shake one hand free of hers, to clear the stray locks from her eyes, but she held fast to him.

"Jake..." She trailed off, as if words no longer sufficed. Maybe they didn't.

Jake threw a wary glance back at the house, its hulking form a blister on the verdant environ. "He's probably still listening. Parabolic mics or something similar."

"Yeah." Her lovely mouth split into a grin. "Parabolic mics? And you claim you're not a spy."

"I'm not." If only he were, he'd whisk her away from here James Bond style. No such luck. He tugged her hands to draw her close, and bent to whisper in her ear. "I have an idea. Someone to talk to."

"A possible ally?" Her hushed tone matched his.

"Yes." With a painful effort, he resisted the urge to fold her in his arms. "But finding this person might take considerable time, and I'll have to travel far from here."

"Go. I told you, don't let me hold you back."

He pulled his head back, ensnaring her gaze. "You never hold me back."

She freed him, in body, mind, and soul. He'd never known—never imagined he could know—the kind of liberation she bestowed on him.

"You know what I mean, Jake." Her shoulders hunched, she scrutinized his neck. "Don't stay here just to be with me. However long it takes, however far you have to go, find a way to end this."

"I will." A lead weight solidified in his gut. "I have to go."

She nodded, her eyes glistening.

He hauled her into his arms for a slow, sweet kiss, rife with longing and anguish. Her soft, yielding lips begged him for more, and he nearly caved in to the need to possess her, to cement this connection, but he peeled himself away from her, inch by heart-rending inch. Tears trickled down her face. He swiped them away with his thumbs, pecked her forehead, whirled away, and stalked back to his car.

Damn Vahl. Jake despised the man, yet he could not wish Vahl had never existed, because then Dawn might never have been resurrected, and his life would still be a bottomless, empty pit echoing with yearnings he couldn't fathom. Dawn showed him the truth, with her sarcasm and suspicion that transmuted into an unwavering trust he struggled, but failed, to comprehend. His incandescent princess.

His soul mate, bound to him by a bond even time could not sever.

As he slammed the car door and cranked the key in the ignition, an epiphany struck, startling him with its intensity. He believed. The timeless connection, the passion that outlasted their physical bodies and endured in some ethereal plane where nothing touched it. When Dawn told him she remembered him from her first life, the one in ancient Egypt, he hadn't really believed it. But now, faced with the agonizing prospect of losing her to whatever Vahl had planned, the reality of their bond crashed through him.

He believed in it. He lived it.

And whatever he had to do, he would save her this time.

CHAPTER FOUR

D AWN SHAMBLED INTO THE LAB, THROUGH AN ORNATE wooden door identical to all the doors in Anton Vahl's house. Only difference was, this portal revealed a scientific laboratory populated with computers, equipment with flashing lights, medical devices, chairs, and an exam table straight out of a doctor's office.

As she walked into the lab, she spied the backside of the door. The wood was a veneer, backed by a thick metal slab.

Three days ago, Jake had left. A pain ignited at the back of her throat when she recalled him storming away from her, his face unreadable even as he fisted his hands and tensed his entire body. She'd wanted to run away with him, escape Vahl somehow, flee to the furthest reaches of...wherever...and hide out for eternity.

Instead, she'd marched back into the house—the mansion—for another go-round of blood tests and scans. Her arms ached from the needle jabs. She rubbed them absently, scanning the lab. Something was different.

Then her gaze collided with the newest object in the lab—a glass tank, rectangular, coffin-like. It hunkered atop a dais, with shallow steps leading up to its side. A pale blue liquid filled the tank.

Her stomach lurched. Her gorge surged high in her throat. She flattened a hand on her chest, as if she might soothe her pounding heart.

A glass coffin.

It was identical to the one she'd awakened inside of almost three weeks ago. She'd nearly drowned in that death box. Jake rescued her, spiriting her away from the Redeo Biotech facility before Saxon, Vahl's underling, autopsied her. Vahl claimed he was different from Saxon, and he hadn't sanctioned the other man's vile tactics, but here she stood face-to-face with the proof of his deceit.

A glass coffin.

She scuffled closer, lured in despite the fear icing her veins with every pulse of her heartbeat. At the base of the dais, she froze. Tiny bubbles fizzed up from the bottom of the tank, lending the blue liquid the festive look of alien champagne.

Her fingers ached. She glanced down to discover she was clutching handfuls of her pink cotton shirt. She released the fabric and smoothed it with her clammy palms, then wiped them over her gray leggings. Jake had run his hands over her the same way the last time she saw him. He'd freed her from imprisonment in one tank, only for her to volunteer to drown in another.

For all she knew, this was the same tank, imported from Redeo.

"It's not what you think."

Vahl's voice startled a yelp out of her. She wheeled around.

He loomed in the doorway, the golden light from the hallway streaming over his dark, wavy hair. A smile played on his lips, though it stopped short of his eyes, where his crow's feet failed to deepen with sincerity. He strode toward her, his muscular body straining the fabric of his crisp white dress shirt. His charcoal slacks hung low on his hips. She might've found him attractive, if he weren't the embodiment of her bondage and suffering.

If he hadn't ripped her away from Jake while claiming he cared about her well-being.

She barred her arms over her breasts. "I am not getting in that coffin."

"Coffin?" His brow knit, his lips puckering. Then realization mellowed his expression. "Ah, the tank. Yes, I can see how you might associate it with coffins and death." He halted close enough to reach a hand up to graze her arm through the cotton of her blouse. "But the tank you woke in was an instrument of life, not death."

"Right. That's why Saxon tried to kill Jake and threatened to dissect me."

Genuine annoyance flickered on his face. "I am not Saxon. He went rogue, violating every tenet of our agreement."

"What tenets would those be?"

"Maintain the integrity of the experiments while behaving in an ethical manner at all times."

She snorted. "Ethical? You're holding me hostage."

"You came with me of your own free will."

A harsh laugh barked out of her. "Because you threatened to blow Jake's head off if I didn't."

"Everyone crafts their own ethical standards." He shrugged one shoulder. "I do what must be done to maintain the integrity of the experiments."

"If you say the word integrity one more time—" She jabbed a finger in the air at him. "—I will beat you unconscious with some of this fancy equipment and then drown you in your precious tank."

Amusement quirked his lips, and he shook his head. "You are a remarkable young woman, but remember this." He seized her upper arms and gave her a hard shake, his voice a gravelly hiss. "I own you. Legally. You will do as I wish or—"

"What? You'll kill me? Torture me?" She squirmed, unable to wrest herself free of his grip. His features contorted into a sneer, and he yanked her into his powerful body, his fingers cutting into her. Swallowing hard, she met his gaze. "Or maybe you'll rape me. Is that what you're really after?"

His hot breaths blasted her face. Her bangs fluttered. "I've watched you with Jake."

The floor seemed to drop away. For a second, she was grateful for his vise-like fingers clamped onto her flesh. Only for a second.

His eyes, inches away, bored into her. His lips parted. "Even fully clothed, you make love to each other. With your words, your lips, your hands, the way you look at each other…" With a sharp intake of breath, he crushed her to him. "I don't understand this. You. Him. The passion and connection you share, even after death. He offers you nothing, while I could've given you every luxury. Why do you love him?"

"I—" How the hell could she answer? Vahl was teetering on a precipice, though what lay below him, she had no clue. Tipping him over the edge seemed like a bad idea. Time for some strategic acquiescence. "I'll get in the tank if you explain what it's for. Please." She fought to calm her breathing. "I'm trying to be amenable, but I have bad memories of a tank like that one."

His gaze impaled her, but then—with an abruptness that stunned a gasp out of her—he let her go and hopped back a step.

"It's known as the CAHR system." He waved toward the tank. "Computer Assisted Hypnotic Regression. It was designed to help victims of traumatic brain injury recover their faculties." He ambled past her, all trace of his sexual heat gone. "Tests have been promising."

"And the tank?"

"In this case, it's for sensory deprivation, which is enhanced by the soundproof construction of this room." He half turned, watching her peripherally. "No harm will come to you."

Her feet had grown heavy, and she glanced at random points on the walls and floor. Not like she had much choice when it came to trusting him.

"I promised to help you regain your memories." Vahl scaled the steps of the dais, resting his hands on the tank's lip, his focus directed into the burbling blue liquid. "I intend to prove I'm a man of my word."

Her fingers fiddled with the hem of her shirt.

Vahl turned around, squaring his shoulders. "I've brought the CAHR system here for you, my dear. Your memories have no value to me, which means I've nothing to gain from this other than your goodwill. Do you wish to try this method?"

For nine days, she'd tried to unearth a way to escape this luxurious prison in the center of the remote desert. Tried and failed. Over and over. No weapon, no allies, no get-away car. If she couldn't break out, then she might as well glean whatever she could from Anton Vahl. To retrieve her memories, herself, and at last understand why she existed, what happened to her, she would risk anything.

She let out a sharp sigh. "Okay. I'll try it."

His lips warped into a triumphant smirk.

Overwhelmed by a sickening sense of déjà vu, she walked up the dais to stand an arm's length from Vahl. "How does it work?"

"First of all," he said, gliding his fingers up and down the tank's rim, "I'm afraid you'll have to remove your clothing."

Naked in a glass coffin, drowning, overpowered by terror.

At least this time it was her choice, and it wasn't as if Vahl hadn't seen her nude body before, since he'd run the Redeo project that revived her.

She gulped, straightened, and lifted fingers that trembled just slightly as she un-hooked the top button of her blouse.

Vahl turned sideways, his gaze intent on the wall behind the tank.

With the last button freed, her blouse slid off her shoulders, fluttering to the floor. She took hold of the rivet of her jeans and pried it loose.

Please, Jake, find a way.

CHAPTER FIVE

J AKE HESITATED OUTSIDE THE FRONT DOOR OF THE MODEST
ranch home in the middle of the woods, high in the Appalachian Mountains. His
body ached from the bumpy ride down a long, winding gravel road that segued into
a rutted two-track. After three days of hunting, he'd tracked down the one man who
might hold the power to aid him. To help him save Dawn.

To save himself.

He scanned the woods, haunted by a lingering fear he'd missed something. How
much more careful could he have been? After leaving Vahl's place, he checked his car for
every kind of tracking device he knew of, but found nothing. Since then, he'd flown on
three chartered planes, switched cars a half dozen times, ditched his clothes four times,
and whenever possible avoided anyplace that might have surveillance cameras. No one
tracked him. He was ninety-five percent sure of it.

Make that eighty percent.

He raised a fist to rap on the plain wood door. It pivoted inward. He started,
dropping his hand.

A gray-haired man with a deeply wrinkled face gazed up at him with bright, pale-
blue eyes. The gentleman kept one arm hidden behind the door, the other tense at his
side. The difference in their heights forced Jake to dip his head to meet the man's
gaze. The older fellow's head barely reached Jake's shoulder height. He'd met Ralph
Westenra a few times during his internship at Redeo, though their interactions had
been brief and formal. Jake knew Westenra left Redeo ten months ago, but the details
had been confidential—until he scoured the personnel files he purloined from the
company. Turned out Westenra quit over "moral objections" to the project.

Jake extended a hand. "Dr. Westenra? I'm Jake Maxwell. You may remember me from Redeo."

Westenra accepted his hand in a cautious shake, his eyes never wavering from Jake's. "Young man, I don't welcome visitors—particularly those with connections to my former employer. Whatever you want, I'm not interested in giving it."

"I think you'll change your mind if you hear me out."

"Why is that?" Westenra shifted, his hidden arm coming into view. He gripped a 12-gauge shotgun, muzzle down, finger poised alongside the trigger.

Jake lodged his hands in his jeans pockets, shooting for a nonchalant, nonthreatening pose. "It's about Project Pleiades."

The shotgun swiveled toward Jake a tad, still muzzle down. "I parted ways with Redeo Biotech almost a year ago. You've wasted your time, Mr. Maxwell."

"Call me Jake." He avoided glancing at the gun, choosing instead to focus on Westenra's face. "You left before the final phase began, didn't you? Did they tell you what happened?"

The scientist's brow furrowed. "Of course not. I no longer have clearance for that."

Jake took a chance. He stepped closer and bent forward. "She's alive."

"To whom are you referring?" The faint quaver in his voice belied his calm words.

"Your specimen. The mummy you and your friends regenerated." Jake waited a few seconds, to let his words sink into the other man's mind. "She woke up."

Westenra stared at him for so long Jake feared he'd lost the battle. Then the man licked his lips and swallowed visibly. Jake would've interpreted the action as hopeful, not rapacious like Vahl, but rather a guarded anticipation. He had no idea what it meant.

The older man pinched the bridge of his nose, wincing, and moved aside. He waved for Jake to enter. "In that case, we have a lot to talk about."

The older man ushered him down a short hallway, into a sunken living room accessed by three shallow steps. Picture windows displayed a view of trees and birdfeeders affixed to metal poles. Westenra motioned for Jake to sit on the L-shaped sofa, while he dropped into an overstuffed armchair positioned across from the sofa, with a glass-topped coffee table between them.

Jake perched on the sofa's edge, hands clamped on his knees.

Westenra positioned the shotgun across his legs. His index finger tapped the stock in an inconstant rhythm.

Tap-tap. Tap. Tap-tap-tap. It grated on Jake's perpetually raw nerves. He ground his teeth, then forced himself to loosen his jaw as he exhaled a long breath.

"Relax, Jake." Westenra eyed him. "I won't shoot unless you've brought a Redeo security detail with you."

"And I'm betting you've got surveillance cameras hidden all over the place, so you'd know if I'd brought a squirrel with me."

"True." Westenra reclined in his chair, his finger no longer tapping. "You were never this tense in the lab. You did your job, chatted amiably when required, and kept to yourself the rest of the time. Never once asked why."

"Why what?"

The other man laid his hands on his thighs. "Why we wanted to resurrect a mummified young woman."

Jake clung to the sofa's edge, fingers driven deep into the plush cushions. His breaths came fast and hard, heaving his chest. *Resurrect.* The word implied they'd meant to restore her to a living state, to full consciousness. But he'd been told the end goal was to return the specimen to a near-living state, to prove desiccated tissue could be regenerated. He must've misunderstood Westenra. "You mean regenerate mummified tissue, don't you?"

"No." Westenra shook his head and chuckled, a soft sound rife with bitterness but lacking malice. "They told you that was the final phase, eh? No-no-no." He leaned forward and plopped the gun onto the coffee table. His glacier-blue eyes zeroed in on Jake's. "That's what the rest of us were told too. It was a lie."

"I don't understand."

"The day I resigned," the older man said, his voice roughened with intensity, "I demanded Vahl tell me what he planned to do with the...remains...once we finished regenerating the specimen. He laughed and said there was no point in lying, because no one would believe me if I told them."

He paused, and Jake's pulse pounded in his veins.

"Vahl confessed," Westenra said, "that his ultimate intention was to resurrect her. Bring her back to life, as a genuine, thinking human woman."

Jake's feet drummed on the carpeting as he fidgeted where he sat. His every nerve had sharpened into a razor point scraping him from the inside out. He needed to know the rest, yet he feared the truth. "And then..."

Westenra shoved his hands into his hair, scrubbing his scalp, head bowed. When he dropped his hands, and raised his head, he looked older somehow. "Vahl claimed he could resurrect her with a magical spell from an ancient Egyptian scroll."

———

DAWN FLOATED IN THE PALE BLUE LIQUID, BREATHING THROUGH A tube, a scuba mask over her eyes and plugs in her ears. Vahl had turned off the overhead lights, and then activated soft white bulbs inside the tank. For the first few minutes—okay, ten or fifteen minutes—she'd squirmed and fought against the breathing tube, overcome by the alien sensation of total submersion. It was like snorkeling, she tried to convince herself. Since she had no memories of snorkeling, though, that didn't help much.

At last, a few moments ago, she'd settled into a kind of Zen submission. Muscles loose. Eyes closed. Letting the liquid buoy her. At body temperature, the fluid slipped over her as a second skin, almost imperceptible. She was poised in outer space, in a void where sight and sound and touch faded away. Her mind coasted into a weightless state of its own, unburdened by worries. For the first time since awakening at Redeo, she found peace.

No. Not the first time. The peace she experienced here, in this tank, paled beside the serenity of lying in Jake's arms. With or without clothing.

She lay naked in this glass coffin. Exposed to Vahl's greedy gaze. On display, like a mummy in a museum.

Well, she had been a mummy, so she supposed this was appropriate.

Still, her skin itched. Her thoughts whirled around a single point—Vahl, outside the tank, leering at her.

Her peace shattered into dust.

What the hell am I doing here? She flailed her arms out, slapping her palms on the tank's walls. Her eyes flew open.

"Be still." Vahl's voice crackled from the speakers in her earplugs.

She swung her head left and squinted through the blue liquid at the blurry figure positioned a dozen feet away, near a bank of electronic equipment she couldn't see now, but had noted before climbing into the tank. Fuzzy multicolored lights seemed to bounce on the equipment, stirred into false motion by the liquid sloshing around her. She couldn't speak, with the breathing apparatus lodged between her teeth.

"Easy," Vahl said, his tone detached. "And try not to damage the breathing tube. Relax your jaw. I promise the tube will not fall out."

She struggled for air, her breaths quick and shallow. Her ears rang.

"Trust me."

She rolled her head to stare straight up again. Shut her eyes. Hauled in one long breath. She exhaled slowly, letting the tension sluice out of her on the breath. Her jaw went slack.

The tube stayed in her mouth, braced by her lips.

"See? You didn't drown."

She restrained a derisive snort. It might dislodge the tube, and besides, she couldn't fire off a sarcastic retort to go along with it.

"You achieved total relaxation for a moment. I saw it. You can get there again, my dear, if you trust me to care for your physical safety in the meantime."

There was the problem. Trusting him.

She had no choice.

Okay. She could do this. He wouldn't hurt her while she was in the tank, because he needed her to feel safe in order for the technique to work and, thus, earn him her goodwill. She trusted him that far—and no farther.

Within a few minutes this time, she floated down into a numb state, divorced from the world, devoid of thought. She drifted there, in blackness, for a long while, the minutes impossible to count, her mind so foggy she couldn't have counted if she tried.

Colors flickered at the edges of her vision. Ribbons of blue, green, red, yellow, and every permutation in between twirled and mutated, coalescing into an abstract painting of an environment too blurry to distinguish. She released her desperation to see, to know, and let her soul find its way.

The colors transmuted into shapes that sharpened into outlines of objects. Her vision swam into focus bit by bit. She was in a room, furnished with tables and chairs, the decorations Egyptian in style. The perfume of flowers permeated the air, exciting her senses. She lounged on a bed, nude beneath a sheet, her bare shoulders and arms exposed. When she stretched, the soft fabric brushed her skin. Her father had imported silk from a far distant land, specially for her. She writhed again, luxuriating in the sleek texture.

The man lying next to her rolled onto his side and draped an arm across her belly. The bed creaked under his shifting weight. "Why are you restless?"

His husky voice made her ache deep inside. "I am not. This sheet pleases me with its softness, that is all."

"No fabric in the world," Bek murmured, rubbing his palm in circles, "compares to your skin."

He peeled back the sheet, skated his palm over her flesh, grazed the heel of his hand across the undersides of her breasts. She trembled with a fevered hunger, one only he could sate. He lifted his powerful body on one arm, propped half sitting, half leaning over her. The golden light from the oil lamps on the walls glistened on his naked skin and accentuated the hard lines of his chest. Instinctively, her hand floated up to trace sinuous lines over his torso. Firm. Warm. Her body roused at the memory of his hard flesh against hers, his shaft driving into her.

If anyone discovered what they'd just done, they would both be executed.

No man touched the pharaoh's daughter, except the husband he chose for her. To consort with her guardian, a mere soldier, was beyond forbidden.

She dropped her hand, her passion doused by a sudden chill.

Bek's brow furrowed. "Raia, what disturbs you?"

"If we are discovered..." She wrapped her arms over her breasts, but the cold persisted inside. "I do not wish to live if harm comes to you."

"Never speak such things." His harsh tone startled her, but the anguish on his face scraped at her heart. She cupped his face with one hand, her finger caressing his temple. He tilted his head into her touch and sighed. "Perhaps we are fools, but the die is cast. My heart, my soul, belongs to you for eternity."

She slid her hand down, her fingertips dancing over his sensual lips. "And I am yours until the stars are vanquished."

He bowed to fit his mouth over hers. She combed her hand through his cinnamon hair, such an unusual shade, and one of the countless things she adored about him. His lips teased hers into parting, then his tongue slipped inside. The flavor of him—honey mead and dates, the remains of which rested on a plate beside the bed—aroused her senses and her body. His hand traveled down, easing her arms away so he might palm one breast. She groaned, her damp sex throbbing.

"Shall I leave?" he purred, his fingers massaging her breast, his mouth achingly near hers. "Is that what you desire?"

"No." Her voice was a whisper, choked by need. She arched into his hand, her breast crushed in his palm. "Never leave me. Never."

"I will not. You have my vow."

His hand drifted lower. His fingers delved between her thighs.

She moaned, her legs opening for him.

The doors exploded inward.

Bek yanked the sheet up to cover her, but it made no difference. There, rigid as a temple column, towered her betrothed. Setka brandished a gleaming sword, his muscled body tensed, his fiery gaze scorching into her.

"You!" He jabbed the sword in Bek's direction. "You have defiled the pharaoh's daughter. For this, you will die—and I shall be the one to cleave your head from your body."

Dawn careened back to the present, her body convulsing. Her heart jackhammered against her ribs, and her breaths wheezed. Blue liquid sloshed around her. Christ, it couldn't be true, what she'd seen, what it meant. It had to be an illusion.

"Calm yourself," Vahl said through the earplugs. An odd tension infected his tone, almost as if he cared whether she drowned.

No, goddammit, he did not care. And what she'd witnessed in her vision or memory or whatever, it was not true.

She summoned all her willpower, drew in slow, deep breaths, and stilled her body. The liquid lapped over the tank's rim as she sat up, tore out the earplugs, and ripped the breathing tube out. No matter what she wanted, the truth rang in her soul. The memory was real, and accurate.

Jake. She needed him, desperately. Where had he gone? Was he okay?

Maybe she could track him down, without leaving this tank. Before her awakening, her soul explored the world, disembodied, in what Jake referred to as her soul travels. That's how she knew so much about the modern world. When she relived the past moments ago, she felt her essence detach from her body. If she could travel to Jake, then she might warn him about her past life experience and discover what he'd learned while away from her.

And oh yes, she could satisfy the craving to see him. Not to touch him, but at least to bask in his grounding presence.

He must know. Whatever this newly unearthed truth meant, Jake should know about it.

Because her betrothed from her previous life was Anton Vahl.

CHAPTER SIX

THE SOFA CREAKED AS JAKE SHIFTED HIS WEIGHT, UNABLE to find a comfortable position. Vahl got his hands on an Egyptian spell to resurrect the dead? Holy heaven. Dawn believed, and convinced Jake, that their destined love revived her, thanks to his unerring devotion to her and a bond stronger than death. What if Anton Vahl was responsible for her rebirth?

Jake swallowed, but the bitter taste in his mouth lingered.

Across the coffee table, Westenra contemplated him with curiosity. "Are you sick, young man?"

"No." Not in the physical sense. But the idea of Vahl summoning Dawn back from the afterlife, snatching her out of her soul journeys, did sicken him. "Do you know for sure Vahl used the spell?"

Westenra shrugged. "Can't say. He had the scroll, but he couldn't read it. His inability to decipher the language seemed to frustrate him beyond reason."

"Did he get someone to translate it for him?"

"I don't know." Westenra rubbed his chin. "He seemed intent on reading the text in the original language, not merely a translation. The pronunciation tripped him up, I gather."

"But couldn't an Egyptologist help him with it?"

The older man shook his head. "According to his own notes, no living person knows how to pronounce the old tongue with the accuracy demanded by such a dangerous incantation. If he misspoke one syllable, it might throw off the whole spell."

Magic. A couple weeks ago, Jake would've laughed at the notion. Today, he lacked the luxury of skepticism. He'd made love to a formerly mummified woman and rediscovered a passion they'd first shared thousands of years ago. With Dawn, he experienced magic in all its incarnations.

Something in him recognized her even as she lay lifeless inside a glass tank. She'd been reborn via supernatural means, of that he was certain. Her memories of a past life stemmed from the deep recesses of her resurrected brain. But his intuitive knowledge of her? He had no clue where it came from. Reincarnation, once a myth, grew more and more plausible every day.

He sat forward, hands on his knees. "Wait a minute. Why did Vahl think he should be able to read a dead language?"

"You would have to ask him that."

Vahl insisted Dawn belonged to him—legally, for sure, but Jake sensed another reason under the surface. What if…no. Absolutely not.

The thought bobbed up again, inescapable.

Jake dug his fingers into his knees. What if Anton Vahl was reincarnated too? Or believed he was?

The hope he was mistaken dangled thin and frayed in Jake's mind.

A hot shiver of awareness rattled him. His heart thudded. His body tensed in anticipation, and he darted his gaze around the room. She wasn't here.

Then why did he feel as if Dawn had entered the room?

He focused on Westenra, against the rush of adrenaline. "Do you, uh, have anything that might help me get Dawn away from Vahl?"

"If you mean information," Westenra said, grunting as he hefted himself off the chair, "I'm afraid I've told you everything I know about Vahl's plans."

"I understand." Jake let his head droop, his shoulders caving in.

"However…" Westenra's promising tone made Jake pop his head up, in time to see the man's lips curve up in a sly smile. "I do have guns and various equipment that might be of use to you."

Jake had a gun. The equipment sounded promising, though. "I'd appreciate anything you can offer."

A caress tingled over his cheek. The breath burst out of him. *Dawn.* Jesus, it was her. His body recognized her, responding to her phantom touch. But how…

"I'll be right back," Westenra said, and trotted out of the room.

Dawn's invisible hands roamed Jake's arms, his chest, and her fingers splayed over his lips. He gasped her name. Her warm, soft body settled onto him, straddling his thighs.

This was impossible. Wasn't it?

Her voice whispered in his head. "Can you hear me?"

"Yes," he sputtered, swamped by a sudden heat. The desire flaring through him was real, though the sensation of her flesh on his was an illusion.

"Listen to me." An urgency tightened her words. "Vahl is not who he says. I experienced a memory from my first life, and...Jake, Vahl was there. I was supposed to marry him."

The thread of hope snapped, and reality crashed down on him with the weight of a ten-ton steel block. He managed to squeeze out words. "Did you—I mean, since you were going to be married, you must've—"

"It was an arranged marriage. I didn't sleep with him. I never loved him, and I never will. I love you, Jake."

He couldn't speak or move. His eyelids closed of their own volition, and he sank back into the cushions, indulging in the fantasy of her delicate limbs wrapped around him.

"You were there too, in my flashback. We were lovers." Her mouth, damp and hot, brushed over his lips. He went hard in an instant, his body starved for her. "We belong together, Jake. Forever."

"But how is any of this possible?"

Her laughter tinkled in his ear. "Magic."

Ice crackled through him. He snapped his head up, eyes open. Despite her ghostly nature, he imagined he saw her face before his. "Dawn, Vahl intended to revive you with an ancient spell."

"Good thing you woke me up first. I wouldn't want some half-ass spell to bind me to Vahl for eternity."

Neither did he. But if the scientist really had restored her living soul to her body, then she might well have a supernatural connection with Vahl. The notion made Jake grind his teeth and fist his hands in the sofa cushions.

"Relax," Dawn assured him, "I know you're the one who brought me back. I feel it. You are inside me every moment, even when we're apart. Whatever Vahl hoped to accomplish, he failed."

"What does he want now?"

"I don't know." The weight of her lifted off him. "I have to go. Vahl's getting anxious about what I'm doing, and I can't let him figure out we've been in contact."

Her presence receded a little. Jake bolted upright, as if he might drag her back to him. "I'm coming for you. Please hang on."

"For you, always."

She was gone.

Her absence shredded him from the inside out.

Westenra traipsed back into the room carrying a wooden box. He dropped into the chair again, the box on his lap. From its depths, he plucked out two black canisters with pins dangling from their tops.

Jake squinted at them. "What's that?"

"Flash bangs." Westenra deposited them on the coffee table. "Grenades designed to stun your opponent with a loud noise and a blinding flash of light."

"Right. I've heard of those." Jake switched his gaze from the grenades to the gray-haired man across from him. "Why do you have them?"

"In case Vahl ever came for me. I have a friend who works for an explosives manufacturer."

Westenra nabbed another item from the box. This one Jake recognized.

"A Tommy gun?" He reached out to touch it, but pulled his hand back. His host set the gun down beside the flash bangs. A thrill rippled through Jake as he surveyed the arsenal Westenra had assembled before him. *Armed with these things, I can rescue her.*

He ran his fingers over the barrel of the Tommy gun. *Yes, I can.*

"That's a handy tool." Westenra extracted one final item from the box. It looked like a large block of off-white clay. He plopped it on the table. "C-4. An explosive. I have detonators for it."

"What am I supposed to blow up?"

"Whatever you need to." Westenra leaned forward, gaze intent on Jake, and told him in a soft, yet fierce, tone, "Every file on the project is housed on servers at Vahl's home. He doesn't trust anyone else to keep them. The scientists at Redeo are allowed to access the files remotely, and modify the data, but the files remain on Vahl's servers. He also has a protocol in place that will release a virus into Redeo's system if anyone tampers with the servers at his compound. Which means if you destroy his computers, you destroy Redeo's too, and erase all evidence of where Dawn came from and how she was resurrected."

"But I copied files from the Redeo servers onto a flash drive."

"I'm sure Vahl discovered the espionage and sealed that security hole."

"Paranoid bastard, isn't he?"

"A person can't amass as much influence and power as Vahl has without developing a healthy sense of mistrust." Westenra pointed at the C-4. "This will eliminate Redeo's claim on our girl and give you control over them. I heard Vahl mention an off-site backup of the files. There must be evidence of its location somewhere in his home."

"I'll find it." Jake considered the objects on the table. "You're just giving me these weapons? No questions asked?"

"Yes." Westenra brought out a device that resembled a price gun from a grocery store, except with an LCD screen. "This is a thermal imaging camera. I bought it for spotting intruders approaching the house, but it should let you see how many people are in Vahl's compound."

"I—thank you." Jake ran his hands over the items on the table. "Why would you trust me with these things?"

"Because I remember you, Jake. You're a good boy."

He couldn't stop the smirk from contorting his lips. "Boy?"

"From an old man's perspective, yes." Westenra slid the C-4 across the tabletop toward him. "But I realize you are mature enough to handle these weapons, and savvy enough to gauge when to use them—and when not to."

"I appreciate that." Jake hovered his hands over the items on the table, disbelieving his own eyes. He snapped his fingers closed and narrowed his gaze on Westenra. "I show up out of the blue and you just happen to have everything I need to break Dawn out of Vahl's compound."

"There's no coincidence about it, son." Westenra braced his elbows on his knees. "I've been waiting for you, ever since I left Redeo. I believed one day you'd come looking for me."

"Why?"

The man linked his fingers loosely, hands dangling between his knees. "I assumed Vahl was insane, with his delusions about the girl. But when I left Redeo, I stole a few files as insurance against Vahl coming after me."

"Just like I did."

"Yes." Westenra gave him a faint smile. "Great minds, eh?"

Jake scratched the back of his neck, averting his eyes. He didn't feel like a great mind at the moment.

"A few months later," the older man said, "I perused the data I'd taken, and found I'd inadvertently copied a folder containing photos from the excavation—of the tomb where the girl's remains were recovered." He shook his head, gaze distant, lost in the past. "Vahl had clearly never looked at them, since artifacts were of no value in his quest. If he had seen the items from the tomb, he would've recognized you in an instant, as I did, once I saw the images."

A fly buzzed around Jake's head. He swatted it away with a violence that swooshed air over his face. His toes drummed on the floor, his shoulders stiffened, and he fought the urge to smash the nearest breakable object. "What images? What the hell did you see?"

"This." Westenra extracted a smart phone from his breast pocket, swiped his thumb across its screen several times, and offered the device to Jake. "These artifacts from the tomb are, well, indicative of something I couldn't have imagined possible before."

Jake slid his palm under the phone. Westenra let go, and it settled into his hand. Warm, from the other man's body heat. He tilted his hand, the screen coming into view.

His blood froze.

122

Though he'd seen the thing before, held it in his hand, somehow the sight of it illuminated on a five-by-three-inch LCD screen cranked the memory back into focus. The phone quivered in his palm.

No, that was his hand shaking. *Christ.*

He couldn't look away. The screen displayed a photo of the same small statue Vahl had shown him and Dawn back in the motel room over a week ago. The statue of a man, painted in lifelike colors. The face was carved in the likeness of one individual.

Me, shit, it's me.

In the motel room, he'd been too distracted by Vahl's threats to truly appreciate the reality of the statue. This wasn't a vague resemblance. The face matched his in every aspect. Dawn had told him she remembered statues from her tomb that looked like him, and though he believed her, he couldn't wrap his mind around the concept.

"Flip the screen," Westenra said.

Jake swiped his finger across it. The image changed. He squinted at it, unsure of what he saw.

"It's the base of the figurine," Westenra explained. "Can you read ancient Egyptian?"

"No." The photo showed hieroglyphs, he knew that much.

"I contacted an acquaintance who's an expert on ancient languages. He translated it for me." Westenra's mouth curved in a knowing smile. "It says 'he will return for her, guardian for eternity, when the dark soul is reborn.' So I knew you'd come to me sometime, assuming Vahl succeeded in resurrecting her."

"He didn't." Jake spat the words, his chest tight. "I did."

"Ah, that does make more sense. You are her guardian, apparently." He canted his head, eyes alight with interest. "And her lover, I presume."

Jake clapped the phone down on the table.

"The artifact has been authenticated," Westenra said. "It's over three thousand years old."

"I know. I've seen it in person."

Westenra's eyebrows lifted. "You have?"

"Yeah, Vahl has it. He showed me and Dawn, right before he—" Took her away. His throat constricted. He coughed, for an excuse to cover his mouth and collect himself. "Anyway, he seems to have gotten interested in the artifacts after all."

"Strange. I wonder what changed."

"No clue, don't care. Artifacts are of no use to me." Jake ran his fingers over the Tommy gun. "Why are you helping me?"

"Fate brought us together." Westenra shrugged, then waved at the items on the table. "I'll show you how to use these, and then you should go. If Anton Vahl has the girl, then there's no time to waste."

The grim certainty in the other man's tone flicked a warning switch in Jake's brain. He locked his gaze on Westenra's. "What aren't you telling me? Do you know what Vahl wants with Dawn?"

"The secrets of resurrection, first of all. But I'm sure you knew that much." Westenra rocked side to side, adjusting his position, and grimaced. "I suspect he has another agenda as well, one rooted in events even he can't fully recall. Somehow, though, the past exerts a powerful pull on him. I never believed any of this would come to pass, and at the same time, I knew it must. Fate has a dark sense of humor."

Jake fought to keep his voice even, despite the frustration tangling his nerves. "What does Vahl want?"

Westenra picked up a flash bang, turning it in his hand. "It's quite simple. Vahl believes you and Dawn betrayed him in a previous life." He balanced the grenade in his palm, upright. "He wants revenge."

CHAPTER SEVEN

AWN SWUNG HER LEG OVER THE TANK'S RIM. HER foot slapped down on the top step, and she swung her other leg out. Water splattered around her. Equipment bleeped and whirred. The scent of disinfectant and dust mingled in her nostrils.

She took a half step. Her body teetered, the room morphing into a Tilt-A-Whirl, and she staggered backward into the tank's wall. It jostled with a *whump-whump* sound as blue liquid sloshed inside it.

Vahl scurried up the steps to grasp her shoulders. "Easy now. Sensory deprivation can be disconcerting."

"No shit." The note of panic in her voice dismayed her, but she could do nothing about it. She earned the right to freak out a tad, thanks to the visceral vividness of her recovered memory.

Well, she'd wanted to remember. And her wish leaped around to smack her in the face.

Limbs weak, she let Vahl assist her down the steps and onto the main floor of the lab. A draft chilled her skin, and she shivered. Vahl handed her a terry cloth robe, which she yanked over her nakedness so fast the fabric swished out to slap Vahl's legs. Why didn't he give her the robe when he rushed up the stairs to her? Gee, maybe he was an insane asshole.

Her sopping hair hung limp over her shoulders and face. She flicked it back with both hands. Water droplets flew out behind her, spattering expensive equipment, she hoped.

A quick glance at her pruned fingers made her ask, "How long was I in the tank?"

"Four hours."

Her hand flew to her neck. Four hours? She might've guessed fifteen minutes, maybe twenty. Not *hours.*

Vahl surveyed her from head to toe with dispassion, as if he hadn't recently glared at her with a black hunger identical to his expression in the memory. From her first life. When he found her in bed with Jake—er, Bek. Cripes, this rebirth stuff was confusing.

What kind of father coerced his daughter into marrying someone like Vahl?

The creep in question raised one haughty eyebrow. "You seem unharmed. Tell me what you experienced."

"Nothing." Like she'd share her vision with him. If he hadn't killed her himself in their past life, he surely oversaw the festivities with demented pleasure.

In the dream, he threatened to kill Jake. If Vahl—Setka, whatever—coveted her for his own, then why kill her?

The present-day version of him grasped her upper arms, his fingers driven into her flesh, and gave her a hard shake. "Tell me."

"Nothing happened. Your plan failed."

"I hardly think so." He tugged her toward him. She dug in her heels, but the liquid pouring off her made her feet slide across the linoleum with a faint squeak. He lifted, forcing her onto tiptoes. Eye to eye, their noses practically touching, he hissed, "Your heart rate spiked. Your brain wave activity too. I know you experienced something while you were in the tank, and you are going to tell me."

"Why should I? What do you hope to gain from all this? More than getting in my good graces, that's for damn sure."

His breath blustered over her face. "You must remember."

Each syllable, enunciated with knife-sharp precision, plunged into her soul. She'd understood he had an ulterior motive, something beyond helping her regain the past she lost to death and resurrection. But his hard tone. The high-tension wires his muscles had become. The deadly current coursing through him. It zapped into her through the air, through his hands on her arms, and the breaths huffing out of him.

He would never let her leave this place.

What, then, did she have to lose? Jake was gone. For days, she'd banked on the knowledge he would come back for her, and she trusted he would sometime, but now she fired a new plea into the heavens. *Please let him stay away.*

Whatever Vahl had planned, she wanted Jake nowhere near it.

He hauled her flush against him. She turned her head away to avoid his mouth. His lips ground across her cheek, and his voice rasped in her ear. "You know, don't you?"

"Know what?"

His laughter made her cringe. "Stop lying to me. I saw the truth in your eyes...Raia."

The room lurched around her as she battled to catch her breath. He knew her old name. The knowledge must've come from past life memories, because every trace of her identity had been scoured from the tomb, from her coffin, from every artifact that might grant her the protection of her name. For in ancient Egypt, words imparted power, and a person's name carried the greatest power of all.

Maybe that's why her soul wandered without purpose for three thousand years. Stripped of her name, she was denied a true afterlife.

No. She'd had a purpose. To find Jake and reunite with him.

Hope lightened her being and shivered over her skin. This was what fate left to her, something to fight for—the man she'd loved for millennia.

Vahl pressed his mouth to her ear, his skin hot and rough. "You are mine. In the past, the present, the future, until the universe crumbles, you belong to me."

"Fuck off, Setka."

He seized her hair and jerked her head back. His eyes bored into hers. "So you do remember me." He raked his tongue over her mouth. She choked back a gag. "Time to step up my plans. You succumbed to the past much faster than I'd anticipated."

"I will never love you." She forced the words out between gritted teeth. "And I'll kill myself before I have sex with you."

With a fake sigh, Vahl shook his head. "I have no interest in your love, my dear. Or your body, though I admit it is quite tempting." He pinched her lip hard between his teeth, wringing tears from her eyes. "What do you think I'm after? I crave your suffering."

She wriggled, but he clamped his arms around her, pinioning her to his torso.

"You know what you did," he said. "But have you regained the memory of what came next?"

Why lie? He seemed to know more than she did. "No. I didn't see that."

"At first, I thought to take your love from you, to execute him before your eyes as punishment for cuckolding me." He kicked her feet out from under her and lifted her higher in his arms to rumble his words into her neck. "Your father agreed to our union as part of an alliance with my people. I was promised a position as vizier to the pharaoh, a role with great status and power."

His teeth grated on her skin.

She thrashed to free her arms, to no avail.

"You ruined my life." His tone had gone feral, infused with an anger too hideous to fathom. "How could I stand for my betrothed bedding another man? Among my people, it is the worst sin a woman can commit." He dropped her onto her feet with a splat. "The pharaoh would never have punished you, so I took you to a private location and meted out my brand of justice on you."

Pain sliced her brain. Images careened through her mind—Vahl beating her, shaving her hair with a dull razor, force-feeding her a poisoned drink that scalded her throat and racked her body with excruciating spasms.

Anton Vahl had murdered her.

She shouted and flailed, but he held fast. "Oh, you fight like a rabbit in a snare. Are you recalling our final encounter?"

"You bastard!"

He grinned, with no mirth, but a hatred as poisonous as the liquid he'd made her drink in another lifetime. "My, how I love it when you squirm."

She went still, breathing hard but passive in his grasp. He loved her struggle? Then she'd rob him of the pleasure, until she found a way to break free of him.

And punish *him*.

Until then, she might as well get a question answered. "How do you know any of this? You weren't resurrected like me."

"No, I was reincarnated. My past life was unknown to me until I reached adulthood. Even then, I was given only snippets of my previous life, enough to propel me into a career in science, in the hopes of understanding my visions." He squeezed her hard. Pains lanced her ribs. "Seeing you, in your regenerated state, unleashed my memories of our shared past. That's when I realized I've spent my entire adult life striving toward one goal—avenging myself on you and your lover."

"Did you kill Jake too?"

"I planned to. But the pharaoh figured out I was responsible for your death, and had me executed. I never had the pleasure of slitting Jake's throat, though I was consoled by watching his grief over your demise."

He strived his whole life? For vengeance against her? But..."Okay, I can almost buy that your research into regenerating dead tissue might've been aimed at resurrecting me so you could punish me all over again. But my tomb was found by accident, by archaeologists who didn't work for you."

"You understand so little." He arched one eyebrow, tipping his head up to peer down the bridge of his nose at her. "I murdered you in your tomb. I knew its location all along, and when our first experiments with regeneration proved viable, I orchestrated your tomb's discovery. I paid a local to tip off a team of archaeologists working in the area. I even used my considerable influence to get them an excavation permit."

He released her. She stumbled backward two steps, and her feet slapped on the wet floor. Her mouth opened and closed, all words trapped in her throat. A lifetime invested in a quest for vengeance three thousand years in the making? It was insane. He was insane.

No surprise, really. He'd been a whackjob the first time around too.

Vahl dusted his hands on his slacks. "Once your tomb was opened, it began."

She clutched her stomach. "What began?"

"The destruction of you and everything you love." His expression blanked, his voice now flat. "And this time, I'll make sure to exterminate your soul. There will be no more rebirth for you." He stalked toward her, his movements fluid, muscles rippling. "I will erase you from the universe, once and for all."

He seized her head in both hands and slammed his mouth onto hers. The lust in his kiss was vicious and not at all sexual. He bruised her with an act of possession, anger, and vengeance.

She rammed her knee into his groin.

Vahl staggered backward, gasping, doubled over with his face twisted in agony.

She belted him in the jaw. Her fist connected with a crack that resonated through her bones. His head snapped up, and he toppled backward to hit the floor in a jumbled heap. She bolted for the laboratory door.

His hand shot out to grab her ankle.

With one swift motion, he flipped her foot out from under her. The momentum of her own body knocked her off balance. She whacked onto the floor flat on her face. A cry exploded out of her. Electric pains shot through her bones and muscles.

Vahl crawled over her on all fours, the heat of his body radiating over her through the all-too-narrow gap between them. He pinned her ankles with one foot, cuffed her wrists with one of his hands, and bent his head to growl in her ear.

"There's no escape, Raia. You stole the power that should've been mine, and this time around you will suffer more than you could possibly imagine." He seized her hair and yanked it. "I've had years to plan my revenge."

She bucked, but he dropped his full weight onto her. Crushed beneath him, she swallowed a whimper.

"And as for Jake," he purred into her ear, "he will come for you, but he'll only be stepping into the snare I've set for him. Then you will watch each other suffer, before I end your worthless lives for all time."

She sank her teeth into his cheek. The tang of blood seeped onto her tongue.

He howled, yanking her head back until stars burst in her vision.

At least he hadn't raped her, in the past or the present. He was clearly more interested in blood than sex. She remembered that from her first life, when Vahl had never even bothered to kiss her and avoided touching her in any manner. She was a means to an end, one her affair with Jake had torpedoed.

He *murdered* her.

Vahl rolled off her, flipping her over, hands still cuffed by his. He shoved a hand into his pocket and pulled out a syringe. With deliberate slowness, he pressed the needle tip into her cheek, just enough to prick the skin and draw blood, then sliced it down her face. The skin stung. A trail of hot blood oozed out in the needle's wake.

He waggled the syringe in the air before her eyes. "This will make you more pliant, but you'll remain conscious. And you will feel everything."

The stinging on her cheek escalated into a burning of such harrowing intensity she fought to stifle a grimace. Oh God. She knew this sensation. She'd experienced it shortly after she and Jake broke out of Redeo, when a cut on her finger mysteriously healed itself.

Except it hadn't healed itself. *She* healed it.

A cold steel ball formed in her gut. Tears threatened, but she bit down on the inside of her cheek to stave them off, unwilling to let Vahl see her terror. He would torture her. Cut, stab, whack until the pain liquefied her brain and dissolved her will.

And her wounds would heal.

Her own body—her own powers—would award Vahl more chances to hurt her than he could possibly imagine. Once he realized she had the power, he might dream up worse torments. If he decided to mine the healing ability from her, as he'd tried to mine the secrets of her resurrection, she would yearn for death. Would it ever come for her? How long could her body regenerate?

Vahl punctured her neck with the needle. Cool fluid poured into her bloodstream. Every muscle went limp. The world blurred around her. Quicksand hauled her thoughts down, down, down.

His mouth sealed over her ear. "You belong to me."

CHAPTER EIGHT

J AKE GRIPPED THE WHEEL IN A DESPERATE EFFORT TO CONTROL
the car's motion, but rocketing down a gravel road at eighty miles per hour
tested the best-built car. This one was not the best. It was the only car
left at the rental agency. The wheels slid and bounced. His teeth clacked
together, so he locked them tight.

Renting a Gulfstream jet on short notice had been easier than it sounded. He
simply dumped a stack of thousand dollar bills on the pilot's desk and promised
a second stack of equal value if the man got him to Nevada in an hour, no questions asked.

The pilot didn't ask. He took the money and met the deadline.

His heart hammered. Dawn needed him. Now that he knew Vahl's true agenda,
there was no time to waste. If the bastard hurt her...

Jake battered his fist on the wheel, biting back a yell.

The car fishtailed. Dust plumed up around it.

He fought the wheel, his foot riding the brake, as the car veered toward the
ditch. No, goddammit, this was not how things ended. Him dead in a ditch. Her
tortured by Vahl. His arms throbbed, but he gripped the wheel harder.

The car skidded to a halt, inches from the drop-off.

He sponged sweat from his forehead with his T-shirt. *Slow down*, his inner voice
urged. No way. Once he was with Dawn, maybe. Not yet.

Grabbing his phone off the passenger seat, he checked the GPS app for his location. It
showed him on a two-track parallel to Vahl's compound, around the backside of it, a couple
miles from the house. Just a little farther.

Did Vahl see him coming?

Jake propped the phone in the cup holder, angled to let him view the screen. He eased the car back onto the road, took a deep breath, and floored the accelerator. The car shot forward, pinning him to his seat. Gravel sprayed up, ticking and thumping on the car's body and undercarriage.

Vahl might see him coming, but he'd never guess what Jake had planned. No equipment on earth conferred the power to read minds.

The dot on the GPS app traveled up the line representing this road. Jake counted down the distance. A mile and a half. One mile. Three thousand feet. Two thousand.

He battled with the wheel. Sweat rolled down his face. The car jounced over potholes, jarring his bones.

One thousand. Eight hundred.

The six-strand electric fence came into view.

Bingo. He jammed on the brakes. The car jolted to a stop and threw him forward against his seat belt. It dug into his chest and shoulder, but the pain barely registered. Up ahead, he glimpsed Vahl's massive hacienda through the screen of palm trees.

He snagged his backpack—now stuffed with Westenra's gifts, plus a few other tools—and flung the door open. He raced in front of the car. As soon as he had Dawn, they'd rocket out of here.

The first device he pulled out was the thermal imaging camera. He'd changed into camo clothes he bought en route, and with the sun dipping below the horizon, he figured he had a better than average chance of surviving this incursion. He'd stowed the flash bangs in a waist pouch and berthed his handgun in a shoulder holster. The Tommy gun was slung over his shoulder on a new strap he'd bought for it. The thermal imaging camera he held in one hand, and fence cutters in the other. He punched the camera's power button.

The multicolored, slightly distorted video outlined objects and the heat they gave off. He spotted six humanoid shapes inside the house. As he took a fortifying breath, he tucked the thermal camera in his pocket and raised the Tommy gun.

Issuing a silent prayer, he forged ahead into the trees.

———

VAHL DEPOSITED HER ON A COLD METAL TABLE, DRESSED IN A HOSPITAL gown he'd dressed her in, like a kid with a rag doll. Her teeth chattered, her body trembling. Not that she'd been able to fight him, thanks to the drug he injected. It turned her muscles into putty, moldable by him, and fuzzed her mind.

Her veins boiled.

Was her body struggling to heal the chemical invasion? Lord, she prayed it was.

A press of a button, and metal cuffs chunked into place over her wrists and ankles. Vahl tapped the cuff on her right wrist. "Electronic locking mechanism. You can't wriggle out of these."

Great. Even if her healing power drove out the drug, she was trapped by technology.

Jake would come back. But when?

She longed to stretch out her newfound mental abilities, to quest for his mind, out there somewhere, and touch him as she had earlier. Hours ago? But it wouldn't work. Her mind was mired, tethered much like her body.

"Where shall we start?" Vahl's tone—his whole demeanor—had reverted to the calm, reasonable persona he projected back in the motel room, when he convinced her to go with him based on the promise he wouldn't harm her. She went with him to save Jake from a bullet to the head, but she'd also believed Vahl. It was stupid, and sick, yet there it was. She believed he meant what he said.

Lies. Vahl had woven a complex tapestry of deceit and fear around her, like the shroud that once encased her mummified remains.

After he murdered her.

He stepped away from her, picked up a spiral-bound notebook from a nearby table, and unhooked the ballpoint pen clipped to the paper. His fingers glided the pen across the page.

"A notebook?" she said. "How quaint."

"Some things are too vital to be trusted to computers."

"Like what?"

He set down the notebook and plucked another object off the table, lifting it for her to see. A stun gun.

The faint, pleasant smile on his lips coiled barbed wires of dread around her heart. He squeezed the gun's trigger, and a tiny lightning bolt arced between two metal spikes on the end of the stun gun. Her body went rigid, the fire in her veins amplified.

"Yes," he said, with detached interest, "this will do for a start. Modern technology has vastly improved the selection when it comes to torture devices."

"You might kill me, but I will come back to get you."

"No. You won't." He turned the stun gun, scrutinizing it. "Not without a body to anchor your soul here."

"All this because you lost the vizier gig? You're pathetic."

His fingers contracted around the stun gun. His hand trembled from the effort. He shut his eyes, his belly inflating with each draft of air pulled deep into his lungs. His shoulders relaxed, his hand too. He opened his eyes to stare at her, without a hint of emotion. "I was executed, you know. Your dear father had me drawn and quartered, with my remains abandoned in the desert—or that was the threat. I imagine the pharaoh did as he vowed." He smirked. "But dear daddy had no idea I'd already stolen into your tomb and erased your name from your coffin, from the amulets concealed in your wrappings, from the wall paintings, from every item that named you." The smirk spread into a cruel smile. "I cursed you to an eternity without an identity."

"I know everything. Your curse failed. You are a failure. Despite everything you did, Jake and I are together again—and we will always be together, no matter what you do to me." She gave him her own nasty smile. "Love conquers all."

He slammed his fist on a metal cart. It flipped over, scattering tools and vials onto the floor. They skittered far and wide.

The lights flickered and winked out.

Darkness deep as death swallowed her. The whirring of the computers dwindled into silence. Her own breaths, and the pounding of her heart, echoed in the tomb-like chamber.

Vahl bellowed.

Her restraints popped open.

The blackness rendered her blind. She could not just lie here. She must try something, anything. Her healing power had eradicated the drug. Her mind was alert, her body energized.

You've got magic powers, girl, use them.

Healing was no help. Her soul journeys couldn't imbue her with see-in-the-pitch-dark abilities. Could they?

Footsteps shuffled toward her. Vahl.

Do something.

She slid off the table as quietly as possible. Vahl stumbled into a cart or some other object. Metal clanged, tools clattered to the floor. He hissed an oath under his breath.

All his noise-making masked her movements. She shuffled through the dark, with the table between her and Vahl. Her outstretched hands became feelers, like the antennae of an insect, her fingers detecting obstacles before she blundered into them.

Vahl pounded on a hard surface. "You won't get out of this room. Whatever your lover has done, you'll both suffer for it." His voice boomed off the walls. "For the rest of eternity!"

He was baiting her, partly. Hoping she'd lash out with words and reveal her location. But mostly, he was stark-raving bonkers.

The tips of her fingers brushed a smooth surface. Not metal. One of the plastic table-tops that housed electronic equipment. She ran her fingers along the table in search of any useful object. A computer monitor. A metal box with buttons and dials. A notebook. It must've been the one where Vahl scribbled his secret things too "vital" to store on computers. She grabbed it, as if a spiral-bound paper were a deadly weapon.

Scuffling. Behind her. Closer.

Her fingers found a pen. A glass disk, probably a petri dish.

Bam. White light flooded the room.

She squinted at the source, throwing a hand up to shield her eyes. A handheld spotlight illuminated the lab from the doorway, which had exploded inward. The door sailed into the room, bounced across the floor with a *thwack-thwack*, and skipped to a stop halfway into the lab. Her gaze traveled from the hand that gripped the light, up the muscular arm, to the beautiful face of the man who'd kicked in the door.

The sight of Jake fluttered a thrill through her chest.

In his other hand, Jake brandished a large automatic weapon. Holy shit, it was a Tommy gun.

Jake edged across the threshold. His head panned left and right. "Where the hell is he?"

Dawn blinked. Glanced around. Blinked again, slowly.

Vahl was gone.

"Maybe there's a secret exit," she said. Vahl might've retreated to gather his forces, or find a weapon, or devise a plan to annihilate her and Jake. A squirming in her gut warned otherwise.

He's here, somewhere.

Jake slashed the spotlight back and forth as he strode deeper into the room. Dressed in green camo from head to toe, he no longer fit the description of the boy next door. With his muscular body taut, his expression determined, and a fiery gleam in his eyes, he was no simple grad student either. He was her hero, come to rescue her from the villain.

All he needed was a white steed.

Her heart swelled. God, she loved him.

The plastic coil of the notebook dug into her palm. She glanced down at the notebook, which she'd forgotten she had, and words on the page seemed to pop out at her. Two sections of foreign phrases were each labeled with English titles. Her fingers were suddenly cold, as goose bumps erupted along her arms.

Death of the Soul, one title said. And the other read, *Reincarnation of the Soul.*

This was how Vahl—Setka—had ensured he'd be reborn, and it must be how he planned on extinguishing her soul for eternity.

Jake waved his hand in a come-here gesture. She raced to him, without reservation, her soul alive with hope and promise.

When he raised a hand toward her, she instinctively reached out to thread her fingers with his. Instead, he thrust a handgun into her palm.

And somehow, that comforted her more than holding his hand.

"Stay behind me," he commanded, and she obeyed. Hard to argue with a breathtaking knight wielding a Tommy gun.

Her gut still squirmed. The slimy worms wriggled their way up into her chest, their trails made of frost. Vahl was here. Hiding.

Jake swept the spotlight across the entire lab. The beam glanced off stainless steel, glinted on polished glass. "Come out, you bastard! There's no place to go. Your men are incapacitated. No one is scrambling to come to your aid."

A clattering reverberated through the room.

Jake swerved the light toward the sound. A metal cart had toppled over, spilling its contents.

"I'm not falling for that," he said.

She huddled behind him, the gun in one hand, the notebook in the other. Dropping the notebook, she rested her palm on his back. Taut muscles flexed beneath her palm. He exuded tension that leeched into her, until she was as stiff and alert as he was. She strained to hear other sounds, but discerned nothing except her own heartbeat and shaky breaths.

With the doorway a few feet behind them, Vahl couldn't sneak past.

A grunt issued from the left.

Before she could turn her head to look, an object rammed into Jake. She glimpsed a flash of silvery metal, then the object—a metal pipe—clattered to the floor and Jake doubled over, clutching his gut.

A force whammed into her chest. Sharp agony speared her.

The knife's handle protruded from her chest. She grasped at it, blood soaking her fingers and shirt, pouring down her chest. Her knees buckled.

Jake caught her. Eyes wild, face blanched, he cradled her in his strong arms.

In the instant before she passed out, she heard him say, "Heal yourself, dammit."

Vahl's laughter echoed around them.

Then everything went black.

⁓

No no no no no. The litany screamed in his brain in an unending loop. Frozen there, with Dawn limp in his arms, Jake stared at the broad-handled knife wedged into her chest, so near the heart it must've at least nicked the organ. He thrust a quivering finger into her neck.

No pulse.

"Heal, goddammit," he snarled. Nothing happened. Pain lanced his own chest, as if a mirror of the blade in her chest had gored his heart. He brushed a hand across her cheek, leaving a crimson trail on her creamy skin.

Why wasn't she regenerating? She could do it, he'd seen her. She fixed her own cut once, for Christ's sake. Why wasn't her healing ability kicking in?

An inexorable power pulled his gaze down to the knife. The blood.

His throat constricted. Blackness flickered at the outskirts of his vision, and he suddenly realized he'd forgotten to breathe.

The knife. A realization rocked him, teetering the world around him. Maybe the weapon needed to be removed before she could heal. But that might make her bleed more.

Screw it. She was already dead—almost dead.

He grasped the handle and tore out the blade. Her body arched, then the knife popped free, and she sank back down in his arms. Slack. Eyes closed. Skin pale as...

Death.

Footfalls clomped behind him.

Jake lifted his head to glare at the man waltzing toward him.

Vahl stopped several feet away. His mouth twitched in a half-contained grin. The flush of excitement colored his cheeks.

Dawn lay pale and lifeless in his arms.

Jake seized the Tommy gun from where he'd dropped it. He surged to his feet, and with one final glance down at the only woman he would ever love, he swung the gun toward Vahl.

A scrabbling noise erupted at his feet.

Both men turned their gazes down to Dawn. Her fingers wiggled, the nails scratching at the linoleum. Her entire body seized. Once. Twice.

Jake forgot all about Vahl. He fell to his knees beside Dawn, flung out his hands to touch her —

"I wouldn't," Vahl said.

Paralyzed, his hands inches from her body, Jake glowered at Vahl. "What the hell are you talking about?"

"Don't touch her." His voice took on a darker edge, rife with greedy hunger, as he uttered the words with exaggerated care. "She's regenerating. Don't you see it?" He folded his arms over his chest and cocked one hip. "This is perfect. Not what I planned, but oh so perfect. I can torture you both, kill her over and over, and every time she will heal herself. I can make her watch you suffer, force you to watch her die again and again. When I finally take your life, she will be a vacant shell. I'll snuff her out, soul and all."

He let out a crazed guffaw.

Jake leveled the Tommy gun at Vahl. "You forget. I've got the automatic weapon."

Dawn gasped. Twitching, she wheezed in a long, hoarse breath.

"Go ahead," Vahl told him, shrugging, "kill me. I will be reincarnated and track you both down again." He sighed in mock resignation. "I've waited three thousand years for my vengeance. What's one more lifetime?"

Jake stared at the man, speechless. He would've loved to dismiss Vahl as a lunatic, but he knew all too well it was true. Souls did get reincarnated. His had. Vahl's had. Who knew how many times such a thing could happen? Would he and Dawn spend eternity battling this perverse bastard, lifetime after lifetime, never free to really live, locked in an endless battle, all because they slighted this son of a bitch once in the distant past?

His shoulders flagged. He slumped back on his heels, his hands dropping. The gun slid down his thighs to clunk on the floor. God no. This couldn't be the purpose of their new lives. It just couldn't.

If he shot Vahl now, would he simply be flipping the hourglass over to start the countdown again?

Dawn moaned.

He couldn't look at her. What was the point? He loved her with such passion, such commitment, his soul clawed its way back to her through the abyss of time and death. And still, he could not save her.

The lights flickered. Computer hard drives whirred back to life. The lights powered on with a buzz.

Vahl barricaded the doorway with his body. "Backup generator. Took a few moments to power up." He braced his hands on either side of the jamb. "You can't defeat me. I'm always one step ahead of you."

Warm, soft fingers slipped over his hand.

Every hair on his body electrified at once. He risked a look. At her.

She smiled, that world-illuminating, heart-lifting smile. Her face beamed with love. For him. He pressed her hand to his chest, then raised it to his lips and kissed each knuckle. The weight on him eased bit by bit. He inhaled the sweet scent of her, savored the taste of her skin, reveled in the feel of her supple flesh.

She was alive. She was his.

Vahl snatched up the Tommy gun.

Jake hadn't noticed the bastard's movements, too entranced by the goddess beside him. The joy of her awakening washed out on a wave of cold realization. They were condemned to never-ending suffering.

No. Her angelic face, it triggered a whirlpool of emotions too intense to name, too glorious to let go of without a bone-shattering fight.

But how did a man conquer his enemy, when the war spanned lifetimes?

Vahl aimed the gun at Dawn. "I'll shoot her in the stomach if you don't do as I say, Jake. She will regenerate, of course, but not without an enormous amount of pain."

Jake set Dawn's hand on the floor. When he tried to let go, she fastened her fingers around his.

"You forget something," she said to Vahl, her voice calm. "You shouldn't leave important documents lying around for anybody to find."

She sat up, wrestled something out from behind her back, and raised the object before her. It was a notebook, folded open to a sheet with words scrawled on it.

Vahl lunged for Dawn.

Before Jake could react, Dawn whipped a handgun up from the floor, pointed it at Vahl, and pulled the trigger.

Vahl jerked. He collapsed onto the linoleum face first, head bent to the side. Eyes wide, he gurgled.

Dawn rose to her feet, looming over Vahl. She flapped the notebook, but her gaze bored into the prone man at her feet. "This ends here and now, Setka. No more lifetimes of misery. No more avenging yourself on us. It's over."

She switched her attention to the notebook and began reciting phrases in another language. It was ancient Egyptian. When Jake met the archaeologists who discovered her tomb, they'd translated some of the phrases carved on her coffin for him. As she recited now, he recognized two words—*mut* and *djet*.

Death and forever.

Tears rolled down Vahl's cheeks, dribbling onto the floor. "This isn't how it was supposed to be." With trembling arms, he pushed up onto his elbows, and spat his words. "You may scatter my soul, but you can't end the curse. I will have my revenge!"

Finished with the incantation, Dawn shook her head at Vahl. "No, you won't."

She targeted the gun at Vahl.

The scientist lashed a hand out to her ankle. His fingers clawed at her. She stomped his foot, and he bellowed.

Jake leaped up to rip the gun her from her hand.

Vahl flung an arm out for the discarded knife, its blade still coated with Dawn's blood. He lanced it through the air toward her, surging up off the floor.

Jake hesitated for a split second, then shot Vahl in the head.

The bastard crumpled. His eyes gaped, empty of life.

Dawn blinked rapidly, her gaze fixated on Vahl.

Jake hauled her into his arms. She buried her face in his shirt, nuzzling him as her arms encircled him. He smoothed her hair, murmured wordlessly, rubbed her back.

After a moment, her head popped up and she aimed her brilliant hazel eyes at him. No trace of sorrow colored her expression, only resolve. "Thank you."

"For what?"

"Saving me." Her smile could've lit the entire state of Nevada on a moonless night. "You're my hero, Jake, and my protector in every lifetime."

He cleared his throat and screwed up his mouth. "I messed up, though. Shouldn't have killed him before I got the information out of him. It's just he was trying to hurt you and—" He met those entrancing eyes of hers. "I could not let him do that."

"I know." Her nose wrinkled. "What information?"

After explaining about Vahl's computer setup, he told her, "I should've made him tell us where the backup site is."

"Might be in his notebook. He wrote stuff in there he thought was too important to trust to modern technology."

"Really." He felt his lips twitch into a near smile. "And you just happened to get hold of this notebook."

One delicate shoulder rose in a shrug. "I stumbled onto while he was bumbling around in the dark." She glanced at the unobstructed doorway, robbed of its huge honking metal barrier, and her brow crinkled. "How did you blow open the door?"

"C-4." He pecked the tip of her nose. "Long story. I'll explain later. Let's get out of here, this place is…unsettling."

She joined her hands at the nape of his neck and rose onto tiptoes. Their faces level, she pressed her soft lips to his mouth in a tender, all-too-brief kiss. "My hero. What's your plan?" she asked.

"We scram." He dug a small, rectangular box out of his pocket. It had a single button on its black surface. "I hit this, and Vahl's compound goes kablooey."

She laughed, a bright sound that lightened his soul. "Kablooey? Scram? Those aren't Jake words."

"I didn't realize I had my own dictionary."

"You do. Most definitely." She ran a finger down the bridge of his nose. "But you've been rewriting it lately."

He took her hand, tugging to urge her toward the open doorway.

It wasn't the only doorway now open to them. They'd just earned a new life.

When they exited the front door of the hacienda a few minutes later, Dawn posed another question. "Vahl's dead, but what if someone else copied files like you did?"

"I'll hunt the scumbag down and terminate him."

"You certainly are macho these days." She curled her free hand around his bicep and fanned her slender fingers out over his skin. "I like the new you. Or maybe it's the old you, from way back when."

"Why is it Vahl remembered the olden days, but I don't?"

"No idea." Her fingertips tickled his flesh. "Doesn't matter if you never remember. The past is irrelevant, all that matters is our future."

She was right, of course. Their past life together had been passionate, but tragic. With Vahl gone, they could write any future they wanted.

He ushered her down the driveway, toward where he'd left his car. Once they reached the vehicle, he motioned for her to climb into the car. After he jumped into the driver's seat and shut the door, he poised his finger over the detonator button.

Dawn frowned. "What about Vahl's employees?"

"I stunned them with flash bangs, tied them up, and quickly explained I was going to blow the place to hell and they had two choices. Stay and die, or flee and live." He didn't even try to contain his smug grin. "They chose the latter."

"You sound like Jake the grad student again, but your actions are the new-and-improved version of you." She settled a hand on his thigh, her fingers flexing, and skidded it higher. Dangerously high. He coughed and pushed her hand away, but she just sighed. "I love both sides of you, Jake. There's no need to be embarrassed about it."

Sliding his hand into her hair, he cupped the back of her head. "Lucky for us, Vahl was a paranoid son of a bitch. It'll all be over in about five seconds."

He flicked the switch.

A boom resonated through the air and the ground, vibrating the car and their feet. A secondary explosion rumbled.

Jake dipped his head to claim her mouth in a deep, hungry kiss. When he pulled away, they were both breathless.

"Let's go," he said. "We're free."

CHAPTER NINE

Three Days Later

DAWN LAY SPRAWLED ON THE BED IN THEIR NEW APART-
ment, arms above her head, naked. The six-hundred-thread-count cotton
sheets glided over her skin when she wriggled. Egyptian cotton. How
appropriate.

The blanket and quilt had been cast onto the floor, along with the top sheet. She lounged
one hundred percent naked with nothing to cover her. The cool draft from the air conditioner
tickled her skin, exciting the hairs. It wasn't the only thing exciting her.

Jake crouched above her on all fours, knees planted at either side of her thighs, his
mouth-watering body a temptation she could not resist. Her hands floated to his chest,
as if pulled by a gravitational force, and her fingers explored his warm, firm flesh. The
spicy, masculine scent of him intoxicated her. His arousal dangled between their bodies,
stealing her focus every time he shifted his hips and it moved too.

"I'm sorry," he murmured, "I should've done this weeks ago."

She skated her hands lower, past his belly button. "Why didn't you?"

"Thought I'd failed you. Thought I didn't deserve—" He sucked in a breath when her
fingers traveled lower still, grazing his shaft. A crooked smile warped his delicious mouth,
the one she hungered to devour. He gave a soft laugh. "Do you want to talk or..."

"Talk later. Option two now." She grasped his hips and tugged. "Please."

He stared down at her breasts. And licked his lips.

She reached for his shaft.

With a low chuckle, he captured her hands, and with one hand, bound them over her head. His strong fingers held her fast, but gently. He lowered his head to hers, their lips nearly touching, his hot breaths wafting over her skin. She parted her lips, as if she might inhale his essence, desperate to consume any part of him she could. He belonged to her, and she to him, forever. No more vengeful ex-fiancés. No more running from Redeo Biotech.

Though she could barely catch her breath, with his sensuous mouth so near hers, she managed to ask the question that plagued her dreams. "Are you sure Redeo is ruined?"

"Yes. Westenra checked in with his friends who still work there, and they said everything's gone. The files on the project—on you—have been destroyed and their computers are fried. Redeo's in a shambles. Vahl was the head of the snake, and without him, the body's flailing in its death throes."

"Uck. Let's not talk about death or Vahl anymore." She nipped his lower lip and told him, in her most sultry tone, "There's only one body I'm interested in at the moment."

One body pulsing with life, throbbing with need, just like hers.

He rubbed his lips across hers. "You better mean my body."

"Always."

"Good." His voice was rough with need. "I want you, Dawn. Can't wait anymore."

"Then don't." She wrapped one leg around his waist. "Please. I need you inside me."

A groan rumbled in his chest. He slanted his mouth over hers, hot, demanding, and she opened to him without reservation, welcoming his silken tongue. He dived deep inside her mouth with hungry strokes, as his hand pinned hers above her head, his need a living energy that suffused them both. His free hand closed over her breast, his thumb flicking over her taut nipple. She moaned into his mouth. He teased her nipple with relentless flicks of his deft thumb.

She ached for him. He was her center, the singularity to her black hole, but instead of devouring the light, he fueled it inside her. She would never leave him, and she knew he would never leave her. A love stronger than time and magic and vengeance bound them together. An unbreakable bond.

He broke the kiss, his brown eyes intent on her. "Marry me."

"What?"

"Marry me." He tweaked her nipple lightly. She whimpered, and his mouth split into a wicked grin. "I want to make it legal. Permanent." He caught her lip between his teeth. Releasing it slowly, seductively, he said, "Say yes."

"But how? I don't have a birth certificate or a driver's license or anything."

"I don't think they care about that shit in Vegas. If they do, I'll get you a driver's license." His hand on her breast drifted down her belly, to the apex of her thighs, his fingers massaging her sensitive mound. She arched her back, drowned in the sensations. His voice rasped in her ear, thick with need. "Say yes. Please, Dawn, say it."

His agile fingers toyed with the little hairs on her mound. Pleasure arced through her in hot, tingling jolts. One of his fingers dipped down to her damp sex, twirled around it, rubbed mercilessly. Panting, she fought to free her hands, but he tethered her there, at his mercy.

She loved it. Because she knew, without a shred of doubt, he would never hurt her.

"Jake." His name was a gasp. "Please."

"Say it." He rubbed faster, harder, sending tremors straight to her core.

Mindless with need, she writhed under his expert touch. When the pressure mounted to near breaking, he pulled his hand away.

He slicked his tongue over her lips.

She bowed up to skim her breasts against his torso—then she moaned, long and throaty. The electric jolts that shot from her nipples straight to her sex seemed to spin out into him too, and he shuddered, exhaling a ragged breath.

"Christ, Dawn," he said. "Just say—"

"Yes."

"Really?"

"Yes-yes-yes, dammit, yes!"

He smiled, the most joyous expression she'd ever seen. "Thank you."

Then he sank his length into her with one smooth thrust. Snug inside her, he paused to gaze at her as if she were the source of everything good in the universe. He released her hands. "I love you, Dawn."

She cradled his face in her palms. "And I love you."

He possessed her mouth with a kiss full of passion and adoration, and as his tongue swirled in her mouth, he drove inside her with the same rhythm. She clung to him, relishing the feel of his muscles rippling around her, his shaft thrusting into her, his tongue forging deep into her mouth. They were joined on every level—hearts, minds, souls, and flesh.

Her climax convulsed her body, so hard and scorching she cried out over and over, riding the waves until he came apart inside her. Spent, he collapsed on top of her. She didn't mind his weight at all, because it proved to her he was hers.

Whatever happened now, nothing would tear her away from him again.

The doorbell bonged.

Breathing hard, Jake propped himself up with his arms and scowled in the direction of the bedroom door, and the living room beyond. "Who the hell is that?"

"Maybe we should find out."

They clambered out of bed, both flushed and sweat-sheathed. She threw on a satin robe, while he pulled on a pair of jeans. They shambled out to the front door.

Jake peeked through the peephole.

His head drew back. His brows converged over his nose. "It's Westenra."

She slapped his arm. "So open the door, dummy."

First, he waved for her to move aside. She complied, mainly because she knew he wouldn't open the door until she did. When he swung the door inward, Westenra looked first at Jake, then at her. His lips curved upward, just a touch.

"What are you doing here?" Jake asked.

"I need to speak with you both." He rested a hand on his face, the smile fading. "It's time I told you the truth."

"About?"

"Who I am. Why I gathered all those weapons." He bobbled side to side, his gaze on the door. "I knew you'd be coming, someday, and so I assembled an arsenal for you. I understood the day would come when Vahl exposed his true identity and went after Dawn."

She inched closer. "How could you possibly know that?"

"Because I have memories of the past too." His eyes turned toward her, then darted away again. He squared his shoulders, nodded, and rotated his head to meet her gaze. "I'm your father."

Her heart stuttered. She swayed into Jake, who caught her in his arms.

"That's impossible," Jake said.

"Isn't all of this impossible?" Westenra shook his head, a sour smile on his lips. "I regained my memories a few weeks ago, though I had inklings before that. I believe it's why I was morally opposed to experimenting on her mummified remains. Some part of me recognized her as my daughter."

Neither she nor Jake seemed capable of speech. He tightened his arms around her, and she laid a hand on his chest.

"May I come in?" Westenra asked. "We have a lot to discuss."

Jake looked to her for the answer.

She gnawed her lip. Her father had betrothed her to Setka—Vahl—but maybe he had a reasonable explanation for his actions. Without a name until today, without a past or a family, she discovered a part of her longed for this connection. To him. To her father.

Jake was her family too. Even if this relationship with her father floundered, even if she learned he'd willingly given her to Setka, she still had someone to lean on, someone who would lean on her in return.

She gave a little nod. "Please, come in."

Whatever awaited her in the future, everything would be okay. Because she had Jake.

Her guardian, her soul mate, forever.

REBORN TO CONQUER

CHAPTER ONE

A s Dawn Maxwell surveyed the Nevada desert around her, she let her mind untether from her body, floating up into the clear blue sky, soaring over the landscape for a bird's-eye view. Though she'd first accomplished this feat while dead, her mummified body rotting in a tomb, the ability still felt strange. Her body seemed to fade away, no longer tying her down, and she flew weightless above the desert, able to scan the surroundings better than even a satellite could.

Watch out, freaky resurrected mummy girl on the loose.

"Are you soul-journeying again?" The voice of her husband, Jake, penetrated the surreal haze around her mind, but she did not want to come down yet.

"Yes," she said, her own voice distant and oddly flat. "Looking for the bunker."

"It's not here. We'll have to check Vahl's other properties."

Circling around their physical location, where their Jeep Cherokee sat parked in front of a metal shed, she gazed down on her husband and her father. Unease prickled her incorporeal skin. *Father.* Though she'd tried really, really hard to think of Ralph Westenra as her dad, she had trouble accepting the idea. Until a couple months ago, she'd had no one except Jake. Now she had a reincarnated father to go along with her reincarnated husband—except they hadn't been married back in ancient Egypt. Anton Vahl—known as Setka in those days—had murdered her before they had a chance.

Despite being detached from her body, her head throbbed anyway. Keeping everyone's names straight, when each of them had at least two, always gave her a headache.

Maybe she should refer to Westenra as His Majesty, since he'd been a pharaoh in his past life. But that seemed even weirder than Dad.

Her attention wandered to the horizon, where the first smudges of storm clouds clung to the tops of the distant mountains. She couldn't hear thunder, but somehow its faint vibrations rumbled through her.

"Come back," Jake urged, a note of distress in his voice. "Please, Dawn."

She swooped down toward the ground, toward her body, and sank into it with a tingly rush of energy. Her vision switched back to the real world, her gaze swinging to Jake. His chestnut hair glistened in the sunshine and his cinnamon eyes were fixed on her. Lips parted, forehead crinkled, he let his shoulders sag. "You're back."

Dawn moved to him, sliding her fingers into his hair. "I'm fine. It's perfectly safe, really."

Not exactly a lie. She didn't know if it was safe or not.

He turned his head, nuzzling his cheek into her palm. "I wish you wouldn't do that. We can find other ways to search."

Jake still didn't like her soul-journeying. He'd told her several times she might get stuck like that one day, but she kept laughing it off as paranoia. Truth was, she didn't know if she could get stuck in her out-of-body state. Never would she admit that to him, though, because he'd forbid her to do it. And right now, they needed all the help they could get.

"Relax." She took her face in his hands and pressed her lips to his. "See? I'm one hundred percent in-body again."

Behind her, Ralph Westenra cleared his throat.

Dawn glanced back at her long-lost father. *Really* long-lost. Until two months ago, they hadn't seen each other in over three thousand years ago. Well, he'd seen her ten months ago—or at least, her mummified remains, displayed in a glass tank inside a laboratory at Redeo Biotech. Her last memory of him was much, much older, and the thought of those days rippled a chill through her. "You have something to say?"

"Perhaps we should give up the search," Westenra said, scratching his scalp as the wind ruffled his gray hair. His blue eyes focused on her. "If we can't find Vahl's hidden repository, the odds are no one else can either."

"Can't take the risk. If anyone finds out about me, about us…" Another chill, harder and more frigid, shivered through her. "Bad things would happen. Again."

Jake settled his hands on her shoulders, squeezing lightly. "Vahl's gone, forever this time. No more reincarnation for that bastard, which means he can never hurt you again."

She leaned back into him, a bit of the tension unraveling. He always knew what she was worrying about, even when she didn't recognize it. "I know, but the data he collected, the files he amassed on me, are still out there somewhere."

Jake slipped his arms around her waist to tug her close. "No one is ever taking you away from me again. You can count on that."

And she knew she could, with unfailing conviction. But the mere thought of becoming a lab rat again had her swallowing against a tightness in her throat. Vahl had vowed to mine the secrets of her rebirth from her body. Would another scientist stumble onto his research and set out to do the same? *Once a lab rat, always a lab rat, eh?*

Jake bent to murmur in her ear. "You're safe."

She shut her eyes and let herself revel in the feel of him, warm and solid, his arms encircling her with his strength, his breaths teasing the sensitive skin just below her ear. Delicious heat burgeoned inside her, the familiar desire that ever simmered beneath the surface. No other man, in any time, held the power to affect her this way. It was...wonderful.

The glow of the sun, bright behind her eyelids, gave way to a gloom that swept over them. Thunder growled. A strange awareness prickled her skin, raising the hairs, and she opened her eyes.

Thunderclouds loomed overhead, swiftly consuming the sky. They hung dark and heavy, purple and blue and gray, like a great bruise in the heavens. A wind whipped up around them, swirling dust and bits of detritus. Jake stiffened against her.

"Do you feel it?" she whispered.

"Yes. I don't understand..."

"Neither do I. But something is coming."

Westenra had twisted his torso around to stare at the storm, one hand raised to shield his eyes. His lips were tight, his face was pinched. His eyes darted, as if hunting for some kind of sign in the clouds.

The wind died in a split second. The storm cloud began to roil and spin, its base morphing into a lumpy mass, darkening to near black.

"In the car," Jake said, dragging her toward the Jeep. They piled in with Jake behind the wheel, Dawn in the passenger seat, and Westenra in the back. Jake seized her seat belt and yanked it down to click it into place. "Hold on. This might get bumpy."

She leaned forward to stare up at the sky through the windshield. Her heart thudded. The entire sky had gone pure black, with whirling tendrils of deep blue and purple fanning out from the base of the storm. A strange energy crackled in the air, even inside the car. The hairs all over her body lifted, and her mouth went dry. Something ancient and evil lurked inside the thunderhead, something terrible beyond imagining, and though she had no explanation for her certainty, the truth of it rang inside her.

Dawn clutched the armrest, nails digging into the upholstery. "It's him, Jake. It's Vahl."

"What?" He cast her a wide-eyed, sideways glance. "He's dead, I shot him in the head. Then I blew up his whole damn compound, with him inside. Vahl is never coming back."

"Not him, not exactly." Bile rose in her throat, searing and bitter. "What he wrought still lives."

"You sound like a bad horror movie."

She shook her head, biting her lip. "I don't understand how I know, but I can sense it. The storm is not just a storm. It's the curse Vahl laid down on us thousands of years ago." She gripped his muscular arm and leaned toward him. "It's alive, and it's coming for us."

Jake's eyes swiveled toward her, unblinking. "That's imposs—"

A bolt of lightning slammed down onto the Jeep's hood. Sparks erupted. The vehicle bounced, fishtailed, as a blast of thunder deafened them. Ears ringing, blinded by the brilliant ghosts of the lightning, she recognized the engine had quit from the sudden deceleration that thrust her forward against her seatbelt. Her pulse roared behind her eardrums. The breath froze in her lungs. She blinked rapidly until her vision cleared, just as the sounds around her faded into perception. A clattering roar masked all but the faintest traces of the high-pitched keening behind it.

Dawn caught sight of the roar's source, straight ahead, and plastered herself to her seat. As if that would help. As if anything could stop it.

Massive and black and spinning like a dervish, a tornado barreled toward them.

CHAPTER TWO

J AKE GRIPPED THE STEERING WHEEL, HIS FOOT STILL RAMMING the brake to the floorboards. He couldn't move. He couldn't speak. His breaths came fast and shallow, and blackness dotted his vision, probably from lack of oxygen. Christ, he could not lose it. Dawn needed him to...What? Save her?

He almost laughed at that, but then his gaze landed on the tornado again. He gulped, his breaths growing shaky, his hands too. He managed to turn his head toward Dawn, and her ghost-white face made his gut twist. He wrenched one hand free of the wheel, clasping her hand. "Can't you fix this?"

Her head whipped around, her impossibly wide eyes locked onto him. "I have healing powers. How does that mean I can stop a freaking tornado?"

The squeak in her voice fractured his heart. He ached to fold her in his arms and somehow protect her from this, but he could do nothing. *Nothing.* Out the corner of his eye, he spied the tornado looming ever closer. The noise escalated until it overwhelmed his senses. *We can't die like this, not after everything.*

Jake wrapped his arms around Dawn and hauled her over the center console into his lap. He squeezed her so tight he felt her sharp exhalation deflate her chest, but he gripped her even tighter, unwilling to let her go, ever. Squeezing his eyes shut, he buried his face against her neck, her hair fluttering from his ragged breaths. The roaring drowned out his own voice as he growled against her skin, "Stay with me, stay with me, it can't end this way."

The Jeep shuddered.

With all the power of his will, however pathetic it was, Jake commanded the storm to vanish. To leave them be. To spare her, at least. Dawn, his soul mate, his sweet and sensual wife, the only human on earth he'd sacrifice his soul to protect. *Take me please, spare her, it's all my fault anyway.*

Silence. It exploded around them with the force of a bomb blast. The Jeep stopped shaking, the wind was vanquished. Jake's heart pounded. Panting, his face sheathed in sweat, he eased his eyelids apart and squinted at the sunshine glaring in his face.

Every muscle in his body went limp. His arms fell away from Dawn as he slumped his head back against the seat. The storm had vanished. The only sign of its existence was a smattering of puffy, gray cumulus clouds.

Dawn sat up, straddling his lap. Brow crinkled, she glanced out the window and her jaw dropped. "Wh—what happened?"

I begged Vahl's curse to spare you and it did. It couldn't be that. No way. Dawn had powers, not him. "No idea."

She squinted at him, her lips puckering. "What aren't you telling me?"

He squirmed under her, the weight of her body pressing into him, rousing his and beckoning him with her heat and softness. *Wrong time, wrong place.* Yet he never could control his reactions to her.

"Jake." She braced her hands at either side of his head, her face inches from his. "Spill."

Oh, he might do that all right, if she kept wriggling her hips over his groin. *Get a grip, man.* He sucked in a breath, letting it out slowly, the air reflecting off her face back onto his. Dawn wore her determined look, and he knew he had no choice. She'd wring the truth out of him one way or another. He sighed. "It's ridiculous. It can't be the reason."

She bent closer, her nose bumping his. "Tell me."

"I begged the storm to leave us alone." He cleared his throat, fidgeting again, which only served to push his hardening shaft into her body. "And it did. Like it listened to me. Which is impossible."

Her lips curved up at the corners in a faint, knowing smile. "Nothing is impossible, Jake. You ought to know that by now."

"You have powers. I don't."

She shook her head, then lowered her mouth close enough that her lips brushed his when she spoke. "You willed me back to life. Or have you forgotten?"

How could he forget the months he'd sat by her tank at Redeo, watching her lifelike-but-lifeless body floating in the blue liquid, fantasizing about what she'd been like when alive. He'd yearned for her to awaken so badly, and then she had. For him. Because of him, Dawn believed. It was insane, though. He had no supernatural abilities.

Dawn stroked the tip of her tongue across the seam of his lips. Her voice was a sultry murmur. "The scientists regenerated my body, but you resurrected me. With your willpower. With your love."

"Maybe, but—"

"Uh-uh." She gave a curt shake of her head, the movement scraping her lips over his, making his erection pulse for her. "No maybe about it, Jake. You woke me up. So why can't you accept that you might have other powers too?"

From the backseat, Ralph Westenra cleared his throat. Loudly. The sound shattered the intimate bubble around Jake and Dawn, but his body still thought they were alone. Jake hauled in a deep breath, fighting to calm his outrageous and thoroughly inappropriate hunger for his wife. No such luck.

Dawn slanted sideways to frown at Westenra. "What?"

He cleared his throat again. In a hesitant tone, he said, "The curse might have gifted you both with metaphysical abilities."

Dawn scrunched her lips. "How could you possibly know that?"

"You let me read Vahl's journal, which included the curse. I read it several times, trying to understand what precisely he'd done to us all."

"And?"

Westenra heaved out a sigh. "I think he overestimated his grasp of ancient magic. He intended to curse you and Jake to suffer for eternity, but I believe he unintentionally imbued you both with supernatural talents."

"I don't get it."

"Think, child. Vahl—Setka gave birth to a living curse, one that seeks to mete out his retribution even beyond his death. But the universe seeks *maat*."

Jake rubbed his forehead with his thumb and index finger. *Maat*? Since reuniting with Dawn, he'd learned a bit about ancient Egypt, so he recognized the word. But its full import eluded him.

Dawn caught sight of his confused expression and gave him a tight smile. Though her gaze never left his, she spoke to Westenra. "*Maat*. You mean the essential cosmic balance between good and evil, order and chaos."

"Yes," Westenra agreed. "To the ancient Egyptians—to our people—*maat* was vital and inescapable. A curse as powerful as this one must find its balancing opposite."

"Fascinating," Jake said. "But how does that explain our having powers?"

"The gift of your powers is the balancing opposite. Order to Vahl's chaos."

Jake's brain hurt from thinking about this insanity. "You think the universe gave me and Dawn paranormal abilities so we could, what, cancel out the curse?"

"Possibly."

God, how Jake wanted to believe it. If he really had awakened Dawn from death, if he had stopped the tornado, then he could at last protect her in the way she deserved. He failed her in his past life. He let her die, murdered by Vahl. Sure, he saved her when Vahl attacked them both a couple months ago, but if he could end this curse and free her forever...

Jake hoisted his wife off his lap, depositing her in the passenger seat. He shoved the driver's door open and swung one leg out, his foot touching down on sandy earth.

"Where are you going?" Dawn asked.

"Taking care of things. I was a Boy Scout, you know."

She smiled, bright and glorious, and his heart swelled. When she smiled at him like that, he felt like he could do anything. And maybe he could. Maybe the bastard who tried to steal away from him everything he cherished had accidentally granted him the power to set them all free. He swore he heard Anton Vahl rolling over in his grave—or rather, the pile of ash where his mortal remains rested.

Jake Maxwell was no longer a useless former grad student.

"I can fix this Jeep like I fixed the storm." Flashing Dawn a grin, he hopped out of the Jeep. She raised her brows. He chuckled. "Trust me, honey, I've got this."

CHAPTER THREE

DAWN WATCHED JAKE STRUGGLING TO POP THE JEEP'S hood, but the metal had been warped by the unnaturally powerful lightning strike and he seemed to accomplish nothing more than wrenching his face into an angry expression while, no doubt, cursing under his breath. Still, her husband refused to give up. She loved his stubborn determination, yet his newfound confidence had her stomach churning.

I can fix this Jeep like I fixed the storm. His words had been infused with a surety she hadn't known from him before, as if he thought he'd become a superhero or something. Dawn rubbed her temples, trying to dispel the ache sprouting behind her eyes. When she'd suggested Jake might've halted the storm, she hadn't meant he was invincible. He seemed to have interpreted her suggestion that way, though.

Great. Now she had to worry about her husband getting himself killed because he thought he was Superman. Groaning, she dropped her forehead into her palm. All those times she called him her hero, she hadn't mean it like that. *I can't lose him, I won't lose him.* She needed to disabuse him of this insane notion he could do anything.

"Worried about Jake?"

Dawn jumped, twisting around to stare at her father. Christ. She'd forgotten all about him. A sick feeling rose in her stomach. She'd been about to make out with Jake, and probably rip his clothes off, while her strangely estranged father sat mere feet away in the backseat. Even when Westenra had spoken up a few minutes ago, she hadn't recognized her own rude and wanton behavior in his presence. Whenever she got close to Jake, the rest of the world receded far into the distance and she kind of lost her head, drowned in the bliss of desire.

"Sorry," she said, a bit sheepish, as she gazed back at Westenra. She felt her lips tighten, most likely because she was scowling at him. "Forgot you were here. Are you okay?"

"Fine." He eyed her with trepidation, as if she might shoot him in the forehead for speaking to her. "Are you all right? You seem concerned, which I assume has to do with Jake."

"I'm not injured, if that's what you're asking." She drew in a deep breath, shut her eyes for a second, and exhaled slowly. "He seems to think he can conquer anything, even this curse, all because we convinced him he's got powers now."

Westenra sighed, his shoulders deflating. "I shouldn't have said anything."

"I chimed right in to agree with you. We couldn't have known Jake would latch onto the idea with so much...gusto."

Her father nodded, eyes closed. "I understand now. How much Bek means to you."

"His name is Jake, and he's my husband. No thanks to you."

Westenra winced and opened his eyes to glance at her, but averted his gaze immediately.

Although Dawn fought to control her anger, it boiled up inside her chest. She fisted her hands on her lap, jaw tight. "How could you betroth me to a psycho?"

"I had no choice." He ran a hand through his unkempt gray hair. "Setka's people were Egyptians, but they splintered off on their own a century before I was born. They became a sort of terrorist cell, hiding out in the far reaches of the western desert, calling themselves the Children of Setesh. By the time I became pharaoh, they'd begun a systematic campaign to destroy the Two Lands with guerrilla tactics."

Dawn studied him as she tried to wrap her mind around what he'd said. The Two Lands meant ancient Egypt. Setka was the original name of Anton Vahl, before he murdered her and cursed all of them to be reborn in different ways so he could wreak his vengeance. Since Setesh had been the god of chaos, these terrorists must've labeled themselves Children of Setesh as a way of demonstrating their intention to tear down the Two Lands.

"Tell me," she said, aiming for a neutral tone that came out a bit tight, "why did the Children of Setesh want to destroy us so badly?"

Westenra hesitated, shoulders hunching, then told her, "They had been commoners in the Two Lands. When they rallied for more power, for more fairness in the governing of our nation, their pleas fell on deaf ears. The pharaoh at the time sought to quash their rebellion, and resorted to slaughtering dozens of them, including women and children, in a nighttime raid. The Children of Setesh never forgave the atrocity, but it took decades for them gain enough numbers and strength to defy us again."

Slouching in her seat, Dawn spotted Jake out the windshield. He'd pried the battered hood up enough to lean under it and fiddle with who-knew-what. She recognized he'd latched onto the idea of having powers because he felt compelled to defend her but ineffectual at the task. She also understood the reasons, at least a bit. In the wake of Vahl's death and her success in recovering some of her memories, she'd longed to get to know Jake better. He'd had a life, in this time, before taking a job at Redeo Biotech. She knew he'd been a communications major, working toward a master's, and that's how he wound up documenting Redeo's experiments on video—and how he'd found her. Yet every time she asked about his family, his childhood, he clammed up. A couple weeks ago, he'd finally opened up to her.

"I was an orphan," he'd confessed, scrutinizing his hands to avoid her gaze. "Bounced from foster home to foster home, never fitting in, always knowing I was an outsider. I learned the only person I could trust or rely on was myself. Got loans for college, worked jobs to pay for everything else."

She'd rested her head on his shoulder, looping her arm around his. "Did you ever look for your birth parents?"

He'd nodded, his gaze full of sorrow. "They died in a car crash when I was six days old. No other living family. That's when I realized I'd always be alone." He turned his head to look at her and his expression changed into something resembling amazement. "Until you."

Jake believed vulnerability made him less of a man. He still couldn't accept she loved him *because* he wasn't invincible.

Reeling her thoughts back into the present, she scratched her neck, knowing she must ask her father more questions, but fearing the answers. The time had come to confront her past, and deal with it once and for all. The truth might arm her with the information they needed to defeat Vahl's curse. Without looking back at her father, she asked, "Where did Vahl—I mean, Setka come into the equation?"

"After the Children of Setesh raided one of our outposts, killing ten of my soldiers, I sent an emissary to broker a peace treaty." His clothing rustled, as if he were fidgeting. "They agreed to a treaty, but only if one of theirs was installed as vizier and wed to—" He coughed. "To my daughter."

"Of course, you signed that deal lickety-split."

"No." He drew the word out on a ragged sigh, sounding more tired than she'd ever heard anyone sound. "I mulled the proposal for days. I consulted my closest advisers, praying to find another way. There was none."

She turned in her seat, almost sideways, and fixed her gaze on his. "Egypt had a huge army. These Setesh worshipers couldn't have outnumbered us." Her throat constricted as a memory flared in her mind, of Setka forcing poison down her throat, of the searing agony that seemed to stretch into eternity, and of the final moment when she realized she was dying—and thanked the gods for it. "Why didn't you wipe those bastards off the face of the earth?"

"How many lives would have been lost then?" A bleakness overtook his expression, settling into his glassy gaze. "I had an entire nation to consider, thousands of lives to balance against—" His words choked off, his eyes cinched shut. "Against your freedom."

"My freedom?" She all but spat the words, a hot ache throbbing behind her ribs, her eyes stinging with burgeoning tears. "Setka murdered me."

Her father drooped his head, his chin on his chest. His voice emerged faint and weak. "I could never have predicted what would happen. I have regretted my choice since the day Setka unleashed his wrath on you." He lifted his head, staring blankly out the windshield. "My only daughter died because of my shortsightedness. I expect no forgiveness, but I hope one day you'll understand the choice I made."

Tears rolled down her cheeks, hot on her chilled skin. Dawn swiped them away with the back of her hand, sniffled, but couldn't stem the tide of anguish crashing through her. "My own father betrayed me. How am I supposed to understand that? You valued other people's lives more than mine."

He stared straight into her eyes. "Sometimes being selfless levies the highest cost of all. Weighing the world's fate against one life…It's a decision I would wish on no one, not even my worst enemy."

The driver's door sprang open. Jake bent across the seat, his feet still on the ground but his focus trained on her, eye unblinking. "What's wrong? You're crying."

Dawn brushed away another pair of tears, straightened, and forced a smile. "I'm fine. Heart to hearts between an ex-mummy and her reincarnated father are stressful, that's all."

Jake pursed his lips, his narrowed gaze shifting to her father. "What did you say to her?"

"The truth. Nothing more."

Dawn reached out to clasp Jake's face in her hands. "He didn't do anything. It's okay. I'm okay."

He studied her for a moment, then nodded, his body relaxing. "All right."

She feathered her lips over his in the barest of kisses. "No luck with the Jeep?"

"Engine's fried." One corner of his mouth twisted downward. "Lightning isn't supposed to punch a hole right through solid metal, but the hood has a perfectly round hole in the spot where the bolt hit."

"That was not normal lightning."

Jake leaned back, retreating from her hands, and rested his arm across the back of the driver's seat. "Maybe the curse created positive lightning. It's much more powerful than the normal, negatively charged kind."

"Not sure even positive lightning would wreck our car like this."

"Yeah." He frowned for a second, then shook his head as if shedding a perplexing thought. "I think only magic will get this heap running again."

"Um…" She bit the inside of her lip and said carefully, "You think you can summon the magic to jumpstart our car."

He shrugged, a small but smug smile on his lips. "Why not?"

"Because until five minutes ago, you were convinced you had no magical abilities."

"Now I believe it." He climbed into the driver's seat and shut the door. "Time to test my superpowers."

She winced. "Jake—"

"Stop worrying." He kissed her cheek, patted it once, and lowered his hand to the ignition switch. "I can handle this."

Dawn grabbed his arm. "Diving in headfirst is a great way to split your skull open."

"It's not a swimming pool, it's a Jeep."

Shutting his eyes, he poked his index finger into the slot where the key should've gone. What, now he thought he could shoot electricity from his finger? Oh God, he really had gone off the deep end. She just prayed enough water would break his fall.

His face pinched, he took slow, deep breaths.

The air crackled around them, imbued with unseen energy. The hairs on her arms lifted in the strange current, and goose bumps cropped up all over her skin. She swallowed against a lump in her throat. Jake scrunched his face up, bent over the wheel, his finger still jammed into the ignition slot.

Dawn squeezed his arm. "Honey, I think it's time to admit defeat."

He grated syllables through his clenched teeth. "Never."

She was about to speak again, but a noise halted her. The Jeep's engine had just rumbled to life.

Jake grinned. "See? Told you I've got this."

Oh yeah, she saw. His newfound abilities didn't bother her—she had some of her own, after all—but his attitude set her nerves on edge. After months of denying he'd awakened her with the force of his will, he'd now embraced his powers without reservation, without common sense. He liked it, a little too much.

And that scared the hell out of her.

CHAPTER FOUR

J AKE GUIDED THEIR REPLACEMENT CAR, AN ALMOST-NEW
Ford Explorer, down the interstate, headed toward the Nevada-Utah
border. The Jeep had kept running long enough for them to ditch it at
a junkyard and purchase the Explorer. Apparently, his powers couldn't
regenerate the Jeep's engine, only revive it for a time. Ah well, he could live with
a few limitations.

In his peripheral vision, he noticed Dawn squirming in the passenger seat. She'd
been uneasy ever since he halted the storm, and particularly since he'd jumpstarted
the Jeep with his finger. Okay, he could understand how those events might unsettle
her. But she ought to be happy. For months, she'd tried to convince him he woke her
up from death and he'd denied it. Now he accepted—hell, reveled in—the truth. And
how did she react?

Don't get too comfortable with your powers, Jake. That's what she'd told him not long
after he restarted the Jeep. She'd also said, *Getting cocky is dangerous.* He was not cocky.
He was...confident. For the first time. Ever. In his life. Or at least, in his current life. Why
couldn't she let him enjoy this?

Maybe she's right, a tiny voice in the back of his mind chided. The annoying
voice kept pestering him, kept poking pinholes in his good mood. Yes, Dawn might
have a point, at least a small one. Still, he needed this. Never before had he possessed the power to defend her against supernatural foes, and it was a gift he had no
intention of returning. He could dial it back a touch, though.

Later.

From the backseat, Westenra coughed. "The next candidate is north of Salt Lake City."

"I know," Jake said, his gaze locked on the road ahead. "Already entered the coordinates into the GPS."

"Perhaps we should be a bit more careful this time."

Dawn snorted. "More careful? We're being stalked by a living curse. How do you suggest we take precautions against that?"

Westenra exhaled a long, loud sigh and then fell silent.

Jake felt Dawn's hand settle on his thigh, warm and welcome. Her fingers plied his flesh, sparking the desire that always simmered just beneath the surface. "We're all exhausted, and it'll be dark soon. Maybe we should stop at a motel for the night."

His wife and a bed? He couldn't turn down an offer like that. "All right. I'll pull into the next one I see."

She retracted her hand. "Thank you."

Jake threw her a sideways glance. Had she just manipulated him into stopping for the night? Why would she? The truth settled in his chest like a granite rock. She was afraid...of him. Well, not precisely him. She feared his confidence, his reliance on these new powers of his, and she must think—or hope—a night off would temper his enthusiasm.

She didn't understand. This wasn't a macho thing. He didn't relish his abilities because they made him feel like a real man, though they sort of did. He relished them because they empowered him to protect her, to care for her, to become the guardian he'd failed to be three thousand years ago. From here on, he could make up for letting her die the first time and make certain it never happened again. He itched to forge ahead, find and destroy Vahl's archives, and bring his wife the peace she'd been robbed of in the past.

But for tonight, he'd give her another kind of peace. He'd pull over at a damn motel and try to stop scaring her with his confidence.

He patted her thigh. "You're welcome."

<hr />

THE SPRINGS IN THE MOTEL MATTRESS CREAKED WHEN DAWN SAT down on the bed. The room was clean, if Spartan, with decor straight out of the 1970s. The TV perched on the low dresser looked just as old, though nothing in the room could predate her. When she heard the shower shut off in the bathroom, she stripped off her clothes, peeled back the covers, and stretched out on the bed. The draft from the air conditioner, cool and dry, wafted over her bare skin.

After a moment, the bathroom door swung open. Jake, wearing only a towel, sauntered out and across the small space toward the bed, his feet shooshing on the worn carpeting. He halted near the foot of the bed. Eyes hooded, he slid his gaze over her naked body. Everywhere his gaze traveled, her skin tingled, and when his attention landed on her breasts, her nipples hardened even more.

He licked his lower lip and said in a husky voice, "Are you trying to seduce me?"

"I have to try?" She pushed up onto her elbows, draping one leg over the other. "Must be doing something wrong then."

"No." He crawled across the mattress on all fours, his muscles flexing with each movement, his towel shifting and loosening until it slipped off his hips. When his body hovered over hers, his erection dangled between them. Jake stared down at her with unrestrained lust. "All you have to do is be here and I'm ready to go."

"My, you are easy."

"Only for you." He ducked his head down to brush his lips over hers. "Thank God your father's in the next room. If we had to share a room with him one more night…"

For weeks, they'd had to share one room because all the motels they'd found were booked up with summer tourists. She and Jake hadn't really been alone in almost a month.

He touched a fingertip to her breast, tracing light circles around her nipple but never so much as grazing the aching tip. Her breaths heaved in her chest. The fiery heat of need pooled low in her belly, and she moaned as his finger tormented her skin but avoided the place where she craved his touch the most.

"Jake." She arched her back, and still he steered clear of her nipple. "Please, Jake."

"Please what?" His finger. Circling. Tantalizing. Maddening.

She grabbed his finger and moved it onto her nipple. "This. Now."

His smile was slow and molten, full of sensual promise. He covered her mouth with his, the kiss hard and demanding and irresistible. She parted her lips for him, and his tongue plunged deep, tangling with hers in a rush of slick, hot hunger. He flicked his finger across her nipple and she let out a sharp moan. He swallowed her cry, his mouth devouring her with every scrape of his teeth across her lips and every thrust of his tongue. She flung her legs around his hips, locked her ankles over his buttocks, and struggled to drag him into her.

A chuckle resonated in his chest and through his mouth into hers, but he held his position above her. He severed the kiss. "Not yet."

"Why the hell not?"

Flashing her a crooked smile, he swiveled his hips, which grazed his shaft over her belly. She gasped. He rocked his hips back, and his erection teased the swollen flesh between her thighs. She whimpered, seizing his arms in a desperate effort to keep from thrashing like a wanton madwoman. She couldn't stop her nails from digging into his skin.

He winced, but then smirked. "Like this?"

Another brush of his shaft over her damp flesh, and she bucked her hips reflexively, but couldn't catch what she craved. He lowered his body onto hers, inch by torturous inch, his skin soft and warm, enlivening her entire body until it was so sensitive she thought she'd climax just from the feel of him on top of her.

"Oh God, Jake," she whimpered. "Please."

He eased her legs apart with his knee, then snaked a hand down her side, between her thighs, to stroke her throbbing flesh. She clutched at him, on fire from the inside out, consumed by the need to have him inside her. His finger toyed with her sex, wringing a desperate cry from her.

The door slammed open.

Jake sprang off the bed, landing on his feet beside it, his body blocking her. She could see the doorway between his spread legs. Arms outstretched in a protective gesture, he stared at the door. It had bounced off the door stop and teetered back and forth, each swing narrower, until it came to rest three-fourths open.

Dawn yanked the sheet over her as she pushed into a sitting position. The doorway stood empty, nothing visible beyond it save for the dark night, broken only by a sulfur-yellow streetlamp in the parking lot and their vehicle, seated within the cone of sickly light. A breeze trickled through the room from outside, the air sticky and tepid, tinged with a fetid odor.

"What is that?" she asked, shielding her nose with her hand. "It stinks like—"

"Death." Jake half turned toward her, his face an impassive mask. "It smells like death."

She twisted the sheets in her fingers. "The curse."

Jake gave a solemn nod.

She swallowed, her gaze drawn to the gaping doorway. "Why isn't it trying to kill us like before?"

"I don't know." He glanced at the door. A muscle ticked in his jaw. "Maybe it's learning."

A frigid chill slithered through her stomach, up into her chest, to coil around her heart. "Learning what?"

"How to terrorize us." He clenched his hands into fists, shoulders bunched, and cast her a frighteningly determined look. "I'll show it who's boss."

"Jake, no."

She flung an arm out to grab him, but he pulled away. Before she could untangle herself from the sheet, he'd spun toward the door and marched straight for it.

"Wait!" She all but screamed the word, but he ignored her. She hurled the sheet aside and sprinted after him. He banged the door shut in her face.

Outside, an inhuman roar blasted through the night.

CHAPTER FIVE

AWN SNATCHED JAKE'S SHIRT FROM THE FLOOR, THREW it on, and yanked the door open to bolt outside. Jake stood utterly naked in the middle of the parking lot, his head tilted back to stare up at the night sky. The odor of rotten flesh and decay permeated the air. Dawn winced at the stench as she raced toward her husband.

When she touched his arm, he rotated his eyes to look at her but did not move otherwise. "It's here. I can feel it. Can't you?"

"Yes." An insistent wriggly sensation wormed through her gut, cold and oily, like the tentacles of a beast from the depths of the Arctic Ocean. Yet they stood side by side in a motel parking lot in Utah, surrounded by the sultry heat of a summer night. She bent her head back to eye the heavens, and though she spotted a smattering of stars, nothing else was visible. No monster. No freaky tornado. Not even a single, puffy cloud.

Jake pushed her behind him, his body rigid, eyes narrowed at the empty sky. "Go back in the room. When it comes for us, I don't want you anywhere near it."

She huffed. "It's a freaking curse. I doubt hiding in a rinky-dink motel room is going to protect either of us."

He jerked his head to aim a furrowed-brow look at her. "Please. Just go inside."

"No." She folded her arms over her chest. "I am not leaving you."

"Dawn." His lips flattened into a line. "Go."

And he called her stubborn. *Sheesh.* Hands on her hips, she shook her head. "There's a reason 'obey' was taken out of the marriage vows. Women don't like being ordered around."

"But—"

She waved a hand at his naked body. "You're the one who needs to go inside, before a cop sees you out here buck naked."

He gritted his teeth, and she swore she heard his molars grinding against each other. Neither of them moved. The death stench persisted, but whatever the curse was up to, it seemed content to hang back. After a tense moment of attempting to stare down her husband, she rushed back into the motel room just long enough to grab his jeans, then hurried back outside to toss them at him.

"Put something on," she said, waggling the jeans in front of him. "If anyone sees you—"

"Yeah, yeah," he grumbled, with a peeved expression, and snatched the jeans from her. After tugging them on to cover his glorious, yet highly inappropriate nudity, he held his arms wide, as if showing himself off. "Happy now?"

She gave a curt nod. "What do you intend to do? Shout at the sky? Curse the curse?"

"It tried to kill us earlier. Not letting that happen again."

"How, pray tell, do you plan on preventing it?"

Puffing out his chest, squaring his shoulders, he fixed her with a look of masculine smugness. "With my powers."

Oh Jesus. Her smart, capable, dependable husband had morphed into a loose cannon. In the space of seconds. Back in the Jeep earlier today, she'd witnessed the instant he'd latched onto the idea he might have powers with outrageous zeal. Where had rational Jake gone? Christ, he'd snapped at last. Off and on over these months, she'd wondered when she might lose her mind in the face of all this insanity. But Jake…She wrapped her arms around herself, rubbing her upper arms. Jake had been her rock, but now that pillar of stability had cracked.

Jake's shoulders sagged. "You hate my powers."

"What?" She blinked at him. "No, of course not. I have powers too, you know."

"I know." He raked a hand through his hair. "But mine frighten you."

How could she explain to him that it wasn't his powers that scared her, so much as his attitude toward them? Gung-ho to the extreme. Reckless. Dangerous. He'd get himself killed. A barbed wire closed around her heart, its sharp tips pricking her soul. She would not lose him. If she had to hogtie him and lock him in a basement somewhere to protect him, she'd do it.

But not before she tried one last time to drag him back down to earth.

Laying her palms on his bare chest, she leaned into him and angled her face up to meet his gaze. His hands came up to cradle her back, though she doubted he realized he'd done it. Gazing at him now, she saw the old Jake—and a slender thread of hope unwound inside her.

"Jake," she said softly, "I love you, and I would never begrudge you your powers. I know having them means a lot to you, but—" She choked down a lump in her throat, taking a deep breath to calm her frayed nerves. "I need you to promise me something."

He brushed a lock of hair from her face with the gentlest touch. "Anything."

"Please be careful." She rose onto her tiptoes, sliding her hands up his chest and around his neck, linking them at his nape. "No more taking off half-cocked, naked as a jaybird, running into God knows what."

Lips puckered, he stared at her.

"I mean it," she said, tapping the back of his head with one finger. "No more Crazy Jake. Hear me? No. More."

He rolled his eyes and sighed. "Fine. I'll be more circumspect from here on. Happy?"

No, she wouldn't really be happy until he was back to normal and this damn curse was eradicated. But for the moment, she'd take what he offered. She pecked a kiss on his lips. "Yes. Thank you."

He tightened his arms around her, pulling her into his body until her breasts were mashed against his chest. His voice was rough with emotion. "You know I'd do anything for you."

"I do." She pressed her mouth to his again, this time lingering there, the warmth of his body and the hint of saltiness on his lips arousing her deep inside. Her nipples went hard, the tips jutted into his flesh. Just as they opened to each other and Jake delved his tongue inside her mouth, footsteps scuffled toward them from behind Dawn.

"Pardon me," her father said, clearing his throat. "Did either of you notice that atrocious odor a moment ago?"

Dawn peeled away from Jake's deliciously hard body. Once again, she'd gotten hot and heavy with him right in front of her father. Her cheeks heated, and she tugged the hem of Jake's shirt down to cover her a little better.

"Yes," Jake said, his gaze drifting past her shoulder. "We noticed."

Dawn sniffed the air. "It's gone. The stink, I mean."

Jake took her hand. "Let's get back inside." He aimed a rueful smile at her. "Apparently, the only way I'll get you indoors is if I go with you."

"Damn straight."

She let him escort her back inside their room. Her father trailed them through the doorway, shutting it. Hands stuffed in his pants pockets, he studied Dawn. "It was the curse, wasn't it?"

Nodding, she dropped her butt onto the bed. "It didn't do anything to us, though. Just stunk up the vicinity."

"Toying with us," Jake said, taking a seat beside her. He slipped an arm around behind her, his fingers grazing her hip.

A tiny shiver rippled through her at the touch, but she straightened her spine and tried to look *not* like she was lusting after Jake. "It's tormenting us. The curse is like a supernatural terrorist. Its main goal seems to be to scare the crap out of us."

Jake hissed a breath out his nostrils. "It tried to kill us earlier."

"No, I don't think so."

He jumped up and began pacing the length of the small room. His hands fisted and unfisted, over and over. "The only reason it didn't kill us was because I stopped it."

Clasping her hands on her lap, she struggled to find a delicate way of explaining this to him. He needed, for reasons she didn't fully understand, to believe he stopped the storm. Maybe he did. But she had a sinking feeling the curse hadn't meant to kill them and it would've ceased its terror tactics before any of them got seriously injured. Jake wouldn't want to hear it.

Still, he needed to hear it.

As he paced past her, she grabbed his hand and urged him to a halt. He gazed down at her without expression, though his eyes blazed—with anger or self-loathing, she couldn't determine which one. She sandwiched his bigger hand between both of hers. "Listen to me. I'm not trying to downplay what you did. I saw you start the Jeep with your finger and I have no doubt you got rid of the tornado. But I don't believe the curse is trying to kill us, not just yet anyway."

"Then what do you believe it's trying to do?" His voice was devoid of any emotion, close to a monotone. "It shot a bolt of supernatural lightning at us."

"The lightning hit the Jeep's hood. The bolt went straight through metal and fried the engine. If the curse had intended to kill us, it could've aimed for our heads."

"What are you saying?"

She bit her lip, then charged ahead. "Think about it. Vahl created the curse. He wanted us to suffer for eternity, not die a quick death. If the curse is exacting his revenge, then it will have to torture us for a good long while before it offs us." She clutched his hand to her chest. "Look what just happened. It let us know it's around, but it did nothing. That's about scaring us, nothing more."

Her father stepped away from the doorway, back into her line of sight. "She's right, son. This makes sense."

"I know," Jake snarled, though she glimpsed resignation in his eyes, rather than anger. He clamped his free hand over the nape of his neck. "I know."

She longed to haul him into her arms and kiss away his frustration and disappointment. With her father here, she couldn't—or rather, wouldn't—do it.

Westenra slumped his shoulders. "What do we do?"

Dawn shot him a sideways glance. "The only thing we can. Keep searching for Vahl's bunker."

Jake bowed his head, his face hidden from her. "In the morning. We all need some sleep."

"Agreed. Till the morning then," her father said, and walked out the door. It clicked shut behind him.

A breath gusted out of Jake as he flopped down beside her, head still bowed. "The plan sucks."

"Yeah." She sifted her fingers through his hair, her heart aching for him. She'd taken away his new toy. Worse, she'd disintegrated his newfound confidence and sense of purpose. *No choice, right?* God, she prayed that was true.

He bent forward, elbows on his knees. "I wanted to be the one who saved you."

"Jake..." She snaked a hand onto his thigh, massaging with her fingertips. "You've saved me more times than I can count. Paranormal abilities don't make you a hero. Your heart and soul do."

Turning his head to the side, he trained his gaze on her. "I wish I could remember our past life. Maybe then I'd know it wasn't my fault he murdered you."

Her heart skipped, thudding against her ribs. He thought he'd caused her death three thousand years ago? She grasped his face in both hands. "Vahl did that, not you."

Sitting up, he shrugged one shoulder. "Neither of us really knows what happened."

"We can't change the past anyway." She leaned in to rest her chin on his shoulder and nuzzle his neck. "What can I do to make you feel better?"

The corners of his lips twitched up. He lifted one brow. "I can think of several things."

A delicious heat flowed through her body and shivered on her skin. "Such as?"

With a sly smirk, he slipped one hand under the shirt that barely covered her. His fingers brushed the curly hairs at the apex of her thighs. "Finish what we started."

He took hold of the shirt's hem and swept it up her body, over her head and off her arms. One hundred percent nude, she shivered in the draft from the air conditioning. When her nipples stiffened, though, it had nothing to do with the air temperature.

She reached for the fly of his jeans.

Before she could grasp his zipper, he surged up off the bed. He yanked the zipper down and whipped off his pants, hurling them across the room to hit the bathroom sink with a *pfft*. He grinned. "Promise not to use my powers to jumpstart you."

She grinned right back. "You don't need magic for that."

Jake scooped her up and dropped her on the bed, flat on her back.

She spread her legs, knees bent, and curled her arms over her head. "Go on then. Have your wicked way with me."

His slow, seductive smile melted her right down to her core.

CHAPTER SIX

O N HIS KNEES AT HER FEET, JAKE GAZED DOWN AT HIS wife—his perfect, wonderful, tantalizing wife—spread out before him, her eyes half closed, lips parted. Her tongue slipped out to moisten her lower lip, and he burned to nibble it. Dawn moved her hips, letting her knees fall wide, and her glistening core was exposed to him. He wet his lips, his focus locked on her swollen flesh that just begged to be tasted.

I don't deserve her.

The thought hit him like a slap to the face. He rocked back, sitting on his heels. A chill whispered through him, yet not even that could diminish his lust for her. Still, the persistent voice in his head kept niggling at him. Dawn had told him she didn't believe he'd stopped the curse when it attacked them back in the desert. All he'd done was dissipate a puny tornado. If he'd done that. Maybe all he could really accomplish was zapping a car engine back to life.

He shoved both hands into his hair, scratched at his scalp, the pain a necessary remedy to the foolish overconfidence he'd indulged in today. Christ, he'd scared Dawn. Refused to listen to her. Ordered her to hide, while he…What would he have done? *No goddamn clue, right?* Dawn said he ran off half-cocked. But he hadn't bothered to come up with one-tenth of a plan, much less half of one. *Idiot.*

No wonder he'd gotten her killed in their first life together.

"Jake."

The soft plea from Dawn pulled him out of his thoughts. She extended a hand to him, her delicate fingers outstretched. He longed to go to her, but—

"Stop it, Jake." She crooked a finger at him, beckoning. "You're supposed to be ravishing me, not obsessing over things that happened three thousand years ago."

He drew his head back. "How did you know?"

"Oh come on." Her throaty chuckle aroused him with the power of a caress. "I know you, and besides, you told me you blame yourself for everything."

She ran her foot up and down his thigh, her big toe brushing his hard shaft.

Coughing, he caught her foot and set it down on the bed.

Her luscious lips cinched into a feigned pout. "Do you want to spend the night chastising yourself, or…"

She wriggled, bouncing her breasts. Lust flared up inside him again, with such ferocity he sucked in a sharp breath. A night of self-loathing, or a night of *her*. No contest.

Jake leaned over her, his hands at either side of her head, his body poised above hers. The feminine scent of her enveloped him, but it was the musky aroma of her desire that made his erection pulse and his body go rigid. He could never want anyone else, not if he lived a thousand lives, reincarnated again and again with no memory of his previous lives. He would always gravitate back to her.

He dipped his mouth within kissing distance of hers, exchanging breaths, taking in a part of her with every inhalation, a blessed fragment of his soul mate. "I love you, Dawn. More than anything in any lifetime. Forever."

Eyes glossy, she reached up to hold his face in her sweet, soft palms. "I love you too. Forever."

And they both meant it literally. Forever was no abstract concept to a reborn princess and a reincarnated soldier.

He took her lips in a slow, erotic joining, nipping at her lower lip, rubbing his mouth across hers in languid sweeps. She sighed against his mouth. When he sneaked his tongue out to trace the seam of her lips, she arched her back, hoisting her breasts up until the firm peaks of her nipples brushed his chest. He devoured her mouth, thrust his tongue deep, demanding a response, commanding her body to take him. She relinquished everything to him, with hungry lashes of her tongue and with her hips thrashing into him, rubbing his cock across her soft belly.

Groaning, he broke the kiss. They were both breathing hard. Passion flushed her cheeks a dusky rose and the intensity of their kiss had left her lips swollen and deep pink. He stared at her for a moment, transfixed by the ethereal yet earthy beauty of her, his angel descended from the heavens. She gazed up at him with reverence, and a molten need that burned in her eyes, as if he were the answer to her prayers too.

The desperate need to demonstrate how much she meant to him drove him to action. He lowered his body onto hers, sliding down her body inch by inch. When his mouth hovered over one rosy nipple, he couldn't stop himself from covering it with his mouth and suckling hard. Her back bowed up, and she let out a long, husky moan. He licked and nibbled his way down her belly, until the silky curls of her mound teased his lips.

"Please," she begged, breathless. "Oh God, please."

He shimmied lower still, positioning his head between her thighs. The intoxicating scent of her desire overpowered him, stealing his breath for a heart-stopping moment. She was so exquisite, like a fantasy come to life solely for him. He would do anything for her. But in this moment, all he wanted was to give her pleasure.

"Jake..." She bent her knees, opening to him, welcoming him.

He captured the taut bud of her sex between his teeth, swirling his tongue around it. She cried out, bucking into him as he tugged and suckled and laved her with his tongue. He tormented her until her body went rigid, her breaths shortened into whimpering gasps, and her fingers clutched at his head. Then he dived one finger inside her.

She exploded beneath him. Her sheath pulsated around his finger, her body convulsed, her scream reverberated off the walls. His erection throbbed, robbing him of the ability to think. Instinct and hunger seized control of him. He rose onto his knees, lifted her hips, and thrust deep into her, pausing there, relishing the hot, wet feel of her around him. It had been too damn long, way too damn long.

"Oh yes," she moaned, gripping his wrists.

He pulled out, threw his head back, and gave in to the burning need, pumping into her harder and faster with each thrust, flesh slapping against wet flesh, until the union of their bodies turned into a wild and desperate mating. Her climax had her body milking him as his back bowed and he erupted inside her.

When his brain finally started working again, he found himself sprawled on his back on the bed with her little body tucked against him, her head on his chest. She painted circles on his skin with her forefinger, round and round, up and down.

He kissed the top of her head.

"Mmm." She braced her chin on his chest, her lustrous hazel eyes on him. "Feel better?"

"Yes." He smiled, running his hand down the curve of her back. "Much."

"Good." She sighed, and the satiated glow seemed to wash out of her, replaced by a somber expression. "Because we need to talk about the curse."

Shit. No time to enjoy the afterglow. Even in death, Anton Vahl managed to ruin Jake's life. One way or another, he would destroy the living curse and free Dawn and himself once and for all.

An idea sprang into his mind.

He trailed his fingers up her spine, loving the way she shivered ever so slightly. No time for that. He laid his hand over hers on his chest. "I have an idea. But you're not going to like it."

Dawn's lips twisted. "Go on."

"I need to recover my past life memories. By whatever means necessary."

CHAPTER SEVEN

THE NEXT AFTERNOON, DAWN STOOD BESIDE THEIR EXPLORER, leaning her hip against the passenger door with her arms folded over her chest. She kept her gaze trained on Jake, who wandered among the trees of this forested plot of land in northern Utah. Scrubby oaks and taller maples surrounded them, while a crystal-clear sky shone azure blue above them.

Ralph Westenra loitered near the Explorer's back bumper, hands stuffed in his pants pockets, shoulders hunched, eyes aimed at the ground.

She wondered what was wrong with him, since he hadn't said five words in a row to her today, but right now her worries focused on Jake. One man at a time was all she could handle. Jake still hadn't explained how he planned on recovering his memories. It was the *by any means necessary* part that scared the hell out of her. Just when she thought she'd talked him out of crazy stunts, he announced his no-holds-barred plan to jog his past life memories.

Her palms ached. She glanced down to find she'd been clenching her fingers so tight the nails dug into her skin.

Jake let out a loud, frustrated groan. He threw his hands in the air, spinning around to face her from twenty feet away. "This is pointless. There's nothing here."

The last set of coordinates in Vahl's notebook had led them here. They had no other clues to go on in their search for the bunker, so she understood Jake's frustration. But still…"It has to be here."

He scowled, squeezing words out between gritted teeth. "It. Is. Not. Here."

"Don't yell at me about it." She pushed away from the vehicle and fixed her best *don't screw with me* stare on him. "Vahl wrote these coordinates down, which means this place was important to him."

Jake slanted his head back to shake it at the sky. "He was a lunatic, Dawn. Maybe he wrote down all these coordinates just to send us on a wild goose chase."

"He never intended for us to see his notebook." She marched up to Jake, halting toe to toe with him. "I know you're frustrated, and we're all sick of this search. But if Vahl noted this location in his journal, it has to be important."

Jake's head dropped, his chin almost on his chest, and he rubbed the back of his neck. "For all we know, he buried his hope chest here."

Dawn took his face in her hands and lifted. When his eyes met hers, she said, "What happened to the man hell-bent on uncovering the truth? Don't give up on me now, Jake."

His eyes drifted shut, his expression turned pained. "All I've accomplished of late is making you afraid of me."

"I've never been afraid *of* you, I'm afraid *for* you."

"Which is almost worse."

She leaned in close, rising onto her tiptoes. "I need you. So stop whining and get back to being the ultra-competent, super-sexy hero I adore."

He looked into her eyes for a long moment, his expression unreadable, then clasped her hands in his, straightened, and cleared his throat. "Let's look around some more. Must be some clue to find."

A wave of relief crashed over her as he set about systematically investigating every tree, every bush, every square inch of earth. This was the Jake she'd come to rely on—smart, capable, determined, powerful. She watched the muscles in his thighs and buttocks flex with his movements, and found her mouth watering at the sight of his muscular body in action. Her mind flashed back to last night in their motel room. Jake on top of her, inside her, consuming her with his passion.

Jeez, she was obsessed with sex. And at the most improper moments.

She rolled her shoulders back. Well, now that she'd sorted out her husband, time to deal with her father.

The one-time pharaoh was still slouching behind their vehicle. As she came around the bumper, his head popped up and his gaze flitted over her face before settling on the trees past her shoulder. She planted one hand on the Explorer, fingers drumming on its rear window.

"What's up?" she asked, in what she hoped was a casually cheerful tone. "You've been awfully quiet today."

A sigh shuddered out of him, and he gave a weak nod. "I know when I'm neither wanted nor needed. Perhaps you could drop me off at the next motel we pass by." A haunted look invaded his eyes, as if he were staring into the distant past and finding only painful memories. "I won't bother you any longer. I've done enough harm to you."

She swallowed hard, a sharp pang stabbing into her chest. Had she really made him feel like a third wheel to be cast off at the nearest dumpster? God, she had. Making out with Jake right in front of her father, blaming him for everything, snapping at him every chance she got, acting like a spoiled princess instead of a mature, three-thousand-year-old woman. Cripes, when had she turned into a raging bitch?

He had betrayed her. She couldn't pretend it never happened. But maybe it was time to move on from the past. If she had the strength to do it.

Dawn took a tentative step toward him. Her throat constricted and a heavy, cold weight settled in her gut. *He betrothed you to a madman.* How could she move past that? Even if she wanted to. She hugged herself, rubbing her arms furiously against a sudden chill. "We need you. It's clear you remember more about our shared past than even I do, and we'll need that knowledge to defeat the curse."

His gaze swiveled to hers, his face gone stony. "Of course. I'll help any way I can."

Why did she feel like she'd gored him with a sword to the gut? She supposed her issues with her father couldn't be resolved today, out here in the wilderness, with a living curse nipping at their heels.

Great excuse, coward.

A metallic bang reverberated off the trees, emanating from past the Explorer's front bumper. Where Jake was. Dawn's heart hammered. She bolted around the vehicle, scanning the vicinity until she caught sight of Jake kneeling on the ground a dozen yards away. He hefted a dirt-and-grass-covered metal slab from the earth. Bits of debris had rained down around him and on his clothes.

Jake grinned at her. "I think I found it."

She hurried to him, slowing her pace as she neared the yawning void in front of him. He stood up beside her and hooked an arm around her waist. She leaned forward to squint down into the abyss. Sunlight cast pale strands of illumination into the hole, and she spotted a steep wooden staircase descending into the depths.

"You did it," she said, beaming a smile up at Jake. "My hero."

He flinched the tiniest bit, but recovered so fast she wasn't sure she'd really seen it. Tugging her tight against his side, he brushed a kiss across her forehead. "Shall we?"

Jake waved one hand toward the staircase.

Westenra trundled up beside her, opposite Jake, and frowned at the hole in the ground. He glanced from the opening to her. "Is this it?"

"Seems like." She extricated herself from Jake's embrace, but slipped her hand into his and linked their fingers. She glanced at each man in turn. "Into the breach?"

Jake released her hand and moved toward the hole, turning to step down onto the staircase. Wood creaked. Jake tested his weight on the step and, apparently satisfied, took another step down into the unknown.

CHAPTER EIGHT

T HE NARROW STEPS LED THEM DOWN INTO A PITCH-DARK space, where their voices echoed off the walls. Jake switched on his phone, using the glow of its white screen as a flashlight. They'd wound up inside a cavernous chamber, rectangular in shape, with metals walls and a concrete floor. The ceiling looked like concrete too. One wall housed a bank of computer equipment, probably hard drives and who knew what else. Multicolored lights flashed. A long, empty metal table hunkered along the other wall.

A buzzing drew his attention to the ceiling, as fluorescent bulbs recessed into the concrete flickered on, shedding sterile white light onto the room. Motion-sensitive lights, Jake guessed as he shut off his phone-light. Vahl must've spent a tidy sum on setting up this bunker.

"This looks promising," Dawn said, sidling up to him.

He curled an arm around her waist, needing to keep her close. They were in the lion's den, though the beast himself was gone. "Let's look around for the backup server."

Now that the lights had come on, he could see the rest of the room. It extended, by his estimate, forty feet in length and twenty feet in breadth. At the far end, perched on a con-crete dais, crouched a coffin-shaped glass box. A chill swept his spine.

Dawn gripped his hand. "Is that…"

"A tank like the one at Redeo, and the one Vahl had at his home." Jake tugged her tighter against him, hoping to reassure her. "No one's shoving you into the tank this time. It's nothing but a relic of a dead man's obsession."

Soft white lights flickered on beneath the tank, illuminating the blue liquid that filled its interior. Dawn stiffened against him.

Westenra scuffled past them, his face blank, his gaze locked on the tank. In a strangled voice, he muttered, "Dear God."

"Yes," Dawn said, her tone hard, "Vahl thought he was a god. But I wouldn't recommend praying to him."

"But why…" Westenra turned sideways to them, his gaze darting to Dawn and back to the tank. "Why would he have another tank here?"

Jake shrugged. "Maybe he planned on bringing Dawn here. Who knows? The bastard's dead so it hardly matters."

Dawn pushed away from him and walked toward the banks of equipment. She lifted a hand to the metal shelves housing the gadgets, running her fingertips along the edge as she traversed the length of the installation.

The tank captured Jake's attention. He stared at the still, blue liquid inside it, remembering how the tank at Redeo had bubbled with effervescent currents that snaked around Dawn's lifeless body. She may have been technically dead then, but she had looked as alive as anyone else in the facility. Vahl had employed a similar tank to force Dawn to regain her memories of being poisoned by him, back when he was known as Setka.

Jake's jaw ached, and he realized he was gritting his teeth again. He inhaled a long, deep breath, releasing it slowly, trying to shed the memories. Thinking about Vahl always made Jake seethe. But for once, those thoughts shined a light on something important. The tank had helped Dawn recover her past life memories. If it worked for her…

He strode across the room, straight to the tank, and rested his hands on its cold metal rim. Why hadn't he realized this before? Maybe fate wanted him to remember, since it brought them to this place, this bunker, this tank. He tightened his fingers over the rim, the tips dipping into the stagnant blue liquid. It chilled his skin. If he could figure out how to power up the equipment that controlled the tank, the water would heat to body temperature. A tingle of certainty swept through him, ushering in a revelation.

This tank may have been created for Dawn, but it was meant for him.

＊

DAWN HALTED NEAR THE END OF THE EQUIPMENT BANK, HER FINGERTIPS grazing over the smooth surface of the computer monitor fitted snugly into the shelves. She felt under the monitor's bottom edge until her fingers bumped over a button. *Eureka.* She pressed the button. The monitor powered up with a faint click, and the screen blazed to life. Icons populated the screen, though she had no idea what any of them signified. Maybe her father would know, since he had worked at Redeo with Vahl.

She started to turn toward Westenra, but movement from the other direction caught her eye. She swiveled on her heels to face the tank...and Jake.

Her heart stuttered. A chill rushed over her, borne on a wave of goose bumps, and every hair on her body went stiff. Jake hunched at the tank, his hands on its rim, his head bowed and his gaze fixed on the blue liquid within the glass coffin.

Coffin. That would always be how she viewed the tanks. How could she see them as anything else, when she had languished in one mere months ago, dead to the world in the most literal sense. Her last living memory, before awakening in the tank at Redeo, was of her coffin lid slamming down over her mummified remains. No one should remember their own burial. No one.

Arms wrapped around herself, she scuffled forward, her feet heavy as stone, until she came up alongside Jake. His determined expression made her gulp against a lump in her throat. A sense of déjà vu warred with a sick dread that burrowed deep into her soul. She raised a trembling hand to touch his arm. When his eyes rolled sideways to focus on her, she asked, "What are you doing?"

"I understand how to recover my past life memories." He stroked a hand along the tank's rim, glancing down at it for a heartbeat before returning his gaze to her. "I can't believe I didn't see it before."

Her face had gone as cold as permafrost, her fingers had turned to icicles. She stuffed them under her arms, to no avail. She didn't want to know, but had to ask. "What do you mean?"

Jake grasped her upper arms. "The tank. It helped you remember, and I'm positive it can release my memories too."

If his hands hadn't anchored her, she would've scuttled away. Her breaths came shallow and quick, and her ears began to ring. *No, no, no.* Anything but the tank, anything. She shook her head hard, rattling her brain and flinging her hair around her face. "No, Jake, you can't. That—that *thing* represents death and pain."

He pulled her closer, his hold loosening a smidgen. His voice took on a tender tone. "I know Vahl used the tank to torment you, but one of these tanks also regenerated you." He cupped her cheek in his big, warm palm, his eyes searching hers. "If it weren't for that tank, I wouldn't have you."

The ice inside her thawed just a bit. Her heart ached at his words, at the truth in them. She feared the tanks because of Vahl, but Jake was right. She wouldn't be with him today without the tanks. But the idea of using one on Jake, of subjecting him to what she'd endured at Vahl's hands...

"It's different," Jake murmured, as if he'd read her mind. For all she knew, he had. His hand warmed her cheek, as his thumb caressed her skin. "I've got you to oversee this procedure, not Vahl. I can't think of a better guide through past life regression."

"Regression?"

"Call it whatever you want." He bracketed her face with both his hands, thumbs brushing over her lips, his mouth close enough to whisper warm air over her skin. "You can teach me how to regain those memories. I know you can."

How could she refuse him? He needed this—or believed he needed it. She had no desire to get back all her memories from her first life, but Jake was convinced recovering those memories would give him closure. What if he remembered everything and still had no conclusive evidence of whether he bore any measure of responsibility for her death? Could he move on, or would the past haunt him forever?

She laid a palm on his chest, curling her fingers. Something else bothered her too. Jake and her father had outlived her, she knew this, but by how long she had no clue. Had Vahl murdered them as well, to set his curse in motion? Or had Jake lived a normal lifespan?

Her stomach sank. What if he'd married someone else? Had children? Vahl's curse might've taken effect once Jake died, forcing him to reincarnate. What if Jake hadn't wanted to reunite with her? Once he remembered everything, he might realize the truth. Maybe the love he felt for her now was nothing but the curse toying with them.

Jake kissed the tip of her nose. "What's wrong?"

She gazed into his cinnamon eyes, her heart clenching. Jake needed the truth, deserved the truth, and she would not deny him out of a selfish desire to keep him with her. If his memories showed him he never had belonged with her, she'd deal with it. Somehow. Even if letting him go destroyed her.

I shouldn't be alive anyway.

Biting her lip, she studied the fabric of his shirt. "I will help you."

He let out a blustering breath, his body relaxing. "Thank you."

"Don't thank me until we see if this works." She dared to look up at him, and tears pricked at her eyes when she saw his shaky smile, full of fragile hope and desperation. She sucked in a breath through her nose, blinking away the nascent tears. "We need to get the tank up and running."

"I can assist you there," her father said from behind her.

Dawn twisted her head around to find him hunched in front of the monitor set into the equipment bank. The screen had changed to a different view. He must've tapped an icon or entered a command, or whatever. She hadn't noticed him moving across the room. Lost in Jake again. Her mouth went dry. If Jake discovered he'd led a better life without her, she wouldn't be lost in him anymore, she'd be lost without him.

She slanted her head, eying him. "You know how to use the computer system?"

He nodded. "It's almost identical to the one at Redeo. I can call up the tank software and get it powered up."

"Do it," Jake said.

Dawn clutched at his shirt. What kind of life could a formerly mummified woman have in the modern world? Jake had given her a life here. If he left her...

She might as well climb back in her sarcophagus and sleep for the rest of eternity. Adrift. Alone. Cursed.

Jake brushed a light kiss across her lips. "Don't worry. This will work."

If only he knew she was praying for the opposite.

CHAPTER NINE

TINY BUBBLES ROSE UP THROUGH THE CRYSTALLINE BLUE LIQUID, now lit from below by soft white bulbs embedded in the dais under the tank's glass bottom. Jake—naked as a newborn—lowered his body into the tank, submerging beneath the lukewarm liquid. It felt slippery, as if it contained a touch of oil. He hesitated with his head above the surface.

Dawn secured a scuba mask over his eyes and nose. Next, she slipped a breathing apparatus into his mouth, and he closed his lips around it, relaxing his jaw to let the apparatus rest there. He'd already stuffed waterproof earplugs in his ears, so she had to mouth her words with exaggerated lip movements. *Okay?* she was asking. He gave her a thumbs-up signal.

Then he dived under the water. His body sank onto the tank's floor, which gave a little, and he realized it was lined with some kind of transparent gel. Vahl cared about the comfort of his test subject? Bullshit. He must've included the gel so the hard glass floor wouldn't damage his precious *specimen*. If the scumbag weren't already dead, Jake would've ripped the scientist apart with his bare hands.

His earplugs crackled. Westenra was turning on the receivers inside the earplugs, which would let him hear Westenra and Dawn, though he couldn't speak to them. After another bout of crackling, the sound cleared up and Dawn's voice transmitted straight into his ears. "Relax, honey, this might take awhile. I'm no expert at it."

As if Vahl had been.

"Comfy in there?" Dawn asked.

Jake made another thumbs-up gesture.

"Good." A pause, then she cleared her throat. "Let's get started."

He noticed the hint of anxiety in her voice and wished he could pull her into his arms and kiss it away. No need, she'd be fine. His wife was stronger than even she realized, and he loved her more than any man had a right to love a woman.

And if he found out his negligence had empowered Vahl to murder her in their past life? Acid boiled in his gut, burning its way up his chest into his throat. He'd demolish that bridge when he crossed it.

"Try to clear your mind," Dawn said in a gentle, lulling tone. "Free yourself of all thoughts and worries—"

Sure, that'd happen.

"—and let your mind drift into a dark and peaceful place."

He shifted position in the dark and peaceful place, sloshing the liquid.

"I said relax, Jake. That means no squirming." A hint of irritation sharpened her voice, but she ironed it out before continuing in her soothing voice. "Listen to my voice and let everything else fall away. You are floating in a tranquil nothingness—"

Where did she come up with this hogwash? He tried to groan, but the breathing apparatus blocked it. Okay, this had been his idea. He should follow her commands and do his damnedest to make it work. Taking slow, deep breaths, he concentrated on her voice and the rhythm of his own breathing. In, out, in, out.

"No worries," Dawn intoned, "no fear, no expectations, just a weightless freedom."

His body lightened, his mind snapping free of the tether that bound him to the tank, to the world. Her voice guided him as he floated up and up, ensconced in tranquil darkness, warm and languid and free.

"Let the currents carry you..."

Falling, falling, without fear of where he might land. A pinpoint of light appeared in the darkness, and he felt himself drawn toward it, ever downward, drifting and falling and spinning into the light as it swelled, glistening a silvery white. A force more powerful than gravity sucked him through the light and hurtled him out into the world. Everything was blurred around him, still rocking, but as his mind settled into the new surroundings, he began to make out shapes and colors in the serene light of the corridor in which he stood.

Not him exactly. He glanced down at his body, the same body he always had, except he wore a white linen kilt with pleats and a leather belt. His feet were bare. As he contemplated the strangeness of his attire, his mind began to shift, adjust, releasing his memories of his time, drawing him into the past as if he were this person, as if he were...Bek.

Of course he was. Who else would he be? He scratched his head, staring at his linen garment. He had another name. But the more he struggled to recall it, the further the knowledge receded from his grasp.

And in that moment, he joined with the past.

⁓

ROLLING HIS SHOULDERS BACK, BEK STRODE DOWN THE CORRIDOR toward the throne room and his new assignment, decreed by King Neferhotep himself. It was an unusual task for a lowly soldier to be assigned, but no man refused the pharaoh.

Bek entered the long, rectangular throne room, and traversed its length—past a grand sphinx and between the columns decorated with hieroglyphs and images painted in bright colors. His plain, mudbrick home seemed pitiful in comparison. The royals truly lived in a different world. The light from oil lamps mounted on the walls flickered through the windowless space, guiding him toward the figure at the far end. She should not be alone, but he supposed this was the reason the king sent him here. Bek marched straight up to his new mistress, halting a respectable distance away.

Her back was to him, her diaphanous gown lending her slender figure a mysterious appeal. Dark red hair spilled down over her squared shoulders to cascade down her back in silky waves. The hair was no wig, he knew, because he could see the part in her hair and a hint of her pale scalp.

He knelt on one knee, head bowed. "My lady."

Fabric swished as she turned toward him, the folds billowing around her ankles, all he could see of her from this vantage. But what lovely ankles they were. She stopped close enough he could've touched her foot without stretching. He slid his gaze over her delicate little toes, the most beautiful he'd ever seen, up and across the arching top of her elegant foot. His focus glided up the creamy skin of her ankles. One glimpse of a smooth calf had him imagining his hand on that flesh, skating up past her knee, to the tender skin of her inner thigh. Not that he could see that much of her. But the fantasy had blood rushing to his groin.

She was a princess, he her subject. The king would eviscerate him for daring to think of his daughter this way.

"You may rise," she said, her mellifluous voice evaporating his forbidden thoughts.

He did not move, his gaze locked on the inner hollow of her ankle. The skin would be soft, somehow he knew this. Soft and warm and yielding. Bek cleared his throat without glancing up. "How may I serve you, my lady?"

She sighed, her largest toe tapping. "I am a woman, nothing more. And my name is Raia, not my lady." She almost spat the honorific, her toe curling, as he imagined her lip might've been. "Call me Raia, please. What are you called?"

"Bek." The instant the syllable left his lips, he wished he could swallow it back down. His name mattered naught to a princess. Yet she had asked...

"I bid you rise, then, Bek."

He barely quashed a smirk. She bid him? First she had no desire to be a princess, and now she bid him to obey her. *Fickle female.* He started to unbend his knee, then froze. "My lady..."

"Raia," she said with finality.

"Um, I—"

Her laughter, soft and melodic, lilted her voice when she spoke again. "Do not worry, Bek, this is no trick. I ask you to stand and speak to me as an equal because I am no better than you or any other subject of the Two Lands."

No better? Equals? Everything he had been taught his entire life told him the opposite. Yet her sweet voice beckoned him, and he found himself unable to resist. He unfurled his body to full height, several inches taller than the prin—than Raia. She gazed up at him with hazel eyes that twinkled in the flickering lamplight, her cheeks blushed with a natural, dusky rose. Her lush lips curved in a welcoming smile.

The gown dipped low between her breasts, exposing a hint of the slopes. He swallowed, hard, and forced his attention back to her beautiful face. The vision of her stole the breath from his body, yet infused him with a life force beyond measure. His heart raced, his body came alive like never before.

"Will you walk with me?" she asked, then bit her lip in the most endearing way. She must wonder if he would refuse, but how could he? Even if she were not the pharaoh's daughter, she was the most stunning creature he'd ever laid eyes on, and he would go anywhere with her.

He nodded, but swiftly remembered his orders. "You are not permitted to leave the palace until the pharaoh's enemies have been routed."

She rolled her eyes. "My father agreed I might walk in the gardens, since they are within the palace walls. That is where you and I shall go." She sidled closer, her conspiratorial smile making his heart stutter. "Besides, I am with my new guardian, am I not? You will let no harm come to me."

And he would not. Ever. He was bound by honor and his king's command to defend her life even at the cost of his own, but that was not why he would do it. Now that he had glimpsed her, spoken to her, immersed himself in her sweet, flowery scent, he would die for her no matter her station. If she were a peasant, he would lay down his life for hers. For Raia.

"Indeed," he said, gesturing toward the doorway, "you are safe with me."

Her brilliant smile set her face aglow, and as she turned toward the doorway, the lamplight glinted off bright green flecks in her eyes. Jewels in a sea of pale gold. "Thank you, Bek. I am grateful you became my guardian. I can tell we are well suited to become friends."

She led him out the door, her hand resting lightly on his forearm. Friends. If she realized what his body and heart wanted from her, she might recant her claim to be grateful for him. But no matter his own desires, he must never act on them. To do so would doom them both.

DAWN WATCHED THE TANK, AND JAKE'S INERT FORM WITHIN IT, her heart pounding harder with every second he stayed submerged in the past. What would he learn there? How would the experience change him, change them?

Her feet moved as if by their own will, shambling toward the tank like an undead mummy in one of those old horror movies. If she'd seen moldering linen wrappings dangling from her limbs, she wouldn't have been surprised. But she remained human, for now.

At the tank, she lifted her hands to grasp the metal rim. The bubbling liquid distorted Jake's face, and she suffered the oddest sensation of gazing through the waters of time, down a shimmering portal into the distant past. She stretched out a hand to the blue liquid. A ripple shivered out across the surface from the point where her fingertip brushed it. A sudden need to touch him rushed through her, and she dived her hand into the liquid, grasping his hand and squeezing gently.

Dizziness swirled through her. She gripped the tank's edge with her other hand as the room whirled around her yet again. Another sensation, alien and yet familiar, sparked in her chest—warm and soothing, intimate beyond description, and...masculine. She sucked in a sharp breath, canting forward to gaze down at Jake through the liquid separating them. He lay relaxed, eyes shut, lips curved in a slight smile.

She was feeling him. Inside her. His essence reached out to her, calling her to join him wherever he'd gone, all but begging her to go to him. Tears stung her eyes, and she caressed his cheek beneath the effervescing water. He wanted her with him in his past life memories. Whether by conscious thought or subconscious desire, he beckoned her. And she would always come when he needed her.

Dawn closed her eyes and surrendered to the call.

CHAPTER TEN

RAIA SAT ON THE GROUND BESIDE BEK, IN THE SHADE OF a sycamore tree, on the eleventh day of their acquaintance. She could scarcely believe she'd known this man for a mere eleven days, as they had come to understand each other like the oldest of friends. A pharaoh's daughter had few friends, and she cherished these quiet moments with Bek.

Besides, he was quite pleasing to gaze at for hours. She tried not to stare at his muscled, bare chest, or his sensuous lips, or the way his linen kilt hugged his hips and powerful thighs when he sat on the ground with one knee bent before him. Oh, and when he smiled…Her body melted.

Bek offered up a fig, holding it near her lips.

Despite the urgent need to draw his finger into her mouth, she shook her head. "I could not possibly eat more."

With a sigh, he popped the fig into his mouth, chewing with erotic movements, as if he hungered to consume her instead. His gaze, fixed on her, heated parts of her she'd never known could grow molten and wet with need. In fact, she had never in her life experienced this kind of desire. Was this lust? *Yes, I believe it is.*

Bek swallowed his treat. His lips slid into a sensual smile, one that kindled a fire deep within her and set her mind to crafting elaborate fantasies of him touching her, kissing her, performing all manner of acts that would get both of them executed. He reached behind his back to pluck something from the ground. Facing her again, he proffered the object to her—a pale purple iris, its long petals arching down, exposing the heart of the flower.

"For you," he said, his voice soft and sultry. "Nothing can compare to your beauty, but this flower is the closest thing."

She blinked, the breath caught in her throat. Never before had he complimented her in such a way. Yes, he'd told her she was bright and clever, a fine companion, and other amiable compliments. But this...His words tingled heat over her skin, from her face straight down her body, where the sensation settled between her thighs. "Bek—"

"Shh." He brushed the iris's petal across her lips once, twice. "I can no longer pretend to feel nothing for you beyond friendship. Can you tell me honestly you feel nothing more?"

"I—" At night, alone in her chambers, she longed for him. Dreamed of him. Begged the gods for a way she could be with him. "We cannot."

One of his brows lifted, just as one corner of his curved up. "Cannot? We both seem quite capable, physically."

A blush flared up in her cheeks. She fanned her face with her hand, but the libidinous power of his words stoke her fire. "Please, this is not allowed. Even our walks together are a risk we should not be taking."

He set the flower down beside her and scooted closer, his thigh grazing hers. One of his arms angled across her lap, with the palm flat on the ground. Braced thus, he bent his face near hers, their eyes locked on each other. "We are alone, Raia."

A shiver of awareness rippled through her. Awareness of his body so hard and close to hers, of his lips hovering achingly near hers. She fisted her hands in the pleats of her gown. Her finger itched to explore his muscles, her mouth watered, her lips burned with the hunger to taste him. To be tasted.

Bek trailed a fingertip along her jaw. "Unless you command me otherwise, I intend to kiss you."

Kiss her? *Her?* She couldn't move. Her breaths grew shallow, her lips parting of their own volition, as if inviting him to take her mouth.

He grazed his lips across hers. That faint contact catapulted a dizzying thrill through her. He explored her lips with his, nipping, suckling, teasing until her head swam and her heart raced. When he slipped his tongue between her lips, she let out a tiny whimper.

"Raia," he murmured against her mouth, "you are a goddess."

Then he claimed her mouth, covering it with his own as he enfolded her in his strong arms. She clamped her arms around his neck, her breasts crushed into his chest. The warmth of him suffused her, and she moaned at the feel of his hard body against her and the sweet invasion of his tongue as it delved deep into her mouth. By the gods, no one had ever told her kissing could be like this. He roused her desire to a mind-numbing level, with every sweep of his tongue against hers and every stroke of his callused palm across her back. Even the fabric of her gown proved no barrier to his caresses.

His lips and tongue fed into her the rich, sweet flavor of the fig he'd just eaten, and the altogether masculine taste of him. He sneaked a hand between their bodies, cupping her breast, and she moaned again, louder this time.

Bek pulled away, panting, eyes glossy and hooded. "Are we still mere friends?"

Breathing hard herself, she struggled for words and found but one. "No."

~

B̲EK STOOD JUST INSIDE THE DOORWAY OF THE THRONE ROOM, hands clasped behind his back, his posture straight and mind alert. Guarding his Raia had become far more important to him than he ever imagined it could. *His* Raia? He had no right to think of her in such a way, yet since they'd kissed six days ago, he could think of her in no other way. She belonged to him, and he belonged to her. He fantasized about making her his wife, about having children with her, spending the rest of his mortal days with the only woman could ever love.

The king would never allow it.

His heart clenched at the knowledge. He'd known before his lips ever touched hers that nothing could come of this bond between them. And yet he also knew he wanted no other, for as long as his soul survived, in this life or what came after it. Perhaps the gods would permit him to share his afterlife with her, if nothing else.

He grunted at his own thought, disgusted with his dreamy fantasies, then recalled with a start he was not alone. Some guardian, daydreaming on the job. He covered his grunt with a cough.

Raia—standing before her father, who was seated on the throne—turned her head to look at Bek. He just stifled his smile, as her glorious eyes met his and her brows drew together, wrinkling her forehead. She gave a small smile, eyes glittering, and then returned her attention to her father. Neferhotep crimped his fingers, scratching his nails on the painted wood of the throne's arms. His expression was guarded, but his eyes seemed haunted.

Bek tightened his fingers around his wrist, where his hands were joined behind his back. For the king to be unsettled triggered a sour taste in Bek's mouth. Neferhotep rarely betrayed emotion. Ever since Raia had received her father's summons this afternoon, Bek had grown more and more unsettled himself. Had the pharaoh learned of their involvement? He had yet to bed Raia—though, by the gods, he burned to—but perhaps someone had witnessed their intimate moments in the gardens.

Neferhotep cleared his throat. "Daughter, we must speak of the Children of Setesh."

"Father," Raia said, chin lifted, and took a step toward the king. "I must speak with you of another matter first. Please."

He gestured with his hand, indicating she may continue.

Raia hauled in a breath, and Bek swore he could feel her anxiety rolling off her in waves. The thumb and forefinger of her right hand tapped together rapidly. "Father, I have found a man I wish to take as my husband."

Bek's heart seized up, then thudded back to life with such force he had to stifle a gasp. She couldn't mean him.

She started to turn in his direction, but the pharaoh's words stopped her short.

"I am sorry, daughter," Neferhotep said, his tone grave. "I have already promised you to another."

Raia stumbled backward a step, her hand flying to her chest. "No. You cannot."

The king sighed and slumped back in the throne. "I can, and I have. The Children of Setesh will not cease their attacks without some acquiescence to their demands. My emissary has brokered a peace treaty with them, but I was forced to make one major concession." His gaze shifted to the floor, and suddenly he appeared far older. "I must wed my daughter to one of their tribe. His name is Setka, and he arrives tomorrow."

"What?" Raia gasped the word, her body going stiff, hands clamped tight. "I refuse."

"You have no choice. The deed is done, and as the king's daughter, your fate lies in my hands. Your wishes carry no import."

Bek fought the sudden, and overwhelming, urge to hurl himself across the distance to the throne and throttle his king. How many battles had he fought for this man, without question, without a care for his own safety? How many injuries had he survived? And yet, the man he had respected—even admired—betrayed his own daughter simply to appease terrorists. For Neferhotep to do this to his only child suggested if he learned of Bek and Raia's intimacy, he would behead them both for certain.

"Father," Raia cried, throwing her arms wide, "you cannot curse me to live the rest of my days shackled to a stranger whose people would murder us all in our sleep if it benefited them. Do you not love me at all?"

The king dropped his head into his hand, and his shoulders deflated further. "I love you with all my soul, Raia. But the good of our people must come before our own happiness."

"Happiness?" she hissed. "I would settle for boredom. But you consign me to a torturous existence, all to please a people who despise us. The army of the Two Lands is far larger than any the Children of Setesh could muster. Conquer them, Father. Conquer them and *save me.*"

The desperate, pleading tone in her voice made Bek's heart ache. He longed to pull her into his arms and comfort her, but he could no longer be with her in any capacity other than as her guardian. As of this moment, she belonged to another.

"Raia," the king said, his voice hoarse, "one day you will understand sacrifice. And then, perhaps, you will realize I've done the best I could."

"But—"

He waved a hand, dismissing her. "Prepare to meet you betrothed on the morrow."

192

She stared at him, frozen, for a long moment. Then she whirled on her heels and stalked out of the throne room. Bek hurried after her, but she moved with such swiftness he could do no more than trail a few paces behind her until they entered her chambers. He dashed through the door an instant before she flung it shut. An arm's length apart, they gazed at each other, and he saw the pain in her eyes, the hurt brought on by her father's betrayal. Her chin trembled, her eyes glistened with gathering tears.

"Bek," she croaked, "this is—I will die if I must—"

He hauled her into his arms and murmured wordless sounds into her silky hair. Her cheek rested on his bare chest, and her hot tears slid down his skin. She sniffled, her hands balled on his chest, pinned between their bodies. She was warm and soft and so fragile. The sweet scent of her perfume, distilled from the blue water lilies in the garden, enveloped him and he inhaled deeply. He relished the unique and womanly scent of her, delicate beneath the perfume.

"I cannot marry this Setka," she said as her body softened against him.

He buried his face in her hair, hugging her closer. "We must leave the Two Lands, together. Perhaps we could reach Hattusha…"

"How? We have no means."

"I will steal anything we need."

She raised her head and her reddened eyes locked onto him. "If you were caught, my father would have you executed. I cannot allow it." When he opened his mouth to speak, she silenced him with one finger on his lips. "Promise me you will live your life. Wed. Raise a family. Be happy—"

"Never." He took her finger between his lips, licking at the tip. "If I cannot have you, I will never marry."

"Oh Bek." She settled one of her slender hands on each of his cheeks. "Please do not say such things. I have no choice. You do."

"You are wrong." He flattened his palms on her back, dipping his head closer to hers. "I love you, Raia. There is no choice for me."

She shut her eyes, but a faint smile played at her lovely lips. When she gazed at him once again, her smile turned sad—to match her eyes. She wrapped her arms around his neck, pressing her supple body firmly against him and rocking her hips into his. His cock shot hard. She fluttered her lips over his and her exhalation tickled his mouth. "If we are both to be damned, then we deserve one night of joy."

With quick flicks of her tongue, she teased his lips.

He slid his hands lower to grasp her behind. "What are you suggesting?"

"Stay with me tonight." She sucked his lip between her teeth, releasing it with agonizing slowness. "My body is yours, my love."

Without a thought or a hesitation, the king's order be damned, he swept her up into his arms and carried her to the bed.

CHAPTER ELEVEN

THE FLAME OF HIS TORCH FLICKERED WITHIN THE ROCK-hewn chamber, casting tongues of light into the darkness around Bek. The shadows slithered away from the torchlight, only to surge back with each retreat of the glow. The darkness always returned. It was stronger than the light, because light always died but shadows lived forever.

Bek lodged the torch into a makeshift sconce on the wall. The workers tasked with hacking this tomb out of the bedrock, deep inside the mountain, had placed such temporary holders along the walls for their oil lamps. Neferhotep had ordered construction of this tomb to begin a year ago, not because he sensed his daughter would die before him, but because she deserved a grand tomb—and grand tombs took years to create. Now her body rested within the simple wooden coffin before him, on its temporary wooden dais.

She was gone. Murdered in her bed.

His chest constricted, aching from deep inside. Bek stabbed his fingers into his hair, his head falling forward until his chin almost touched his chest. His eyes burned. His gut kept twisting, as if a serpent writhed within him, gnashing its fangs into his flesh. If he found—no, when he found—the party responsible for Raia's death, he would rip the man to shreds. It was a man, it had to be. A woman could not have wreaked the damage Raia's attacker had inflicted on her fragile flesh.

Visions flared in his mind, of the moment he had entered Raia's bedchamber and come upon her…body. He clenched his jaw hard, pangs shooting out through his skull. She had lain atop the sheets, naked, bloodied from numerous wounds, her beautiful eyes wide and her expression frozen in the final moment of terror. Her mouth gaped, and a dark liquid dribbled from one corner of her lips down her chin. A goblet sat upright on her chest, the remnants of the same dark liquid puddled in its depths.

Where was *maat* now? What good could come of this tragedy to balance the evil act?

"Wesir!" he shouted. Spittle spewed from his lips as he shook his fist at nothing, knowing he could never see the great god of the underworld. "You cannot take her. Anpu, her soul is not yours to judge. Not yet. May you all be consumed by Amaunet the Devourer for allowing this travesty!"

Again, his mind flashed back to the scene of Raia's death. The wounds had not sapped her life force. Looking upon her lifeless form, Bek realized the truth. Someone had beaten, then poisoned, her.

Even as he huddled here in her unfinished tomb, the fire of anger seethed within him. It seared his heart, scorched his lungs, and soldered his muscles until his body felt rigid as the stone walls around him. Nothing mattered except punishing her murderer.

Bek slammed his fists onto the coffin. He pounded on its blank lid, beat and beat until the wooden legs of the dais beneath it cracked and splintered. He stopped then, his heart thundering. After failing to protect her in life, he would not fail to safeguard her remains by shattering the dais so her coffin clattered to the floor and broke open. *No.* Raia deserved better. She deserved to live, not to die, not like this. She should have borne children, daughters with her gold-and-emerald eyes.

He threw his head back and bellowed at the ceiling.

"Ah, the lover's grief is exquisite."

He spun to face the man who sauntered into the tomb from the corridor beyond. Setka—the one Neferhotep had commanded his daughter to wed—observed Bek with a slightly amused expression.

Bek clenched his fists, shoulders bunching from the effort. Through gritted teeth, he hissed, "You have no right to be here."

"She was my betrothed." Setka waved a hand, as if his cat had died instead of his soon-to-be wife. "I thought I should pay my disrespects."

"Your what?"

The emissary of the Children of Setesh chuckled. "You truly have not discerned the truth yet, have you? Ah well, I suppose a great hulking beast such as you can be expected to understand nothing more complicated than how to batter down a palace gate."

With a heart-stopping suddenness, the meaning of Setka's words exploded in Bek's mind. He surged forward, halting within spitting distance of his enemy. "You murdered Raia. You beat her savagely, then forced her to drink poison."

"Indeed I did." Setka brushed his palms across each other, then swept his fingers over his shoulder as if removing dirt from his skin. "Tombs are such dank and dusty places. Too bad your beloved will have no Book of the Dead painted on these walls to guide her into the afterlife. In fact, she will have no accoutrements at all."

Bek lunged a fist at Setka's gut. His hand smacked into an invisible wall. Pain ricocheted through his bones, from his fingers all the way up his arm. He choked back a yell, stumbling away from Setka.

The murderer chuckled again, his eyes alight with pleasure. "You cannot touch me, beast. My magic is far too strong, for I call upon the powers of Setesh himself. Chaos is my ally."

For this man to call upon the god of chaos and summon the darkest magics, he must be utterly insane. Had Neferhotep known this when he bound his daughter to Setka? He could not have. Despite the king's faults, Bek could never believe Neferhotep capable of such treachery.

Magic. Bek had believed in it, in the abstract sense, but to experience it…He massaged his aching hand. Both his hands trembled, though not entirely from pain or exertion. Spells and incantations were real, and tangible. How could he fight this?

Setka must pay. If it killed him, Bek would ensure the man suffered an agony equal to what he had wrought on Raia.

"Why? Bek demanded. "Why kill her? You did not even know Raia."

"She is the pharaoh's daughter." Setka rubbed his chin, then tapped his finger on it. "It was an elegant plan. I wed her, and soon after the king is felled by a tragic accident."

Of course. Bek scowled. "You kill Raia and assume the throne for yourself."

"After a decent interval," Setka said. "No one must suspect. And besides, I would have time to sire a child—which is, of course, the only valuable contribution a woman may make to the world."

The only valuable contribution? Bek bared his teeth, snarling like an animal. A feral instinct in him had roared to life at Setka's callous statement. He would have impregnated Raia with his spawn, then murdered her after the child's birth. Bek fought the impulse to hurl himself at Setka and throttle the man. It would have been a wasted effort, because the man's magic would prevent it.

Must kill him somehow. Make him suffer a thousand agonies.

"Bek, Bek, Bek," Setka chided, shaking his head. That vile little smile stretched his lips. "You ruined my lovely plan. Fortunately, I was spying on Raia and learned of your dalliance with her. I had to adjust my plan."

"You could not spy on her. The palace is secure, I made certain of it."

"My methods evaded your detection, oh great protector."

Bek ground his teeth. "How?"

Setka sighed. "Magic, naturally."

The gods must have abandoned Raia, abandoned him, left the entire world without their oversight. Nothing else could explain it. *Maat* was supposed to balance the scales, yet where was the balancing good? The goddess Maat herself must have fled.

"The king is dead," Setka said in a bored tone. "I sneaked into his bedchamber—by magical means, of course—and slit his throat."

Bek jerked as if Setka had struck him. The king, dead? It could not be.

Setka retreated a few steps, reached around the corner of the doorway, and retrieved a sword. He brandished its blood-stained blade, his lips peeling back in a predatory smile.

"As for you," Setka said. "You will be the last to die, and the first to suffer."

Drawing his dagger from his belt, Bek assumed a fighting stance.

Setka laughed. The harsh sound echoed off the rough-cut stone walls. "Still, you do not understand. Once I dispatch you, I shall invoke a curse of my own devising. The three of you shall endure an eternity of anguish at my hands." His voice grew hard, his words spat from curled lips. "Never-ending torment, as recompense for stealing my birthright. My people should have become kings, but instead we were banished to the desert to fend for ourselves. I could have reclaimed what is rightfully ours, but you—" He slashed his sword in the air directly in front of Bek. "You had to defile my property. I consulted Setesh for guidance, and learned Raia would bear your child. *Yours.* It should have been mine."

His child? Bek staggered sideways a half step, his heart racing. She would have borne his son or daughter—their child. This man robbed them of their future.

Setka sneered, his knuckles white around the sword's hilt. "I had to punish the lot of you."

Bek glanced back at the coffin. His throat thickened, his chest ached. "What will you do with her remains? Burn them?"

"No, no, no." Setka set the sword's tip on the earthen floor, his palm resting on the hilt. "She is the key to my vengeance, the bedrock of the curse. I will ensure her body is mummified and sealed in this tomb—with no funerary rites or decorations, of course. Her soul will be bound to her body, but she will never find peace in the afterlife. Her soul belongs to me."

A fury like nothing he had ever experienced erupted within Bek. He roared, wielded his dagger, and charged at Setka. The other man smirked. Bek slammed into the barrier, bounced off it, the energy of the magic flinging him across the chamber into the coffin dais. His head struck hard. Lights sparked in his vision as the room tilted around him.

Setka stalked up to him, sword in hand. "Darkness always conquers the light."

He plunged the sword into Bek's heart.

CHAPTER TWELVE

J AKE SPRANG UP IN THE TANK, HIS HEAD AND CHEST OUT OF the water. Blue liquid surged up over the tank's rim to splash down on the dais and spill out across the concrete floor. As the last drip-drips subsided, he wiped the liquid from his eyes with the back of his hand—and went cold. Dawn slumped over the tank's left side, one arm limp in the water, her cheek on the metal rim, eyes shut.

He laid a hand on her cheek. "Dawn."

Features crimping, she fluttered her lids apart. Her confused gaze darted back and forth several times before settling on him. "We're back."

Back? He scooted closer to her, his butt still on the tank's gel floor, and slipped his arm around her shoulders. "What are you talking about? Are you okay?"

"Mm-hm." She propped her elbows on the tank's rim to lift her torso off it. "You kind of pulled me into your past life memories. I even experienced one from my own perspective. It was weird."

With the last phrase, her voice took on a dreamy tone. Her expression had gone soft and dreamy too, as if she were sliding back into those memories. He had no idea how he'd pulled her into his remembrances, but since they both apparently had supernatural powers, who was he to question it? Still, her odd demeanor plucked at his nerves. He clambered out of the tank, slapping first one foot, then the other, down on the wet concrete floor. Liquid dribbled off his body, but he didn't give a damn that he was naked. He grasped Dawn's shoulders and turned her toward him, lifted her off the dais, and set her on the floor in front of him, maintaining his hold on her.

She blinked slowly. Her eyes became clearer, her face less slack. She blinked again, more rapidly, focusing in on him. Her features pinched, she sucked in a shaky breath as tears rolled down her cheeks.

He brushed them away with his thumb, but held her fast with his other hand. "What's wrong?"

"Nothing." She smiled, an expression so bright and alive his heart swelled to see it. But still she was crying. He dropped his arm to her waist, tugging her close. Her wet clothes clung to her curves and damp hair was plastered to her cheeks. She flattened her palms on his chest. "It's just I was worried—Doesn't matter now. Forget it."

Frowning, he cupped her face in one hand. "It matters to me."

She bowed her head, giving him a fantastic view of the part in her hair. "I thought maybe you moved on after I died, had a wonderful life with someone else and loved her more than me. It's selfish, but I didn't want it to be true."

He pressed his lips to the crown of her head, smiling against her hair. "I could never love anyone else. It's always been you, and only you."

"I know." She tilted her head back to aim those stunning eyes at him. "We belong together."

"Damn right we do."

"Jake." She chewed her lower lip and averted her gaze. "Did you get the answers you were looking for?"

"You should know. You were there with me." He sighed when she gave him a peevish look. Much as he hated talking about himself, and especially his feelings, he realized she needed to know how he'd interpreted the memories. How he'd felt. What revelations he found in them. He folded his arms around her, holding her gently. "Setka—or Anton Vahl, whichever you want to call him—he used magic to accomplish his goals. I couldn't have protected you from his spells and curses. He had a goddamn invisible wall around him so I couldn't even strangle the bastard."

"Which means?"

The love on her face triggered a wave of warmth in his chest, like the light of eternal devotion shining down on him. Poetic nonsense, but he could not deny the truth of it. Not anymore. He'd known since he first saw her face he belonged with this woman, but now he understood the depth of their connection, a bond that survived death and rebirth and the undying hatred of one sick fucker.

"It means," he said, "I never failed you."

She stroked a hand over his cheek, her fingertips trailing off his jaw one by one. "Told you so."

Grinning, he bent to kiss her. "Now if we can figure out how to defeat the curse…"

"I know how."

"You do?"

"It was something Vahl said to you in my tomb." She stepped back from him, roving her gaze up and down his body. She ran her tongue over her lower lip. "Maybe you should put some clothes on, honey. I mean, I love to look at you this way but my father might not approve."

They both swung their attention to the equipment bank, where Westenra had stood when Jake entered the tank and traveled back to his past life. The man was gone.

Dawn's eyes widened. "Where is he?"

A scream fractured the silence.

Before Jake could stop her, Dawn bolted for the stairs. He rushed after her, and just as she clambered up the top few steps, lightning pierced the sky above the opening. Thunder detonated a split second after, rattling the stairs and the computer equipment below. Dawn climbed out onto the ground outside.

"Wait!" Jake shouted, but she ignored him. By the time he scrambled out of the bunker hatch, Dawn was hurtling across the clearing toward a figure at its center. The sky above roiled with black and blue and green clouds. Lightning bolts lanced down into the forest, striking with a hiss and a crackle. Not far away, but out of sight, trees cracked and the *whoosh* of their bodies tumbling down echoed through the woods. The wind whipped through the clearing in tornadic currents.

Ralph Westenra stood motionless, head bent back, shoulders slumped.

A bolt of lightning slammed straight into his chest. The light blinded Jake for terrifying seconds, but he rushed onward anyway, desperate to catch up to Dawn. She screamed, and his blood curdled in his veins. *You can't have her, you son of a bitch.*

Whiteness spotted his vision, but he made out the figures of Dawn and Westenra on the ground. The older man lay prone, still as death, eyes open and wide but devoid of life. Dawn hunched over him on her knees, sobbing, shaking him, babbling nonsense.

Jake fell to his knees beside her. He jammed a finger into Westenra's neck. A chill overtook him, freezing him to the core. He dragged Dawn into his arms, pressing her face into his neck. "I'm sorry, it's too late. He's gone."

A sob wracked her body. "H-he can't be. I was s-so mean to him and he never knew—"

Yet another sob choked off her words. He cradled her, rocking her in his arms until her crying eased up enough that she no longer shuddered from the power of her sobs. He stroked her hair, murmured soothing sounds, kissed her temple.

All the while, his gaze stayed glued to the inert form of her father. His clothing was scorched, melted to his chest where the bolt had struck. It seemed to have tunneled through flesh and bone and internal organs to—

Holy shit. Jake gulped back his gorge, as it surged up in his throat. The lightning incinerated the man's heart.

Dawn wrenched out of his embrace to confront the mortal remains of her father. She squeezed her lips together, clearly fighting back more tears. Sucking in a deep breath, she exhaled it in one long huff. "I can fix this."

"Fix it?" Jake studied her face, the grim determination there, and his heart sank. He reached for her, but she shook off his hands. He scrubbed his face with his palms. "Sweetie, he's gone. You can't resurrect the dead."

"Can't I?" She lifted her chin, gaze sharp and clear. "I have the power of healing."

He seized her shoulders and forced her to face him. "You have no idea what might happen to you if you try to resurrect the dead. It could kill you."

"You said I brought you back from death. Back when you were poisoned by those Redeo creeps." She bored her gaze into his. "You told me I burned death out of you."

"I know but this is diff—"

She twisted out of his grasp. Before he realized her intention, she'd slapped her palms on her father's scorched chest. Eyes squeezed shut, she screwed up her face with intense concentration. The wind still whirled around them, whipping her hair into a writhing mass of auburn waves. Her breaths grew labored, her chest heaving.

Jake moved to grab her, but froze inches from touching her. His fingertips tingled with a sizzling energy that emanated from *her.* He yanked his hands away and sank back on his heels, entranced by the vision of her, filled with a mixture of terror and awe. White lights sparkled around her, enlarging and spreading out to surround Westenra's body. The energy engulfed Dawn and her father, until Jake could see neither of them through the blinding curtain. He flung up a hand to shield his eyes, squinting, his heart pounding against his ribs. Jesus, was she actually doing it?

The light extinguished, so quickly Jake's eyes needed a moment to adjust. His gaze fell on the two of them, and his jaw dropped.

Ralph Westenra pushed up into a sitting position, blinking, glancing around in con-fusion. His body had healed, but his clothing remained scorched. He rubbed his cheek, but then his face paled and his expression crumbled. Jake tracked the other man's focus to the limp figure on the ground beside him. Dawn. She lay still, crumpled on her side with her knees bent, her skin gray, lips pale.

No. Jake scrambled to her and hauled her into his arms.

The sky grumbled. Lightning coruscated. Wind swirled around them, casting de-bris in every direction. The clouds mutated to a fathomless black, and the stench of death permeated the air.

Jake clutched Dawn to his chest. No heartbeat pounded in her chest. No breaths escaped her lips or nostrils. She lay limp, jaw slack, eyes closed, skin…cold.

A roaring erupted overhead, accompanied by a rattling and thwacking, like a runaway locomotive barreling out of the sky toward the ground.

Dawn was cold. Lifeless.

No, goddammit, this was not how it ended. They hadn't survived past lives and rebirth only to die like this, victims of an evil bastard's living curse. Vahl would not win. Not as long as Jake had a breath left in him.

He froze. Glanced down at Dawn's slack face. He had more than breath left in him. He had magic powers, for shit's sake. Dawn insisted he'd brought her back to life back in the lab at Redeo. He awakened her then. Why not now?

A giddy kind of panicked glee seized him. He wrapped his arms around her, shut his eyes, and willed her to come back to him.

Because this was not the end. Not by a long shot.

CHAPTER THIRTEEN

THE SOUNDS RETURNED TO HER FIRST. WIND HOWLING. THE storm roaring. Jake's hushed pleas uttered straight into her ear.

"Please come back, please come back, you can't leave me, I need you."

Dawn wrinkled her nose as the stench washed over her. Then she began to feel—the wet grass under her fingers, the heat of Jake's body mashed to hers, the rain pelting her skin.

With a near-explosive suddenness, the storm died. Silence descended around them, save for the pitter-patter of the rain. She peeled her lids apart to gaze up at Jake. His eyes were shut tight, his face wrenched in a desperate expression.

She moaned as aches and pains came back to life inside her.

Jake's eyes flew open. His lips quivered, curving up into a weak smile. "Are you really…"

He raised a trembling finger to her cheek, hovering it millimeters from her skin.

She smiled. "What'd I miss?"

He collapsed into her, his face buried in her neck. She looped her arms around his neck and combed her fingers through the hair at his nape. "It's okay. I'm not dead anymore."

But she had been. And dying had hurt like hell.

Jake raised his head, his gaze flitting over her face as if he couldn't quite believe she was really alive. "Christ, Dawn, I lost you."

"Got me back, though." She pressed a kiss to his lips, letting her mouth linger on his. "This is the second time you've brought me back to life."

"Let's not make a habit of it." He made a little noise, almost a laugh, then hugged her so tight she couldn't breathe. When he eased off a bit, she inhaled and he stared at her with a look of wonder. "You're here."

"Yep." She glanced over her shoulder, and her heart swelled at the sight of her father kneeling there. He gave her a tight smile. She returned the expression and told him, "I'm glad you're okay. And I'm really sorry about the crappy way I've been treating you."

He shook his head. "Never mind that. You saved my life, dear, though I'm not at all certain I deserved it."

"You did." She managed to turn slightly in Jake's iron embrace, to face her father. "I understand now, what you meant about sacrificing the ones you love for the good of the world. Sometimes we have to be willing to give up what we want most for the greater good." She bit her lip, then added, "I still don't like what you did, but I get why you did it."

He rubbed his brow, mouth slack, and stared at her. "You can't forgive me."

She leaned into Jake, relishing the solid feel of him. Her savior, in every lifetime. To her father, she said, "I understand your actions, because I had to make the same kind of choice. When I realized the only way to stop the curse was for me to die."

"What?" Jake all but screeched the word. "You didn't tell me."

Dawn patted his cheek. "Would you have let me do it if you knew?"

His lips twisted, and he hissed out a breath. "No."

"That's why I didn't tell you."

"Um," her father said, raising a finger, "I don't understand. How did your death end the curse?"

She glanced to Jake, then back to her father. "I shared Jake's past life memories when he was in the tank. When Vahl confronted Jake in my tomb, after he'd killed me and you, he bragged about his amazing curse." She turned to Jake, looking straight into his eyes. "He said I was the bedrock of his curse. That's when I understood. Without me, it would collapse."

Jake swallowed visibly. "If you died, the curse would be defeated. Death conquered evil."

"Not quite." She combed her fingers through his hair. "Love conquered evil. My death destroyed the curse, but my resurrection shattered Vahl's evil plan for vengeance. We conquered that slimebucket once and for all."

Jake grinned, but the expression faded swiftly. "The server. We still haven't gotten rid of the evidence Vahl kept about you and your regeneration."

"Ah." Her father scuttled in a half crouch across the grass toward them. "I found the server. Vahl, paranoid madman that he was, included a self-destruct mechanism in the bunker. Once we hit the button, the entire bunker will implode. No more server, no more record of Dawn's resurrection or the process that regenerated her." Dawn must've looked amazed—she certainly felt it—because he shrugged and added, "I had time to kill while you two were reliving the past."

Jake got to his feet, hoisting Dawn up with him. "It's time to put the past to rest and move on with the rest of our lives."

"Amen to that," she said.

Westenra nodded. And then he did something that left Dawn gaping at him slack-jawed. He grinned.

They all filed into the bunker, somehow needing to witness the pushing of the button as a group. The curse had started and ended with them, and it seemed fitting the records of her resurrection should also be destroyed with the three of them present. The men in her life insisted Dawn hit the button.

She hesitated for a half second, her finger over the red button recessed into a console beside the monitor. Then she punched it.

A countdown timer appeared on the monitor. T-minus two minutes.

They hurried out of the bunker. Just as they reached their vehicle, a muted boom rumbled through the forest and the ground trembled. Back the way they'd come, a cloud of dust plumed up from the treetops.

It was over. Forever.

Dawn danced her fingertips up Jake's chest to his throat. "We have some work to do if we're going to have those three babies."

"What three babies?"

"The ones my intuition tells me we will have." She slid her hand around to his nape. "Soon."

He pulled his head back, lips parting. "How could you know?"

"I have magical powers, silly." She laughed, bumping her nose against his. "I can feel it. We are going to have a family, provided we get started on the baby-making." She skated a finger over his lips. "Are you up for the job?"

He threw his head back and laughed. "You have to ask?"

A hand lighted on her arm, and she glanced at her father. "Is there a chance I could—I mean, may I be a part of your life?"

She flung an arm around his shoulders and pulled him in for a hug, even with Jake's arm now curled around her waist. "Yes, of course. You're going to be a grandfather and I expect you to spoil our children rotten. Got it, Dad?"

He nodded, a broad smile enlivening his features. His blue eyes sparkled.

For the first time since awakening inside Redeo Biotech, she felt human and whole. She had a family, with her father and Jake, and soon they would welcome new members. Everything was perfect.

She beamed at her father and husband. "Let's go live our lives. We are free."